GATHERING
SHADOWS

Books by Nancy Mehl

GATHERING SHADOWS

NANCY MEHL

BETHANYHOUSE
a division of Baker Publishing Group
Minneapolis, Minnesota

© 2014 by Nancy Mehl

Published by Bethany House Publishers
11400 Hampshire Avenue South
Bloomington, Minnesota 55438
www.bethanyhouse.com

Bethany House Publishers is a division of
Baker Publishing Group, Grand Rapids, Michigan

Printed in the United States of America

Library of Congress Cataloging-in-Publication Data
Mehl, Nancy.
    Bathering shadows / Nancy Mehl.
      pages cm. — (Finding Sanctuary ; 1)
      Summary: "Wynter Evans came to the town of Sanctuary looking for an-
swers. Can Mayor Reuben King help her discover the truth about her brother's
disappearance?"—Provided by publisher.
      ISBN 978-0-7642-1157-7 (pbk)
      1. Journalist—Missouri—Saint Louis—Fiction. 2. Broadcasting—Mis-
souri—Saint Louis—Fiction. 3. Missing Persons—Fiction. I. Title.
PS3613.#4254G38 2014
813'.6—dc23   2013047197

Scripture quotations are from the Holy Bible, New International Version®. NIV®.
Copyright © 1973, 1978, 1984, 2011 by Biblica, Inc.™ Used by permission of Zondervan.
All rights reserved worldwide. www.zondervan.com

Cover design by Dan Pitts

Author represented by The Steve Laube Agency

14 15 16 17 18 19 20   7 6 5 4 3 2 1

To my friend Darlene Papke:

She is clothed with strength and dignity. She speaks with wisdom, and faithful instruction is on her tongue. Her family and her friends arise and call her blessed. Many women do noble things, but you surpass them all. A woman who fears the LORD is to be praised. Honor her for all that her hands have done, and let her works bring her praise at the city gate.

Proverbs 31:25–31 NIV Paraphrased

These scriptures say it better than I ever could.
You've touched many, many hearts with your life.
I'm so thankful to be one of them.
I love you.

PROLOGUE

He observed the youngster ride his bike to the end of the block where the street dead-ended. Then, after looking around carefully, the man slowly drove his car over to where the boy stood staring at something on the ground. He parked a few yards away and watched as the boy wiped tears off his face.

The man rolled down his window.

"Excuse me," he said. "You're Ryan Erwin, aren't you?"

The boy stood up straight and stared wide-eyed at the man, his expression guarded. He blinked furiously, obviously not wanting the man to know he'd been crying.

"Yeah, I'm Ryan."

The man smiled. "I'm Bill Martin. I live on the next block. You've seen me before, right?"

Ryan frowned, his forehead wrinkled in thought. "I . . . I don't know . . ."

"Sure you have. I own the big black Lab."

The boy's expression brightened. "Oh yeah. I know that dog. You own it?"

The man nodded. "That's Sadie. She recently had puppies,

and one of them is missing. I wonder if you've seen it?" The man reached over to the passenger seat and grabbed a photo. "Here's a picture of Waggles. He got out this morning. I'd sure hate for him to get run over. He's just a little thing." He held the picture out.

Ryan nudged the kickstand on his bike down and approached the car.

"He's cute, isn't he?" the man said, his smile pasted firmly in place. "My kids are heartbroken." He pulled the photo a little closer to him. "You have a dog, don't you?"

The boy nodded. "Yeah, a golden retriever."

"What's his name?"

"We named him Ollie, after Laurel and Hardy. My dad . . ." Ryan took a deep breath. "My dad thinks they're funny."

"I like that name."

The boy came up even nearer to the car.

"Ryan, do you think you could do me a favor and help me look for my puppy? I'd hate to go home and tell my kids something happened to him."

The boy studied the man's face once again, then stared down at the photo of the small black Lab puppy. Finally, he nodded. "My teacher told me not to talk to strangers, but I guess since I know you, it would be all right."

"I'm glad you know about stranger danger. It's very important to be careful." The man's smile widened. "Why don't you leave your bike here? We'll look for Waggles, and after we find him, I'll bring you right back."

"Sure," Ryan said. He glanced back once at his new blue racing bike as he ran around the car and got into the passenger seat.

An hour later, Ryan's father found the bike.

But Ryan was gone.

CHAPTER
ONE

"You look like you've seen a ghost."

Megan's voice made me jump. I looked up to see her standing beside me. I hadn't heard her come in. "Sorry. Guess I drifted away for a minute."

She stared back at me with a strange look on her face. "You're about the whitest person I've ever known, Wynter. When *you* get pale, it's scary. Something about those pictures upset you?"

I shook my head. "No. Just looking them over." I cleared my throat and turned back to the photographs that lay scattered on the large mahogany conference table. "Where did you say you got these?"

"From my mom. She took them about six years ago." Megan plopped down in the chair next to me. Her brown eyes sparkled. "She lives in Madison County." She pointed at the photos. "This town is about ten miles from her. The people shop in Fredericktown, where she lives, so she sees them quite a bit. They don't like people taking their pictures, but Mom snapped these from her car as she drove past them. I doubt they were happy about it."

"They're Amish?"

She frowned. "No. Mom said they're Mennonite. Not as strict as the Amish, but I think they share some of the same beliefs. Don't know if this place would fit into your report, but since you're putting together a list of unique Missouri towns, I thought you might find the pictures interesting." She pulled one of the photos closer and peered carefully at it. "My mom says the whole town isn't religious, but most of them live very simply. You know, horses and buggies, stuff like that. Mom has a friend who moved there just because she wanted a more uncomplicated life. She's not Mennonite though." Megan shrugged her thin shoulders. "I don't know much else."

I fingered through the photos once again. They showed people riding in buggies. Most of the men wore hats, while the older women had some kind of head covering. I couldn't stop my fingers from trembling.

"Are you sure you're okay?" Megan asked again, her voice tinged with worry. Her dark eyes sought mine. "The flu's going around. Maybe you've got it." She pushed her chair back a bit, causing me to smile.

"No, I'm fine. Too much coffee this morning, I guess."

"You do drink more coffee than anyone I've ever known."

I nodded. "What's the name of this town?"

"Sanctuary. Cool name, huh? But I doubt it's on any map." She flipped over one of the pictures. "I wrote down some directions so you'd know how to find it." She shook her head. "I haven't had time to do any other research. Sorry. Ed's got us jumping. The new owners are due in at the end of the week. No one knows what will happen after that."

I didn't respond because there really wasn't anything to say. According to a friend at another station in town, new owners could be a blessing—or a curse. Usually the latter turned out to be true. Corporate hotshots, convinced they knew more than anyone else, loved to clear the deck and "bring new excitement" to existing television stations. Often the best people were lost in the shuffle, while new, inexperienced reporters and on-air personalities drove loyal viewers to a competing station. It had already happened twice at KDSM before I was hired. I was hopeful this transition would be smooth.

"If you look online, it's possible you might find a phone number for someone who actually lives in Sanctuary," Megan said, going back to our previous discussion. "You could stumble across a resident who could help you." A smile lit up her ebony features. "Who knows? Maybe this will turn out to be an adventure."

"Maybe." I returned her smile. "I'm hoping this idea will turn out to be interesting enough for Ed to sign off on. With a little luck it could end up being a franchise. You know, like John Lewis's *People of Missouri*." John Lewis, a reporter at KJML, another station in St. Louis, had vaulted himself into an anchor position after putting together a weekly piece about unique people who lived in our state. Although I enjoyed my job as a reporter, I secretly hoped this story would move me up too. Like John, more than anything, I wanted to sit in the anchor chair.

"Missy is so jealous," Megan replied, grinning. "She really wanted the next assignment. When Ed agreed to let you put this concept together and present it, she turned three different shades of green." She laughed. "Even her carefully applied makeup couldn't hide her jealousy."

"She's been gunning for me ever since she started. I'd hate to know what she's really thinking behind that fake smile."

"I'm sure it's not suitable for prime time," Megan quipped.

"I agree." I reached out and touched her arm. "Thanks, Megan. You've been so supportive. I really appreciate it."

"That's what friends are for." She got up and left the conference room, slowly closing the door behind her.

Her words echoed in my mind. Were we really friends? I guess she was closer to me than most of the people in my life. I tried hard to keep a distance between me and my co-workers. Working at a television station was a competitive situation at best. Everyone fought for their spot, and no one, including me, ever felt safe.

I'd started at KDSM as an intern while still in college. I was excited to be officially hired right after graduation. Including my internship, I'd spent almost three years at the station. Maybe it wasn't one of the largest stations in St. Louis, but they had a good reputation, and several successful anchors at the big stations had been hired from here.

Megan Parsons, a production assistant, had been friendly from my very first day. We had a lot in common. We were both twenty-three, and we both came from broken homes. Like me, Megan was raised in church, although I'd stopped going when I was a teenager. Our biggest differences were in our appearance. Megan's dark skin, eyes, and hair were an antithesis to my pale complexion and light-blond hair.

Realizing I'd allowed my mind to wander, I pushed worries about my job away and pulled out the picture that had sent shock waves through me. I stared at the face of the young boy caught by the camera as he rode past in a buggy. It was clear from his shocked expression that he wasn't expecting to have his picture taken. I could feel my heart beat faster, and I found it difficult to catch my breath. The features were so familiar.

Could it be Ryan? Was I just seeing what I wanted to see? Ryan was seven when he was taken. There was something about the eyes—and the hair. The boy wore a black, wide-brimmed hat pushed back on his head. His widow's peak was clearly visible. Just like Ryan's.

"Ready for our meeting?"

Ed Grant, KDSM's news director, strode into the room, and I quickly pushed the picture underneath my notebook.

"Yes, sir. I've done quite a bit of research, and I think this would make a compelling piece."

He sighed as he lowered his massive body into the chair across from mine. The chair squeaked under the pressure, and as he scooted into place, sounds emanated from underneath him that I prayed came from sliding across the leather seat.

"I'm not convinced this is newsworthy, but Leon says we need more stories with local interest. Our new owners are pushing for it. I guess this idea is as good as any other." He sighed again, obviously not happy dealing with a new corporate entity. Ed's job at KDSM was tentative, as was our general manager's. Leon Shook was a great GM, and no one wanted to see him leave. But in a previous shake-up, the news director and the general manager had been the first to go. What we could get in their places worried everyone.

"I believe this piece could be popular if we get it right," I said. "I have quite a few suggestions. Some are obvious, like Defiance and its Wine Country Gardens, and Fulton, which has a piece of the Berlin Wall. Then there are all the ghost towns left behind when the mining companies moved out. You know, like Morse Mill. Also, Columbia is interesting because it's home to a lot of ex-Amish. There was a special on TV a while back that mentioned . . ."

Ed held his hand up. "That story's been done and overdone. Besides, Columbia's too big. I want small towns. Out-of-the-way places. Spots that even Missourians don't know about. And nothing about that Amish town, Jamesport. We just did a story about them."

I cleared my throat, trying to quell my nervousness as I pushed some of the pictures Megan had given me across the table.

"In that same vein, here's a possibility. A small town called Sanctuary. Residents are mostly Mennonite. It seems to be inhabited by people looking for a simpler life."

Ed took the pictures and riffled through them. "I've never heard of this town, and I thought I knew every nook and cranny of this state."

I sat back in my chair, hoping it wouldn't make the embarrassing sounds that had come from Ed earlier. Since I only weighed a third of Ed's three hundred pounds, thankfully there was only silence.

"What do you think?" I asked.

I was greeted with a cold stare followed by a shrug. Actually, from Ed, that was a sign of unmitigated approval.

"What do you need?"

I pulled the photos back when he shoved them toward me. "I'd like a couple of weeks to tour these towns. I'll need to interview people, do some research."

He crossed his arms across his chest and looked bored. Once Ed made up his mind to do something, his interest waned. "You'll need a photog."

"Why don't you let me look around first? I'd hate to waste anyone's time. Once I find towns that fit the bill, I'll call you. Then you can send someone."

He shook his head. "Waste of valuable time." He stood to his feet. "You have one week to get it done. I'll see who's available. Why don't you leave on Saturday the twenty-fifth? That gives you two weeks to make contacts and get things set up. Be back a week from the following Monday. That will give you ten days to get this thing done. If it's good enough, we'll run it in July."

July was a minor sweeps month. Not as important as February, May, or November, but I had to take what I could get.

I cleared my throat. "I'm wondering if this could turn into a franchise. We could highlight one town every week. There are a lot of interesting places in Missouri. And lots of special events. We might . . ."

Ed held his hand up again, a sign that I should stop talking. "You're getting ahead of yourself. Why don't you go to . . . what was it? Sanctuary? See what's going on. Get something on film and send it to me. If it looks good, we'll talk. If it doesn't excite me, get out of there; go to four or five other towns. We'll go over the footage and put something together. Ten days, Wynter. That's it."

Although I wanted to point out that it was really only nine days, I didn't dare criticize Ed's math abilities. Arguing with him was a mistake. In his present frame of mind, it could cost me this opportunity. I didn't say another word, just nodded my agreement.

As the door swung closed behind him, I gazed once again at the picture of the teenage boy. Nine days with a photographer tagging along. Was I chasing shadows? Or had my parents and I quit too soon? Was Ryan still alive?

Had I actually found my brother?

CHAPTER
TWO

"Don't see why I pulled this project."

Stuck in a car for two hours with a petulant photog was pure torture. Zac had only been with the station for a couple of months, so there hadn't been much time to get to know him. Unfortunately, I was learning a lot more than I wanted to. From the time he'd crawled into my car, he'd done nothing but talk about himself. He was only a year younger than I, but he reminded me of a rebellious teenager.

"Maybe you'll end up enjoying this," I said, fairly sure he wouldn't. "You moved to Missouri six months ago. This will give you an insider's view."

He raised one eyebrow and let his jaw drop. "Inside of what?" he said finally. "Back roads, roadkill, and wild boars?" He snorted. "I'm more interested in the nightlife in St. Louis. This is *definitely* not why I came to Missouri. How far away is this place from St. Louis anyway?"

"Almost ninety miles south. If you're thinking you can run back and forth to the city from Sanctuary, forget it. You're stuck, so you might as well make the best of it," I said, trying to keep my temper in check. "You'll get lots of assignments you don't like. It's the nature of our jobs."

He reached up and turned the rearview mirror toward himself and checked his image.

"There's a mirror on the back of your sun visor," I said.

He shrugged and pushed the rearview mirror back toward me. While I moved it back into place, he flipped his sun visor down and stared at himself. He looked carefully at his hair, which I found odd, since he'd pulled it all back into a ponytail. What was there to fix?

"I don't see why we have to go to this . . . Sanctuary place first," he said as he put the visor up. "We've already passed several of the towns on your list."

"I explained it to you once." I took a deep breath and let it out slowly, trying to stay calm. "Research is easy with these other places, but there's nothing about Sanctuary online. It's the one town we'll have to investigate ourselves. Boots on the ground."

"Boots on the ground?" he repeated. "What are you, ex-military?"

I shook my head. "No, my dad was. He used the expression a lot. Guess I picked it up."

"Wow, he must be fun at holiday meals."

"I have no idea. He divorced my mom when I was sixteen. A year after that he got a new family. Guess they meant more to him than I did. We don't talk much anymore."

Zac didn't respond. Just yawned and looked out the window.

Why had I said that? I never talked about my personal life. Besides, Zac was the last person I wanted in my business.

"It doesn't matter anymore." I shrugged. "I don't even think about him. My mom's been mother and father to me ever since he remarried. He's not important."

"Uh-huh."

At first his rude tone irritated me, but I didn't really care what Zac Weikal's opinion was . . . about anything. All I wanted to do was get to Sanctuary. I needed to find this kid who looked so much like Ryan. In my gut, I was certain once I saw him up close, I'd know he wasn't my brother. Yet something inside pushed me forward. My family had never had closure. Ryan's disappearance had been the catalyst that ended my parents' marriage—and destroyed my family. I had to follow this lead. Had to know the truth.

"Are we going to check into the hotel first?" Zac asked. "I'd like some time to chill out."

"No, we're meeting someone in Sanctuary. A lady named Martha Kirsch. She runs the library. I called her and set up an appointment. I hope she'll help us get the story we need."

"Mennonites read?"

"There are all kinds of Mennonites. In fact, John Traylor, the evening news anchor? He's Mennonite."

"But he doesn't wear a funny hat or anything. Hey, and he's on TV? I thought these people didn't watch TV."

"You're talking about Old Order or Conservative Mennonites. A lot of them don't. Sounds like Sanctuary is made up of all kinds of people. Some of them don't belong to the Mennonite Church at all. According to Martha, the one thing residents in Sanctuary have in common is that they're all looking for a more uncomplicated life." I let out a deep sigh. "I can understand how they feel."

"Oh, come on. You? You seem like a city girl, and you're a bulldog at work. Everyone knows you'll end up in the anchor chair one of these days."

His statement surprised me. "What? Are people talking about me?"

He shrugged. "Don't get offended. It's just that you act so . . . driven. It's obvious."

"Maybe so."

My GPS warned me that a turn was ahead, so I concentrated on watching the road. Zac was right. I did feel driven. Sometimes I wondered why. I loved the energy at work, but once I left the station, I sought peace and quiet. I spent my time reading and even did some writing—something I didn't admit to anyone. Sitting in my favorite chair with my feet up and writing on my laptop with Mr. Henderson, my cat, snuggled up next to me brought me the feeling of tranquility I craved. Over the past year, my social life had slowed to a crawl. And that's the way I liked it.

Zac suddenly let out a long and prolonged sigh. "I hate being around religious people."

I glanced over at him and frowned. "You knew we were going to a Mennonite town, right? I don't need you coming across as antagonistic with these people. Why did you take this assignment?"

He shrugged again and looked out the window. I toyed with the idea of turning around, taking him back to the station, and getting someone else. But Ed would expect me to get this situation under control.

"Look, Zac, I have no idea why you don't like religious people, and frankly, I don't care. But I expect you to act professionally while we're in Sanctuary. Can you do that?"

He turned back toward me. "Not a problem. I filmed those nut jobs from Kansas when they protested at the funeral of a soldier. I wanted to grab them one by one and bash their heads in, but I didn't. I kept my cool. If I can handle them, I can deal with people running around in goofy clothes, acting like they're better than me."

I had to smile. "No one wanted to beat those Kansas jerks more than I did, but I don't understand why you have an attitude about people in Sanctuary. People you haven't even met yet."

"Religion is something men made up so they'd feel better. A fantasy designed to make us think there's something more to life than there really is."

I checked the GPS again. We were still a couple of miles from our turnoff. "Okay, but I still don't get it. What if someone wants to believe there's more to life than what we see every day. It's their business, right? They're not hurting us."

"It's not that. No skin off my nose if they want to believe a lie."

I took my eyes off the road long enough to stare at him. His jaw was working furiously. Obviously the subject of religion was a hot-button topic for him.

I turned my attention back to the highway. "You didn't answer my question," I said bluntly.

"It's personal. I have my reasons. Can we just leave it like that?"

"Sure, as long as you don't cop an attitude in Sanctuary. I need these people to be . . . cooperative."

"So what do you think will happen when the new station owners take over?" Zac asked, abruptly changing the subject.

"I have no idea. I think Leon and Ed have more to worry about than we do. I *am* concerned about our anchors though. Almost every time someone new takes over a station, they think they need to empty the anchor chairs. We have a good team. I'd hate to see any of them leave."

"I overheard someone say you could end up taking Cindy's place at five and six."

The car swerved a bit, and I slowed down. Before I could

respond, the GPS voice announced it was time for a right turn. I turned accordingly and then turned again. It was as if civilization disappeared once we left the highway. Dense trees lined both sides of a narrow two-lane road. I could see a few houses, but they sat back a long way, surrounded by trees and foliage.

"What are you talking about?" I asked finally, once I was certain we were headed in the right direction. "Who said that?"

"A couple of reporters were discussing it. Have no idea where they got the information."

I forced myself to concentrate on my driving. According to my GPS, the last turn to Sanctuary was only 1.8 miles away. I pushed down a tickle of exhilaration. Ed hadn't said a word about it to me. Before I got too excited though, I had to consider the source. Overhearing office gossip wasn't really reliable. Just as quickly as the rush of euphoria came, it left. I couldn't trust this information. Besides, I liked Cindy Drake. She was always nice to me and had gone out of her way to help me when I first came to the station. It was true that she was getting a little older, but she was dedicated, thorough, and extremely professional. In my heart, I believed the station would be making a grave mistake if they let her go. As much as I wanted to anchor the news, I didn't want to see Cindy lose her job.

I suddenly realized Zac was waiting for some kind of response.

"I'm not comfortable talking about this," I said. "And I'm not going to hope someone like Cindy gets fired."

Zac grunted. "Without the killer instinct, you could get eaten alive. Tough business, you know."

I kept quiet, but his words echoed through my head. Did I have any "killer instinct"? Did I even want it? The idea of being an evening news anchor was all I'd ever hoped for, but now, when the reality got a little too close, the prospect made me feel uneasy.

"Looks like you've got a call," Zac said, staring at my cell phone, which was in a holder mounted on my dashboard.

I glanced down. Sure enough, the light was flashing. I'd forgotten and left it on silent again. I'd missed a call from the station. I quickly picked up the phone. With one hand, I entered my voicemail code while I kept my other hand on the wheel. Then I put the phone up to my ear.

"Wynter, this is Ed. I thought you said you cleared this story with the muckety-mucks in . . . what was it? Sanctuary? We just fielded several calls from some religious nuts who are extremely upset we want to film their little backwater hole in the ground. Forget 'em. I don't need the headache. You've got lots of other towns to visit. See you in ten days."

"Nine days," I mumbled under my breath. I slipped my phone back into its holder.

"Anything important?" Zac asked.

"Nope. Not at all."

I slowed down when I saw the sign pointing to Sanctuary. As I took the turn, the butterflies in my stomach morphed into condors.

CHAPTER

THREE

"Might as well tell you right off that some people in Sanctuary aren't happy you're here."

Martha Kirsch stared at us over the rims of her narrow glasses. Everything about Martha was narrow. Her face, her long nose, her body. Even her eyes narrowed as she looked us over.

"I don't understand," I said. "What changed since I talked to you the other day? You seemed excited that we were coming. You said you wanted a chance to share your town's history."

"I . . . I *was* excited. But then word got out, and everyone started complaining."

I pointed at the large front window in the small library. "I see horses and buggies, but there are also quite a few cars. Obviously not all of your population is Old Order or Conservative. So why would *everyone* be opposed to our story?"

She shook her head, and the chains attached to her glasses jangled. "This town is very special—to everyone who lives here." She sniffed, something she'd done more than once since Zac and I entered the building. Although the library looked clean, there was a musty smell. The building was old. Probably built in the

1800s. The aroma of an ancient building combined with old books could have been distasteful, but not to me. It reminded me of the library back home in Chicago where I'd grown up. I'd loved that library, frittering away many happy hours wandering through the aisles. There were tables where patrons could sit and read, but I spent my time sitting cross-legged on the floor next to tall shelves full of books. No one seemed to mind, and I was never asked to move. The library workers understood the lure of a good story and the magic of finding just the right spot to tuck oneself away to read.

"Just who is it that doesn't want us here, Mrs. Kirsch?"

Another sniff. "That's *Miss* Kirsch, thank you. Most of our residents are Mennonite, although there are only a few families that shun electricity and automobiles. Still, they don't like being in the spotlight. And then there are the others."

"The others? What others?"

The woman took a deep breath and scowled at me over her glasses. "Some people come here because . . . because they need privacy. They don't want to be photographed. I shouldn't have told you to come. I was wrong."

Martha's attitude was beginning to grate on my nerves. "Look, I don't mean to be disrespectful, but I went to a lot of trouble to arrange this visit. I intend to stay."

She rubbed her arms as if cold, but the inside of the library was almost as warm as the air outside.

"I must apologize for Martha." A deep voice boomed from behind me, and I turned around to find a man staring at me. I immediately thought of a young Ewan McGregor. Blue eyes, cleft chin, a stubbly beard, and shaggy dishwater-blond hair streaked with golden highlights. He was dressed in jeans and a blue-and-white checked shirt. His bronzed skin obviously didn't come from a tanning salon. His resemblance to one of my favorite actors made me gulp with surprise. I'd had a crush on McGregor ever since he'd played a young Obi Wan-Kenobi in the *Star Wars* saga. Who'd have thought I'd meet Obi Wan in a small Missouri Mennonite town?

"I don't need you to apologize for me, Reuben King," Martha said, accenting her words with another sniff. "You might be our mayor, but I think I can speak for myself."

"I'm sure you can, Martha," he said soothingly. "But telling a visitor they're not welcome doesn't do much to promote hospitality, does it?"

Even though Reuben was much younger than the aged librarian, she seemed to wither under his light reproach.

"I . . . I'm sorry," she said, directing her attention to me. "I don't mean to be difficult." Although her words sounded conciliatory, her expression relayed a very different message.

"I understand. Please be assured that we'll be very respectful to the residents of Sanctuary. We're not here to intrude. We think your town is unique. I'm sure no one knows more about its history than you. I hope you'll allow us to interview you, Martha."

Looking somewhat mollified, the librarian's eyes darted back and forth between the mayor and me.

Reuben smiled. "Thank you, Miss . . ."

"Evans. Wynter Evans," I said quickly. My cheeks felt hot, and I hoped with every fiber of my being that my face wasn't red.

"Nice to meet you, Wynter." He looked questioningly at Zac. To be honest, I'd forgotten Zac was even in the room.

"I'm sorry," I said. "This is Zac Weikal. He's my photog. I mean, photographer."

Reuben stuck his hand out. "Glad to meet you, Zac."

After shaking hands, Reuben smiled widely at both of us.

"Now tell me what I can do to help you."

The chastised Miss Kirsch slunk away toward her desk. Frankly, I was relieved and thankful that Reuben had some influence over the cranky librarian.

"Actually, we'd love to talk to you," I said. "Find out more about Sanctuary. Maybe visit with some of your residents. I realize not everyone will want to be on camera."

Reuben nodded. "That's true. I must ask you not to take or publish videos or pictures without the permission of the people involved. If you'll agree to that, I don't think anyone will have a problem with your presence here. And that applies to all of our residents, not just the Mennonites."

"I thought only Old Order Mennonites avoided having their picture taken."

"There aren't many Old Order Mennonites left. Most of the Mennonites in Sanctuary are conservative. They live simply, but almost everyone here uses electricity. You'll see some horses and buggies, but the large majority of our people drive cars and trucks. You'll find a mix of lifestyles and beliefs here."

I frowned at him. "I guess I'm not seeing much difference between Sanctuary and any other small town."

When Reuben laughed, his eyes sparkled. Anyway, I think they did. I felt like a silly schoolgirl in his presence instead of the confident professional I believed myself to be. I shook myself mentally. *Get a grip, Wynter, before you make a fool of yourself.*

"I think we're rather special, but why don't we talk more over dinner?" He glanced at his watch. "It's a little after three. Where are you staying?"

"The Mountain Inn in Fredericktown."

He frowned. "That's quite a drive. Why don't you stay here?"

Zac made a coughing sound. I knew staying in Sanctuary was the last thing he wanted to do.

"I looked for motels closer, but I couldn't find any."

"Esther Lapp has a big house on the edge of town. Since her children moved out, she's all alone. I'm sure she'd love to put you up. Esther's lived in Sanctuary all her life and was raised Old Order. She'd be a wealth of information for your story."

"I don't know," Zac said slowly. "I need electricity. And a TV."

Reuben grinned. "Esther has electricity. Can't help you with the TV though. Esther won't have one in her house."

I held my hand up before Zac could voice another objection. "We're not here to watch television. I think your suggestion sounds wonderful. I'll call the motel and cancel our reservations. Of course, we expect to pay Esther for her hospitality."

"Then you'll have a problem on your hands," Reuben said. "Esther wouldn't think about taking a dime of your money. She loves company."

"The motel in Fredericktown will charge us for a day," Zac interjected. "You won't be giving them twenty-four hours' notice."

"No big deal. Overall, we'll save money." When he started to complain again, I gave him my best withering look. Although I had no idea how threatening it actually was, it seemed to do the trick. Zac's mouth snapped shut, but his pouty expression stayed firmly in place.

I walked over to Martha's desk and thanked her for her help. She barely acknowledged me, giving me an almost imperceptible nod. It didn't bother me. It was clear Reuben was going to be a much better source of information anyway. He called Esther while I contacted our hotel. I had to step outside to get a decent cell phone signal. By the time I had enough juice to attempt my call, I was well out into the road. Several people passing by stared at me curiously. I wondered how many visitors they actually got in Sanctuary.

The manager at the hotel was extremely nice and canceled the reservation without charging me anything. That would keep Ed happy. I'd just turned off my cell phone and was preparing to go back inside the library when a buggy pulled up next to me and a young man got out. He looked like an older version of my brother, Ryan. Our eyes met, but there was no recognition in his expression. He smiled briefly and then turned to help an older woman out of the carriage.

"I'll pick you up in an hour, Mother," he said, leaning over to kiss her cheek.

"Thank you, Elijah," she said with a smile.

I stood there in shock. I'd been in town only a short time and had already met the person I'd come here to see. I watched as the woman walked up the steps and went into the library. Then I turned back to see the young man get into the buggy and ride off. The love between them was evident. That boy didn't look like someone who had been kidnapped and held against his will. Had I made a mistake in coming here? Was I risking my job on a wild-goose chase? A voice in my head told me to get out of Sanctuary. But another one whispered that I should stay. I decided to listen to the second voice.

FOUR

We followed Reuben to Esther's house. A large two-story structure with a huge front porch, it reminded me of my grandmother's home in rural Nebraska. Before we had a chance to knock on the front door, it swung open. A small elderly woman welcomed us with a wide, friendly smile. She wore a dark-blue dress with a small floral pattern. Her hem hung to just above her ankles. Her gray hair was wrapped in a bun, and a black covering sat atop her head. I introduced myself and Zac, and she welcomed us inside as if she'd known us all our lives.

I tried to concentrate on everything she said, but the image of the young man I saw outside the library overwhelmed my thoughts. I'd have to tread carefully. If that boy wasn't my brother, I could ignite a situation that could disrupt his life—and mine. Ed wasn't going to be happy that I'd ignored his directive to skip Sanctuary, and finding out I was stalking a teenage Mennonite boy would probably cost me my job.

I tried to concentrate on what Esther was saying as we followed her up the stairs that led to the second floor.

"Zac, you will stay in Benjamin's room." She swung open a

door on the left side of the hall. The room was spacious and comfortable. A large iron bed stood against the wall. It was covered with a beautiful quilt, the kind my grandmother used to make. There was an oak dresser with several drawers, and in the corner sat an overstuffed chair with a matching ottoman. The antique floor lamp next to it helped to create a wonderful cozy nook to read a book. As if confirming my evaluation, Esther pointed to a large shelf near the door that was stuffed with books.

"Benjamin is a reader," she said with a smile. "These are only some of his books. The ones he couldn't take with him. Please help yourself, Zac. They are yours to enjoy."

I shook my head at Zac when he rolled his eyes. Thankfully, Esther didn't see him.

"It's a lovely room," I said. "We're so grateful."

To his credit, Zac wiped the smirk off his face. "Yes, Mrs. Lapp. It's very nice. Thank you."

Esther nodded happily, pleased with his response. "I'm so glad. And please, call me Esther," she said. "Mrs. Lapp was my mother-in-law." Esther wrinkled her nose and grinned. For a brief moment, she looked like a young girl. "She never thought I was good enough for her son. We were married only twenty years before he died, but every single year was happy."

"I'm sorry he passed away so young," I said.

Esther's eyes flushed with tears. "I am too, honey." She sighed and regained her composure. "But I know we will spend eternity together, and that knowledge keeps me praising God every day. No reason to feel sorry for myself."

I glanced over at Zac. His raised eyebrow told me he found Esther's conviction fanciful.

He put the bag with his camera and equipment down on the bed. "I'll go to the car and get the rest of our stuff."

I nodded. "Thanks. I appreciate it."

"Now for your room," Esther said, smiling at me. "It belonged to my daughter, Rebecca. She's married now. She lives with her husband and four children in Springfield."

"You must miss your children."

Esther was quiet for a moment. When she spoke again, it was almost a whisper. "More than you know."

"I-I'm sorry."

She shook her head and managed to smile at me. "I have a dear friend who lives next door, Janet Dowell. She's alone too. We kind of look out for each other. Having a close friend really helps the loneliness."

"Is she Mennonite too?"

"No. We differ in some of our beliefs, but we're one in the Lord. I've never known anyone who can talk about God the way Janet does. Like they're best friends. But that's the way it should be, isn't that right?"

I nodded and followed her out of Zac's room to a door at the end of the hall, her question ringing in my ears. I actually understood what she meant. My grandmother had been like that, talking about God as though He was someone she could call up on the phone and talk to whenever she wanted to.

"You probably think it is silly to keep my children's rooms just like they were when they lived here," Esther was saying. "But I hope my grandchildren will like staying in the same room their mother or father grew up in." She put her hand on my arm. "Besides," she whispered, "I like to remember them as little children, even though I know they're grown-ups now."

Ryan's room flashed in my mind. Mom kept it just the way he'd left it until my father sold the house out from under us and forced us to move. I don't think Mom ever forgave him for that.

It was only one item in a long list of thoughtless incidents per-petrated by my father that eventually led to my parents' divorce.

"Are you all right, honey? I know I talk a lot. I don't mean to prattle on and on."

Esther's voice snapped me back to the present. "No, that's not it," I said quickly. "I'm sorry. You said something that reminded me of . . . someone."

"Someone you miss?"

Startled, I blurted out, "My brother. I haven't seen him in a long time."

I'd had no intention of telling anyone in Sanctuary about Ryan. My father's voice floated through my thoughts. *"Loose lips sink ships, Emily. Best to keep your secrets close to the vest."* I didn't understand what the *vest* comment meant, but I knew it was important to keep quiet about my brother. My comment was said innocently enough, and I couldn't see any way it could cause problems. But I'd have to be very careful from here on out.

"I'll pray for you and your brother," Esther continued in her sweet voice. "Just remember that God will keep your loved ones safe—whether they're in this world or in the next. Love is never lost."

"Thank you." I pointed at the door, trying to distract the el-derly woman from her current train of thought. "You said this was Rebecca's room?"

Esther studied me for a few seconds before removing her hand from my arm. "Yes, it was. I hope you like it." She pushed the door open.

Expecting a plain, unadorned room much like Zac's, I was surprised and pleased to find a lovely bedroom full of feminine touches. A tall bed with a carved mahogany headboard stood against the wall, windows on each side. There was a matching armoire near the door and an old fainting couch against the far wall. A dark-wood table next to the bed held an antique lamp with a Tiffany-style shade that matched the rich colors in the room. The couch was covered with maroon brocade, and the magnificent quilt on the bed tied in with the burgundy and forest-green colors in the wallpaper.

"Oh my," I said, stunned by the gorgeous room. "It's so . . ."

"Not Mennonite?" Esther interjected. She laughed lightly. "Mennonites love fine craftsmanship. This furniture was fashioned by my father, and my mother made this quilt."

Esther had just mentioned the colorful quilt when a gray-striped cat suddenly jumped up on the bed and lay down as if it belonged to him and we were the intruders.

"Clyde!" Esther said. "You get down off that bed."

Clyde gave his mistress a dismissive look, yawned, and promptly closed his eyes.

"Did you hear me, young man?" Esther said as she reached for him.

"Don't make him move on my account," I said quickly. "I love cats."

Esther stopped and looked at me with concern. "Are you sure, honey? Some people are allergic."

"Well, I'm not. I miss my own cat when I have to travel. Having Clyde around will make me feel better."

"Well, if you're positive," she said hesitantly.

"I'm absolutely . . ."

Before I could get my next words out, another cat jumped up next to Clyde. This one was small with white and red fur.

"Maizie!"

"Um, how many cats do you have, Esther?"

"Only four. Clyde, Maizie, Frances, and Sam. Sam is the

oldest." She shook her head. "Uncaring people drop off pets in the country, leaving them to fend for themselves. We take them in. You'll find a lot of dogs and cats in Sanctuary."

I smiled at her. "Just one more reason for me to like this town."

"And you're sure the cats won't bother you?"

I reached over to pet Maizie, who stretched her legs out as far as she could to enjoy being rubbed. "Not at all. They'll make me feel right at home."

Esther took a deep breath. "I'm so glad. They're my family now. I don't know what I'd do without them."

Although I didn't say it, I understood. My cat, Mr. Henderson, kept me from feeling alone. When I got home from work, there was always someone to greet me. Someone excited to see me. Mr. Henderson loved to cuddle, and he spent many hours lying in my lap while I watched TV. He also slept on my bed at night. I couldn't imagine life without him.

"I think you'll enjoy staying here," Esther said. She sighed as she gazed around the room. "Rebecca was very happy in this room."

"I'm sure she was."

Esther pointed to a small stool against the wall. "You might want to use that stool to get in and out of the bed. Some of the older beds are taller than today's more modern beds."

"Thank you, Esther, for all your generosity. After we get settled in, I'd love to talk with you more about Sanctuary. I bet you know a lot about this town."

She was silent for a moment, and when she spoke again, I was surprised to see a guarded expression on her face. I'd chalked Martha's attitude up as paranoia, but Esther? What was she worried about? What was it about Sanctuary that made everyone so nervous?

"Why don't we talk after breakfast tomorrow?" she said. "I heard you make dinner plans with Reuben, and I go to bed pretty early."

"That sounds fine. What if we stay out late? Do you want to give me a key?"

Esther chuckled, her previous good humor restored. "This is Sanctuary. The door won't be locked. You just come on in whenever you get back."

"Okay. Thank you."

We heard footsteps coming down the hall.

"That must be Zac with your luggage," she said. "There are two bathrooms on this floor. A full bath across the hall and a small half-bath down at the other end. I'll make sure you have clean towels. You're welcome to use the kitchen anytime, day or night. Help yourself to anything you see. I'll get to the store tomorrow and stock up. If there's anything in particular you want, just let me know."

"That's so kind of you," I said, "but why don't you let us run to the store for you? It's the least we can do."

Esther smiled. "You just concentrate on your story. I'm sure you'll want to finish as soon as possible so you can leave town."

I looked closely at the diminutive woman. Was that a hint to get out of Sanctuary? "Hopefully, it won't take us long to get what we need. I don't intend to leave until we do."

Esther's smile disappeared. "Just be careful, honey," she said softly. "Some people are willing to protect their secrets at all costs." She walked out the door just as Zac came in.

"Where do you want these suitcases?" he asked.

"Put them over there on the floor," I said slowly.

"Looks like I can't toss them on the bed. You seem to have visitors." Zac put the suitcases against the wall.

"Yes, Clyde and Maizie. There are two more running around here somewhere. Hope you like cats."

"I like all animals. It's people I have a problem with." Zac sat down on the bed next to the two very comfortable cats. Clyde eyed him somewhat suspiciously, but Maizie immediately jumped up on his lap. Zac laughed and petted her. She began to purr loudly. This was the first time Zac had reacted positively to anything since we'd left the station.

"You've got another small bag," he said. "I'll bring it up with mine." He looked up at me and frowned. "You look upset. Something wrong?"

"I don't know. I think Esther just politely encouraged us to get out of town. Something about protecting secrets."

"Wow." He cocked his head and raised his eyebrows. "This place is weird. And I don't mean just because it's religious." He shook his head, causing his auburn ponytail to sway back and forth. "There's something else here. Something . . . disturbing."

"Probably just small-town paranoia." I could hear the uncertainty in my voice. Esther's comment had shaken me, but it wouldn't do any good to raise Zac's suspicions.

He stared at me for a moment. "Is there something you're not telling me, Wynter? We're here just for the story, right?"

His question caught me off guard. How could he know? Was I that transparent? "I have no idea what you're talking about. We'll get our interviews, and then we'll leave. That's all there is to it."

"All right. It's just that . . . well, you've been different ever since we got here." He rubbed Maizie behind the ears once more before getting to his feet. "Dinner with that Reuben guy tonight, then tomorrow we'll shoot and get out of here, right?"

"I intend to spend some time with Esther tomorrow. We'll

see. Better plan on being here a couple of days. We have to make sure we've got everything we need."

"Okay," he said, drawing the word out. "Just keep me in the loop, will you? I don't like being on the outside."

I watched him as he left, Esther's words ringing in my head. *"Some people are willing to protect their secrets at all costs."*

FIVE

"So what do you recommend?" I asked as I perused the menu at Randi's Oil Lamp Restaurant. According to Reuben, there were two restaurants in Sanctuary. The other one, The Whistle Stop Café, was only open for breakfast and lunch. Randi's was it for the Sanctuary resident who wanted to eat supper out. It was a charming little place with mismatched vinyl tablecloths and red and yellow plastic mustard and ketchup bottles. The air was heavy with the aroma of grease and grilled onions.

"Randi's got some great dishes," Reuben said with a smile. "Her cabbage casserole is incredible. And if you like liver and onions, you'll never have any better than hers."

Zac had decided to stay back at Esther's and clean his camera equipment. Honestly, I was relieved. His attitude grated on my nerves. Not having him around allowed me to relax a bit.

I happened to glance back toward the kitchen and noticed a man staring at me from a large pass-through window. An older man with sparse, graying hair and the features of a basset hound. His expression was less than welcoming. Surely visitors to Sanctuary weren't that unusual. I broke my gaze away from his and turned my attention back to ordering.

"Well, I'm up for liver and onions," I said.

Reuben nodded. "Sounds good to me too."

I glanced up and caught him looking at me. Every time I looked into his blue eyes, my heart beat a little faster. I had to remind myself that I wasn't here to pick up a Mennonite boy-friend. I had something much more important to accomplish.

"So tell me about Sanctuary," I said. "When was it founded? Was it always Mennonite?"

Reuben started to say something, but I held up my finger. "Wait a minute. Do you mind if I record this? I don't want to trust my memory."

"Sure, that's fine," he said, "but it's a little intimidating. What if I say something I want to take back later?"

I smiled. "Then I'll erase it. It's not like our conversation will end up in court or anything."

"I'm afraid that would be a pretty boring court case. Nothing very exciting ever happens here."

I fumbled through my purse for my phone. After several attempts, I finally gave up. "Must have left my phone in my room. Guess I'll have to do this the old-fashioned way." I pulled out the small notebook I always carried with me, along with a pen. "I'll just take notes. It will help us decide what we want in the interview." As I put my notebook on the table, I couldn't help but look back toward the kitchen once more. The cook was still there, but he was looking the other way. Good.

Before Reuben had a chance to respond, a young woman came up to our table with an order pad in her hand.

"Hey, Reuben," she said. "Who's your friend?"

"Evening, Randi." Reuben nodded toward me. "This is Wynter

Evans, a reporter from a television station in St. Louis. She's here with a photographer to do a story about Sanctuary. Wynter, this is Rachelle Lindquist," Reuben said, "the owner of this fine establishment. We all call her Randi."

"Nice to meet you." Her words were welcoming, but the look on her face echoed her cook's. Fortunately for her sake, she was much better looking. "Hope you won't make us all out to look like hicks," she said. "We're not, you know."

"We have no intention of presenting Sanctuary in a bad light," I said. "We're here because you have a unique town. This is just a human-interest piece, not an exposé. You have nothing to worry about."

The guarded expression on Randi's face slipped a bit, but the look in her eyes made me feel slightly defensive. What was it with these people? As soon as the thought entered my mind, the reality that I was here with ulterior motives hit me. I felt a quick stab of guilt.

"I'll hold you to that."

"Your cook seems upset," I said. "He's been giving me the evil eye ever since I sat down."

She shrugged. "Not my problem. Guess you'll have to take it up with him."

"Knock it off, Randi," Reuben said. "Wynter is our guest. Let's treat her with some respect."

"Respect is earned, Reuben," she snapped back. She swung her gaze back to me. "So what do you want to drink?"

Reuben and I ordered coffee.

"We'd also like to get something to eat," Reuben said. "Can you hold the poison?"

For the first time, a small smile flitted across Randi's face. "Yes, I think I can do that. I suppose you want the usual?"

Reuben shook his head. "No, I think tonight I'll try the liver and onions."

Randi's expression registered her surprise. "You never order liver. What's up with that?"

He grinned and looked at me. "Guess I'm just in a mood to try something new."

Randi pointed her pen at me. "And you?"

"Uh, liver and onions, please."

She raised an eyebrow but didn't say anything. Just wrote down my order. Then she grabbed our menus and walked away.

"Sorry about that," Reuben said as soon as Randi was out of hearing distance. "She's a little opinionated."

"A little?" I said with a smile.

He grinned. "I get your point." He cocked his head toward the kitchen. "Don't worry about August. He's our local curmudgeon, but he's harmless. I was just kidding about the poison, you know."

"I wasn't really worried about poison," I said. "But there are other rather disgusting things cooks can do to food if they're unhappy with you."

"Trust me. August isn't the kind of person who would do something like that. He takes great pride in his cooking."

"Well, that makes me feel a little better," I said, trying to smile. Despite Reuben's assurances, I decided to keep a close watch on the angry cook.

"So you were asking about how Sanctuary was founded," Reuben said. "Do you want me to talk about that now or after dinner?"

"Now's fine. Just tell me what you can. I'll stop you to ask questions when I need to, if that's all right."

He nodded. "Sounds good."

Before he had a chance to say anything else, Randi suddenly showed up with our coffee. "Here you go," she said. She took two cups of coffee off her tray and set them on the table.

I thanked her, but she didn't respond. Just tossed her head and walked away.

Reuben shook his head and chuckled. "Okay, one more time."

"Don't worry about it. Interruptions are par for the course. I'm used to it."

He took a sip of coffee and then put his cup down. "How did you become a reporter? Was it something you always wanted to do?"

I laughed. "Wait a minute. I'm supposed to be asking *you* the questions. Not the other way around."

"Hey, turnabout is fair play. You answer my question, I'll answer yours."

"Okay. No, not really. I got interested in high school after a local reporter spoke at one of our assemblies. Her life seemed interesting." I shrugged. "That's all there is to it. There wasn't any earth-shattering revelation or voice from the heavens telling me I'd found my calling." I smiled at him. "Can I ask an unofficial question before the actual interview begins?"

He nodded. "That's permissible."

"I'm surprised Sanctuary has a mayor. Especially one so young. How old are you?"

"I'm twenty-nine. I'll be thirty on Christmas Day."

"A Christmas baby, huh?"

Reuben laughed. "Yes. At least I know I'll never have to work on my birthday."

"I was surprised when we first met. I read something about Mennonites not believing in local government."

"You're right. It's only an honorary title. The state and county make decisions that affect us. Someone has to deal with them. The town chose me to do that."

"They voted for you?"

"Not really. We held a town meeting and the pastor of a local church stood up, suggested my name, and asked if anyone had a problem with using me to deal with whatever the local government threw our way. No one objected, so I was elected. Although I don't know if *elected* is really the right word to use."

I grinned. "Wow. I'm impressed. It sounds like a landslide."

"Well, more like gradual erosion. There wasn't anyone interested enough to stop it."

"You're pretty funny for a Mennonite."

Reuben's eyebrows shot up. "And what do you think a Mennonite is?"

"To be honest, I thought all the women would be wearing long dresses and head coverings—"

"They're called *prayer* coverings."

"Oh, sorry. Prayer coverings. And the men would be dressed in black pants, long-sleeved white shirts, and big black hats."

He nodded. "You're not entirely wrong. Some conservative Mennonites dress that way, but not all Mennonites are conservative. The modern Mennonite church isn't much different than most mainstream churches anywhere in the country."

"What are the differences?"

"A commitment to nonresistance and the belief that the church and the state should be separate."

I frowned. "But isn't that part of the problem in the world today? People trying to take God out of everything? Our schools and our government?"

He shrugged. "That's an argument you'd have to take up with someone who's Mennonite."

My jaw dropped. "I . . . I assumed—"

"I was Mennonite?" He shook his head. "No. I respect our Mennonite neighbors, but I'm not Mennonite. I attend a non-denominational church."

"Well, that's what I get for making assumptions."

He smiled. "Maybe we should get back to our interview."

"Okay. Here's my first official question. Can you tell me how this town was founded?"

He nodded. "German Mennonite immigrants came here in the 1800s. It was called New Zion back then. As the years progressed and residents died, it became what it is now. Still strongly Mennonite but integrated with people of other beliefs as well."

I hesitated a moment. "Something's bothering me. Esther said something about people living in Sanctuary having . . . secrets. Do you know what she meant?"

Reuben's mouth tightened just a little. "Sorry, but it's my turn." He stared at me for a moment. "You have the greenest eyes I've ever seen. Do you wear colored contacts?"

I smiled at him. "No contacts. Real eye color. Which is odd because everyone else in my family has brown eyes. They also have dark hair. I'm the only blonde."

"Anything your mother and father didn't tell you?"

"No. Just one of those weird genetic things. My mom was blond as a child. Now I get an extra question."

He started to protest, but I held up my hand. "You got an extra question. Turnabout is fair play."

He grinned. "Okay, just this once."

"Randi seemed a little . . . unfriendly. Is it just because she doesn't want us here, or is there something else?"

He colored slightly. "Oh, that. Sorry. We dated for a while, but it didn't take long for us to realize we weren't right for each other. We're just friends now."

I wasn't sure Randi was convinced they were *just friends,* but at least I knew her antagonism wasn't totally because of our story.

"Okay, we each got an extra question," I said. "Now, abide by the rules. Answer my original question."

"All right. People come to Sanctuary for many different reasons, Wynter. Some are simply tired of big-city life and big-city problems. Sanctuary is like . . . like stepping back into the past. We don't have crime here. No bars or liquor stores. No smutty book or video stores. We don't lock our doors. We believe in old-fashioned values, and God is welcome everywhere. We don't try to shut Him out the way the world does."

"But what if someone moved here and wanted to open a bar— or a smutty bookstore? Wouldn't they have the right to do it?"

"I think it's my turn."

I held my hand up. "Wait a minute. This is related to my other question. I should have the right for a follow-up."

He laughed easily; fine laugh lines crinkled at the corners of his eyes. "Okay. You win." He took another sip of his coffee as he considered his answer. "So far no one has tried to do anything like that. Why would they? There wouldn't be any support. Even if someone tried to open an . . . inappropriate business, how would they pull it off? There's nothing for sale here. We're all too protective of this town."

"So you're telling me that no one—meaning not one person—ever tried to buck the system?"

"Well, Randi used to joke about serving beer in her restaurant, but that's the extent of it. Like I said, she wasn't serious. Folks who live here know the rules."

"Rules? Are there really rules?"

He quickly shook his head. "No, maybe that wasn't a good way to say it. There aren't any written codes that we live by. No *Ordnung* like many Amish communities have. But we know what Sanctuary is—and we keep a close watch over it. It's as simple as that."

"But then . . ."

"Wait a minute. It's got to be my turn by now."

I smiled. "Okay. Go ahead."

"Is your name really Wynter?"

His question alarmed me. How had he zeroed in on the one thing I couldn't talk about? Warning bells went off in my mind. I'd have to be careful.

"No, it's not my real name. It's my on-air name. I picked it because I love winter. In fact, I was born in the middle of a snowstorm in a small Missouri hospital. There was only one nurse on duty that night, and she actually delivered me. The doctor didn't make it in until hours later."

"I like that story," Reuben said. "So what's your real name?"

"Follow-up?"

He nodded. "Follow-up."

"It's Emily."

His eyebrows arched in surprise. "A good old-fashioned name."

"I guess."

"Did you change your last name?"

"A little. Not much." I shook my head. "That's off-limits."

"Okay. Did you change your name because you didn't like it? Or was there another reason?"

"Off-limits," I said again.

Reuben studied me as if he could read my thoughts, and it made me uncomfortable. What was it about this man?

"I guess it's your turn," he said, watching me closely.

I tried to look as nonchalant as I could, even though his piercing gaze made me nervous. "Let me ask about your more conservative residents. I noticed a family out in front of the library today. The boy's name was . . . um, I think it was Elijah. He dropped his mother off at the library. They were dressed in Mennonite garb, and they rode up in a buggy. Can you tell me something about them? How they live?"

"I can tell you about them, but I'll warn you right now that they won't be seen on camera."

"Because they're conservative Mennonites?"

He nodded. "They don't believe in getting their pictures taken, and that would certainly apply to video."

"Okay, let's just use them as examples then. Tell me how they live. It will help me to understand people like them."

Reuben started to respond, but before he could, a man walked up to the table.

"Hey, mayor," he said with a smile. "Who is this pretty lady?" His bright blue eyes were inquisitive but kind. Longish thick black hair framed a handsome face. Obviously, Sanctuary was home to some good-looking men. If any of the single women I knew got a look at these guys, Sanctuary's visitor population would likely explode.

"Wynter Evans, meet Jonathon Wiese."

"Welcome to Sanctuary, Wynter," Jonathon said. "I heard journalists were in Sanctuary. You're the talk of the town."

I shook his hand and smiled up at him. "Seems like most of that talk is pretty negative. So how do you feel about it?"

"I think it's great. Sanctuary is a wonderful place. Should make an interesting spot in your feature. I doubt seriously if we're going to be run over by tourists or people wanting to move here. This town is certainly not everyone's cup of tea."

"With the recent popularity of Amish and Mennonite fiction, you might be surprised."

"They'd have to find a way to support themselves. There aren't any jobs in Sanctuary. We're far enough away from larger towns to make working there and living here impractical."

"Sounds like you've thought this out."

He chuckled. "You're right. I have."

"Jonathon would be a great person for you to interview," Reuben said. "He used to live in a strict Mennonite town in Kansas. He left there because he wanted more freedom."

"So you came here?" I said, with surprise. "Why not go somewhere more . . . modern?"

"Desiring more liberty doesn't mean I was ready to throw away my roots. I just wanted to stretch them a bit."

At that moment, Randi showed up with our plates. "Hey, Jonathon. Are you joining these folks for dinner?"

"No. Just stopping by to meet our guest. And to give her this." He held out a folded piece of paper in front of me. "I found this stuck on the windshield of the Prius outside. I was told it's your car. Thought I'd better bring it to you. It's a little windy, and I was afraid it might blow away."

"Thank you. I can't imagine what it is."

He shrugged. "I have no idea. Maybe it's from someone who wants to be interviewed for your special." He stuck his hand out. "Well, it was nice to meet you, Wynter. Let me know if I can help you in any way. You can catch me at the church during the day."

I shook his hand and smiled. "Thanks, I appreciate it."

"Nice guy," I said to Reuben as Jonathon walked away.

"Yes, he is. And he meant that about helping you."

"You all need anything else?" Randi asked.

"More coffee when you have a chance," Reuben said.

"Sure."

As soon as Randi walked away, I opened the folded piece of paper Jonathon had given me. Written in large block letters, someone had written GET OUT OF TOWN NOW OR YOU'LL BE SORRY!

CHAPTER
SIX

Even though I was tired and the bed at Esther's was comfortable, that night I had a hard time getting to sleep. The words in the letter kept running through my brain. Reuben had basically dismissed it. "We may be a Mennonite town," he'd said, "but we still have teenagers that like to pull pranks. There isn't anyone you need to worry about in Sanctuary." Maybe he was right, but I wasn't convinced. Esther's odd warning, combined with the note, pointed toward something darker. Something disquieting.

After lying in bed for an hour or so, I finally got up and decided to transcribe the notes I'd written at the restaurant to my computer files. I settled on the fainting couch, my laptop balanced on my lap. I was typing away when I felt something. Or maybe it was a movement caught by my peripheral vision. A quick look out the window next to me revealed a figure standing outside in the street, looking up toward my room. Fear gripped me, and I froze. The lamp was on, so whoever it was could clearly see me, yet I couldn't make out anything except an outline of a man.

I forced myself to move, putting down my laptop and swinging my legs over the side of the couch. Then I got up, clicked off the lamp, and went back to the window. A quick look outside revealed nothing. The street was empty. Had I really seen someone, or was my imagination working overtime? After sitting in the dark for another hour, I finally crawled into bed, falling asleep out of pure exhaustion.

Saturday morning I awoke to the aroma of bacon frying. Not my normal morning experience. A cup of yogurt or a granola bar was my usual breakfast fare.

The beautiful old bed was very comfortable, and my body craved a couple more hours of sleep. After staying under the covers for a few extra minutes while trying to shake off the last remnants of sleep, I finally sat up and lowered my feet onto the step stool. I definitely needed it to get out of the unusually high bed. The clock on the small table near the door read seven-thirty. Late for me. I usually got up by five every morning. Esther had told us breakfast would be ready at eight, so I got out of bed, quickly got dressed, and fixed my hair and makeup. I didn't have time to use my curling iron, so I fashioned my hair into a long braid.

After getting ready, I went over to the window and looked out. A few people were walking down the street, but no one was staring up at me. There was a lamppost across the street in the same spot where I thought I'd seen someone. Had my imagination turned the lamppost into a person? I shook my head. "You need to get a grip, Wynter," I said softly.

Although I was prepared to dismiss the idea that a man had been watching me last night, I was still upset about the note stuck on my car. And there was the problem of Zac. He was ready to leave town, and I was ready to see him go. Unfortunately, getting another photog now would be problematic. I couldn't ask Ed to send someone else. He'd know I was in Sanctuary. Somehow I had to keep Zac stable. Acting like I believed the note wasn't a serious threat was my only choice. My instincts told me the cook at Randi's restaurant wrote it. I noticed he'd taken a couple of breaks last night. Hopefully, he was exactly what Reuben had said—a cranky curmudgeon, no different than a toothless dog. Lots of bark but no ability to bite.

I was on my way downstairs when I heard Zac's door open. Good. The last thing I wanted was for him to offend our hostess by being late for breakfast. I really liked Esther.

"Good morning," she said cheerfully as I entered the dining room. "Have a seat. Everything is ready."

I surveyed the large oak dining table, loaded with platters of bacon, sausage, eggs, pancakes, fried potatoes, biscuits, gravy, and jam.

"I hope you're expecting a lot of company for breakfast. There's enough food here for twenty people."

She waved her hand at me dismissively. "I love to cook. Sometimes I ask my friends over for dinner, but I don't get to cook breakfast very often. This is a treat for me."

She pointed toward a chair, and I sat down, wondering how in the world I could make a dent in the huge feast.

"Wow. Something smells great."

Zac came into the room, his eyes wide with surprise. I hoped he was a big eater. If not, we would probably disappoint our hostess.

"You sit here, Zac," Esther said, pointing to a chair across from me. "I'll get some coffee and be right back."

"You'd better be hungry," I whispered to him. "I'm not really a breakfast eater."

"We're both going to have to rise to the challenge," he said. "We can't hurt her feelings."

I looked at him with surprise. "Since when did you start caring about anyone in this town?"

He grunted. "I like Esther. She's a good person." He picked up a napkin from the table and put it in his lap. "By the way. We need to talk."

"About what?"

Zac glared at me. "About why we're here when Ed told you to take Sanctuary off our list."

My mouth went dry. How could he know? Ed certainly wouldn't have shared information like that with a photog. Esther saved me from coming up with a response when she reentered the room carrying a carafe.

"Here, let me get that," Zac said, getting up from his seat.

"Thank you, Zac. It is a little heavy."

My mouth almost dropped open in surprise. I caught myself just in time. Zac had manners? Who knew?

Zac put the carafe down while Esther perused the table.

"I hope I didn't forget anything," she said softly.

He smiled. "Just more people to eat it all."

"I know I overdid it, but I wanted your first breakfast in Sanctuary to be a good one."

I nodded, but my mind was still focused on Zac's revelation. What should I tell him? How could I explain?

Esther sat down and folded her hands. "Would you like to say grace, Zac?"

My dumbfounded photog turned red. "Uh, I don't really . . . I mean, I'm not sure how . . ."

"I understand," Esther said. "What about you, Wynter? Do you pray?"

"Sure," I said, sounding more confident than I felt. It had been a while, but I gave it my best shot, asking God to bless our food and the woman who had welcomed us into her home. During my prayer, I snuck a sideways glance at Zac. His eyes were wide open and fixed on me. I almost stumbled over my words and had to force myself to concentrate.

"Thank you, dear," Esther said when I finished. "Now, both of you help yourself."

I spooned some scrambled eggs onto my plate, along with a couple of sausages and a helping of fried potatoes. Zac got a little of everything.

"This is delicious," I said after a couple of bites. "My mother used to make big breakfasts on the weekends, but that was before . . ." I choked back my words. I'd almost said *before my brother disappeared.*

"Before what, dear?" Esther said.

"Before . . . my parents' divorce."

Esther shook her head. "I am so sorry, Wynter. That must have been very hurtful for you."

"You get over it. Life goes on."

"But children need . . ." Esther was interrupted by a loud knocking on her front door. "Oh my," she said, getting up. "I can't imagine who that could be."

As she hurried off, Zac pointed at me. "We're not finished. I want to know what's going on."

Angry voices stopped any further conversation. Martha, the lady from the library, burst into the room, her face crimson and her expression angry. Reuben trailed behind her.

"There you are," Martha sputtered. "I should never have told you to come here. This is all my fault. I can't believe you could do something so . . . heinous."

I stood to my feet. "What in the world are you talking about?"

Martha stomped over to the table, a laptop in her hands.

"There's the evidence right there. Proof that you're trying to ruin our town."

I gazed down at the small screen and saw a picture. Upon closer inspection, I realized it was taken in Sanctuary. It was a photo taken out on the street, and it included several individuals. Their faces were clearly visible. I clicked over to several more candid shots of Sanctuary residents. People who obviously had no idea they were being photographed.

"Where did these come from?" I asked, flabbergasted. "I've never seen them before. We certainly didn't take them."

"Oh, really?" Martha snapped. "Just look." She reached over and scrolled down, revealing the sender's e-mail address.

"That's the station's address," I shook my head. "I'm totally confused. I had nothing to do with this. I didn't even bring my camera."

Martha scrolled down again and pointed at the e-mail message. "This is clearly a response from someone at your station confirming they received the photographs *you* sent. They say they just cc'd the library so you would be sure to get the information. Thank goodness they did, or you would have gotten away with it!"

It was true that I'd e-mailed Martha several times before coming to Sanctuary. It would make sense for someone at the station to copy an important message and send it to the library, since, as far as they knew, it was my only contact here. But how would that even happen? Ed had told us to forget Sanctuary, so he wouldn't have done it. Could it have come from someone else? It was highly unlikely. The only other person at the station who knew about Sanctuary was Megan, and this message hadn't come from her. She would have used her own e-mail account— and she would have included a personal note. Of course, even if I could figure out a way it *could* have happened—it didn't matter, since I hadn't sent the pictures in the first place. It was clear that someone was out to sabotage our efforts.

"Look, I have no idea what's going on, but I had nothing to do with this. As I said, I didn't even bring my camera."

"Well, I know you have a phone," Martha said. "I saw you using it."

"Of course I have a phone, but I didn't take any photos with it."

"Do you know where it is?" Reuben asked.

I shrugged. "I assume it's in my room. I haven't looked."

"Can you get it?"

"Sure." I wasn't sure what he was thinking, but I hurried up the stairs. After a brief search, I found my phone on the floor next to the nightstand. That explained why I'd missed seeing it last night. I grabbed it and went back downstairs. No one was talking as I entered the room. Martha still looked angry, Reuben's expression was solemn, and Zac looked bored.

I held up my phone. "I found it. It fell on the floor. That's why I didn't put it in my purse last night."

"Did you check it for pictures?" Reuben asked.

I frowned at him. "Of course not. Why would I?"

"Humor me," he said. "Take a look."

I sighed and brought up my pictures. My mouth dropped open. There they were. The same pictures that were sent to the library.

"I . . . I don't understand," I said, my voice barely above a whisper. I looked over at Reuben. "You have my word. I didn't take these. And I certainly didn't—" Suddenly something occurred to me. I pulled up a list of the last numbers I'd dialed. Triumphantly, I handed the phone to Reuben. "I didn't make any calls to the station yesterday at all. This proves I had nothing to do with those photos."

"Then why are they on your phone?" Martha said slowly. Her expression was celebratory, as if she'd caught me in a lie. "Are you saying someone stole your phone and snapped these pictures? That's pretty farfetched, isn't it?"

All I could do was nod. I knew how it sounded. "I have no idea how it happened, but someone is certainly going out of their way to cause trouble."

"No one in Sanctuary would do such a thing," Martha said with a sniff, her nose in the air.

"Well, it seems very convenient. You want us out of town, and these shots show up on your laptop. Odd, isn't it?"

Martha's already red face deepened until I began to worry about her blood pressure. If she had a stroke, I'd probably be blamed for that too.

"That's a lie. I would never—"

"Okay, that's enough," Reuben said. "We need to sort this out calmly." He put his hand on Martha's shoulder. "The important thing is that no one is going to get the chance to use these pictures." He looked at me. "Can you get rid of them? Make sure they don't go any further?"

"I'm not sure where they came from, but I assure you it'll be taken care of. If anyone from the station actually did see them, I'll instruct them to delete them immediately."

Reuben nodded. "Thank you. But before we proceed with your story, we need to have a serious talk. If we can't find a way to ensure people's privacy, we'll have to call this whole thing off."

"I understand. I really do. But you have my word. I'm not behind this."

Reuben studied the pictures closely. "I believe you. If these pictures really were taken with your phone, you couldn't have done it. First of all, as you said, you didn't have your phone last night. But even if you had, you didn't leave the restaurant until after dark. These were taken while it was still light." He straightened up. "You're definitely being set up." He pointed at the irate librarian. "Martha, go back to the library—and don't spread this around. I mean it."

She straightened her back and glared at him. "People have a right to know what's going on."

"Normally I would agree. But if word of this gets out, we might not be able to figure out who's behind it. And I want to know."

Martha started to protest, but he shook his head.

"Not now. You know me, Martha. I won't let anyone hurt this town. Especially not for a story that doesn't really need to be told. But *someone* took those pictures. Then they made sure you saw them. Obviously they didn't care if they threatened our peace of mind or put this sanctuary at risk. In my mind, they're more of a problem than these nice people." He nodded toward Zac and me. Esther, who had been quiet since Martha stormed in with her computer, added her agreement.

"I believe that is very wise counsel, Reuben," she said. "Deceit and manipulation should not be taken lightly."

Esther's words were like a knife in my heart. I hadn't been honest with anyone since I'd stepped foot in Sanctuary. Whoever took those pictures wasn't alone in their attempt to manipulate these good people.

"Go on back to the library, Martha," Reuben admonished.

Although it was obvious she wasn't happy with this turn of events, Martha grabbed her computer and stormed out of the house.

Reuben sat quietly for a moment before taking a deep breath and staring at me, an odd look on his face. "There is only one person who could have done this, Wynter. You know who that is, don't you?"

It took me only a few seconds to realize the truth. "You're right." We both turned our heads to stare at the person sitting next to Esther. "It's you," I said. "You did this, Zac."

CHAPTER

SEVEN

"Denying it won't work."

We sat alone at the dining room table. Reuben had already left, asking me to call him later. Esther had excused herself to clean the kitchen so Zac and I could be alone.

"You can't prove—"

"Stop it. It had to be you. I have no choice but to send you back to the station."

He glowered at me. "But then Ed will find out the truth. That you went to Sanctuary after he told you not to. We seem to have a standoff here."

I sighed and put my head in my hands, thinking. There was no way I could leave yet. But how could I stay and still keep my job? I had no choice. There was only one thing left to do.

"Okay, Zac. I'm going to tell you the truth. Why I'm really here. After I'm done, I want you to explain why you felt the need to take those pictures and try to sabotage this story."

He shrugged. "Whatever."

I took a deep breath, praying I wasn't making a mistake I couldn't rectify. "When I was thirteen years old, my seven-year-old brother disappeared. At first, my parents thought he'd been kidnapped and was being held for ransom. We were rather wealthy back then. My father owned a large mortgage banking company. So they waited for a phone call. It never came. Then the bodies of young boys stared popping up about fifty miles away from where we lived in Chicago. The police were convinced the same serial killer took Ryan, even though his body was never recovered. My father believes he's dead. That was almost ten years ago. For years after he went missing, I woke up with nightmares. Terrible dreams where he was calling to me, and I was trying to find him."

"No one ever mentioned this at work," Zac said, his voice heavy with skepticism. "Seems something like that would be common knowledge at a news station."

"Ed knows. I told him when I first came to work at KDSM. He's never revealed the truth to anyone. When I got out of college, I changed my name from Emily Erwin to Wynter Evans. I got a new name because . . . well, I needed a fresh start. A new identity. I didn't want to be known as the girl whose brother was kidnapped. Can you understand that?"

"I guess. But what does that have to do with Sanctuary?"

"I . . . I saw a picture, Zac. Of a young man who looks a lot like Ryan. He's here. In Sanctuary." I held my hands up as a sign of surrender. "It's very possible I'm deluding myself. Everyone else gave up on Ryan years ago. But I . . . I just can't. I still have those dreams. I still hear him calling me. How can I ignore that?"

"Wow." Zac's normally insolent expression softened. "You said your father gave up on your brother. What about your mother?"

"We don't talk to her about Ryan. She had a breakdown after

he went missing. My father couldn't deal with it, and they split up. Losing Ryan destroyed my family. My father and I rarely speak, and my mother . . . well, we're close, but it's not the same. She's better now, but when we're together, it feels like someone's missing. We remind each other of Ryan, I guess."

"I-I'm sorry, Wynter. I had no idea."

"I appreciate that. But now I need the truth from you. Why did you take those pictures and send them to the station?"

He sighed. "Because I'm a selfish idiot." He stood up and walked over to the window behind us. "Missy Spencer told me that if I ruined this story for you, she'd make sure I got all the plush assignments at the station. I took those pictures yesterday, sent them to the station and then called and asked them to copy the library so we'd know they received them."

"I can't believe you'd actually do something like that."

He turned back toward me. "Well, believe it. Missy knows you're being considered for the anchor chair. She wanted to knock you out of the running. She figured if you blew this story, she'd become Ed's first choice."

"I knew she hated me, but I had no idea she'd go to these lengths."

Zac came over and sat down again. "I should have told her to take a hike, but it seemed like a smart career move. Somehow, I lost sight of the fact that you're a human being with feelings and . . . problems." He shook his head. "You may not believe this, but I was raised to care about people. My mother . . ." He cleared his throat and looked away for a moment. After a deep sigh he said, "My mother is a Christian. She tried to teach me to put other people first. Guess I didn't listen."

"But you said you hated being around religious people."

"It's a long story, and this isn't the time for it. The important thing is that we're finally being honest with each other. And I'd like to help you, Wynter. Really. No more tricks, I promise. I'm sorry for being such a jerk. It's not who I really am."

"I don't know if what you did can be fixed, Zac."

"I sent the pictures to a friend of mine, Amy, another photog. After she sent the e-mail, I called her and asked her to dump the pictures and delete the e-mails. I didn't want this thing to be traced back to me. That's when I found out we weren't even supposed to be here."

"What if she tells Ed?"

He shook his head. "She won't. We keep each other's secrets."

"I hope you're right," I said. "I won't leave Sanctuary until I know for certain that young man isn't my brother."

Zac stared silently at me for a moment. "Wynter," he said finally, "if Ed knows the truth about your past, wouldn't he understand why you need to be here?"

"When he hired me, I promised to put the past behind me. Ed made it clear he wasn't looking for someone who was so wrapped up in her own story that she couldn't be trusted to put the interests of the station first. You know Ed." I lowered my voice. "'The story comes first. It's all about the story.'"

My attempt at sounding like Ed made Zac smile. "But you have a real lead. That should make a difference."

"No, I don't. I've found a boy who looks somewhat like my brother. That's it. I have no reason to believe he's Ryan. This is probably an exercise in futility. It's just . . ." I bit my lip, unwilling to continue.

"That you have to know."

I nodded. "I intend to proceed very carefully. I'm not looking to destroy my career. Nor do I want to cause these nice people any trouble. I need to do some digging. Some investigative reporting. I've done it before for a story. Now I'm doing it for myself. If I find out this teenager, this Elijah, isn't Ryan, we'll finish the story, head out of here, and get back to the station. No harm, no foul."

"But how long can we remain in Sanctuary before Ed gets suspicious?"

"I don't know. We'll probably have to take a few quick trips to some of the other towns on our list while we're here." I lowered my voice so I wouldn't be overheard. "I've seen Elijah only once. Somehow I've got to get some time with him—or with someone who knows him."

Zac's eyes darted toward the closed door to the dining room. "Seems to me Esther would be the best source for your questions. She's lived here forever. She'd know when Elijah came to Sanctuary."

"You're right. But I've got to be careful. I'm afraid if I show my hand . . . let anyone know why I'm really here . . . they'll kick us out."

"What about calling the police?"

I shook my head. "Not yet. Not until I'm sure he's Ryan. You heard Reuben. There are people here who value their anonymity. I don't want to endanger them for no reason."

Zac forced back a yawn. "Sorry. Didn't sleep too well last night."

"Guilty conscience?"

"Yes. And believe it or not, I do have a conscience. Just haven't listened to it much lately. By the way, have you wondered why people are hiding out here? I mean, this town doesn't look like the kind of place where hit men and Mafia bosses would retire."

"Yeah, I've thought about it. My guess is the name *Sanctuary* means something. Maybe some folks are here for their own safety. If I've actually found Ryan, I wonder what will happen to this town. The truth could cause a media firestorm. Who would I be putting in danger?"

"I see your point. So what's our next move?"

I smiled at his use of the word *our*. "Zac, you need to think about this carefully. If Ed finds out I didn't follow orders, we could lose our jobs. Maybe you should head home. Tell Ed you're sick or something."

He shook his head. "No. I want to stay. For the first time in a long time, I feel like I'm doing something that matters." He cocked his head to the side and gave me a lopsided grin. "You and me, Wynter. Sherlock and Watson. Nick and Nora Charles. Castle and Beckett."

I chuckled. "We may be more like Laurel and Hardy, but I appreciate it, Zac. Really. I'll be careful. Try to protect both our jobs."

"That's good enough for me." He folded his arms across his chest. "Is there anyone else who could help us? Someone who might know something about Ryan's abduction?"

"Just one person, but I dread calling him."

Zac raised his eyebrows. "Who is that?"

"My dad. He knows everything about the case, and his memories of Ryan are much clearer than mine. But I really don't want to contact him unless I have to."

"Okay. Whatever you say."

Zac reached for his coffee cup and took a quick sip. Then he set his cup down on the table. "So, Sherlock. The game is afoot?"

I smiled at him and nodded, but doubts filled my heart. Had

I just made a serious mistake? Could I really count on Zac? For a woman who didn't trust many people, I'd just delivered myself into the hands of a man who had tried to betray me once already.

My hand shook slightly as I took a sip of cold coffee. I'd made myself vulnerable, and I didn't like it. Not one bit.

EIGHT

"Do you think Martha will keep quiet about the pictures?" I asked Reuben. We'd stopped for lunch at The Whistle Stop Café after a walking tour of Sanctuary. Reuben had introduced me to several people who'd agreed to let me interview them. I was charmed by the small town and its eclectic residents. It was clear that this piece of our story would be very interesting. Boiling it down to a few minutes would be tough.

The Whistle Stop was almost an exact duplicate of The Oil Lamp, except the owner, who seemed to be working all alone in the restaurant, was softer and sweeter than Randi. And when she went to the kitchen to cook, she didn't glower at me the way August had.

I'd left Zac at Esther's. He'd phoned Reuben in person after breakfast and confessed to taking and sending the pictures. I knew it was hard for him, but to his credit, he was completely honest and took full responsibility for his actions. However, he wasn't quite ready to face Reuben yet and had elected to skip lunch to do some online research about Ryan's disappearance. Since I was still full from breakfast, I ordered a small salad.

Reuben was already on his second helping of chili. His lean frame contradicted his zest for food.

"Yes. I explained what happened. She was upset but also relieved that the pictures didn't go any farther than her computer. I'm thankful Zac admitted the truth about what he did."

I nodded. "I am too, but—"

"You're not sure you can trust him now?"

"Exactly."

Reuben frowned. "He took a chance, you know. Telling you everything."

"I know." I sighed and shook my head. "I have a very hard time trusting people."

"And why is that, Wynter? Someone hurt you?"

I stared into his cobalt-blue eyes. "Long story. Not very interesting."

"It is to me."

I cleared my throat to give myself a moment to think. How much should I tell this man? In the end, I went with the partial truth.

"My parents divorced when I was sixteen. The divorce left my mother scarred and my father absent. He remarried, got a new family, and walked out on his old one. I guess I'm not in a rush to put myself in another situation where I can be rejected again."

Reuben's eyebrows shot up. "That's pretty intuitive. Most people don't understand why they react the way they do."

"Sure," I said with a quick smile. "I may be damaged, but at least I know why."

Reuben didn't laugh at my attempt to lighten the tone of our conversation. "I've found trying to protect yourself from pain usually makes it worse. Life hurts sometimes, Wynter. But getting caught in the past can destroy the good life God has planned for you."

I grunted. "Maybe God only has a plan for special people. I've decided to take over my life and do what I want with it. If He doesn't like it, He'll have to tell me."

Reuben put his spoon down. "That sounds pretty cynical."

"I-I'm sorry. That didn't come out the way I wanted. I mean, I believe in God. I'm not trying to be rebellious; it's just that I can't give control of my life over to someone I don't understand."

"Do you go to church?"

"I used to, when I was a kid. But I quit going after . . . after my parents' divorce. I don't feel the need to be part of organized religion. Too many hypocrites there."

Reuben smiled. "Maybe that's why we need churches. To help the hypocrites."

"My mother says the same thing. She keeps asking me if I'm back in church. I know it upsets her when I say no." I speared a big, juicy piece of tomato with my fork. "I'll find a church someday, I guess. But right now, I'm too busy."

Reuben didn't say anything, just went back to his bowl of chili. For some reason something my Sunday school teacher once said reverberated in my head. *"We should never be too busy for God, children. He wasn't too busy to give His life for us."*

Why in the world was I thinking about that now? I shook my head as if I could jiggle the unsettling thought out of my brain. It didn't work. It kept echoing in my mind while Reuben talked. I tried to listen, but by the time my thoughts were clear again, I was lost.

"I'm sorry," I said finally. "Could you repeat what you just said? I get a little distracted sometimes."

"Sorry. I have a tendency to drone on and on."

"No, it's not you. Really. You were saying something about the people who live in Sanctuary?"

"Yes. I was explaining that no one here is hiding out from the law, if that concerns you. We don't shelter criminals."

"I wondered about women hiding from their abusers. This would be the perfect place to start over. If you like small towns."

Reuben nodded. "That might be true. And releasing the wrong information could put someone in danger."

I couldn't hold back an exasperated sigh. "Then why are we here?"

Reuben smiled slowly. "Martha's initial enthusiasm opened the door. Several of us tried to shut it, but it was too late."

My mouth dropped open. "You were one of the people who called my station?"

"Yes. I asked your boss to reconsider using Sanctuary for your special. From what he said, I assumed he'd agreed. I was surprised when you showed up."

"When we met, you didn't act surprised. I got the impression you wanted us here."

He shrugged. "You were already in town. I was afraid asking you to leave would just make things worse. You know, reporters smelling a story. I figured if we gave you what you wanted, within reason, you'd leave. It seemed like the safest choice."

"I didn't come here to exploit this town, Reuben."

"I know that now." He nodded quickly and stared down at his bowl.

"You could ask us to leave, you know. It would be the safest choice, wouldn't it?"

He wiped his mouth with his napkin and met my gaze. "I don't want you to go, Wynter. I like you, and I want some time to get to know you a little better." He blinked several times but didn't break eye contact. "Maybe that sounds selfish."

The usual protective wall that automatically went up when a man expressed interest in me stayed in place for a reason I couldn't begin to understand. Finally I said, "No. Not really."

There was a long silence, but it wasn't the least bit uncomfortable. Instead, it felt restful. Calm. Suddenly, the last time I saw Ryan popped into my head. *Stay focused, Wynter. You're here to find your brother. Nothing else matters.*

We finished our lunch and left, walking back through town toward Esther's. It was a lovely spring day. A light breeze kept us cool, and the smell of honeysuckle surrounded us like a soft, sweet perfume. Reuben took me to a quilt shop that was closed when we'd first walked through town. I met Rachel Stolz and her mother, Beatrice. Their quilts were lovely, and I decided to buy one before I left Sanctuary. Being conservative Mennonites, they declined an on-air interview but agreed to let us get some footage of the store and some of the quilts.

We'd just left when a stocky woman walked up to us, a big smile on her face.

"Howdy, Mayor," she said loudly. Although she addressed Reuben, her eyes were glued on me.

"Hello, Rae," he said. "Visiting a patient in town?"

She nodded. Short and round, hair cut like a man's and dressed in overalls, she exuded a kind of enthusiastic presence. She stuck out her hand. "I'm Mady Rae Buettner. Everyone calls me Rae."

I took her hand and shook it. Strong grip. "Nice to meet you, Rae. Wynter Evans. I'm from a television station in St. Louis, here to do a story on Sanctuary."

She let go of my hand and nodded. "I heard you were in

town." Her broad smile widened. "You don't look like much of a threat."

I laughed. "Thank you. I don't feel like one."

"Rae is our town's veterinarian," Reuben said. "She not only takes care of our pets, but she also looks out for our horses and livestock."

"I love animals," Rae said. "It's people I'm not too fond of sometimes."

"I understand," I said with a smile. "I'm a cat person."

"What kind of kitty you got?"

"A Persian. Named Mr. Henderson."

Rae clapped her large hands together. I noticed that they didn't look completely clean. "After Sally Rogers's cat in *The Dick Van Dyke Show*?"

I grinned. "Yes. I love to watch reruns of that old show. Most people don't make the connection."

Rae put her head back and guffawed. "Most people aren't as old as me, honey." She pointed at Reuben. "You need to get Lazarus in for his booster shot, Mr. Mayor. I expect to see him next week, you hear?"

Reuben smiled at her. "Yes, ma'am. I'll call and set up a time."

"Good." She patted me on the back. "Nice to meet you, honey. Hope you get whatever you need for your story."

"Me too. Thank you, Rae."

I watched the large woman lumber away. She stopped and talked to several other people on the street. She seemed to be well-liked by the residents.

"Nice lady," I said to Reuben as we began walking.

"Not only nice, but a real blessing to this town. Some of our residents are farmers. If they need help before they sell their harvest, Rae carries them. She's taken care of several animals for free. I've never seen her turn away an animal that needed help. We had to use a vet in Barnes before Rae got here almost two years ago. He wasn't as compassionate as she is."

"I guess that's why so many people like small towns. That feeling of family."

"Yes, it's why we look out for one another. Rae doesn't go to church, but she's still a valued member of this town. People accept her as she is."

"Sanctuary's certainly not a big town, but with the many farm animals and pets, how can one woman take care of all of them?"

"She doesn't. Esther's friend and neighbor, Janet Dowell, helps out. Janet's a vet. They both stay pretty busy."

"Esther mentioned her. Said she's a close friend."

"She is. Janet stays to herself, but she and Esther have a special bond."

The cautious look on his face led me to suspect Janet was one of Sanctuary's *special* people. "I take it Janet's not someone I should interview?"

Reuben frowned. "I would appreciate it if you didn't approach her."

"Look, Reuben. I'm certain I can include Sanctuary in our special and protect everyone's privacy at the same time. We'll do a little about how the town was founded. Maybe use Martha, since she runs the library and is such a history buff. Then we'll show some of your businesses, talk to a few people who want to be on camera, and that's it. No sweeping shots. No group shots. Up close and personal. That should ensure we don't get the wrong people on film."

"I think I can round up a few more interviews for you," he said. "Why don't you let me take care of that?"

"Sure. Thanks. You know, it would be great if we could get

at least one person on camera that is more . . . conservative. I know that might be a problem, but we're presenting Sanctuary as a Mennonite town."

"I told you that most of our citizens *are* Mennonite."

"I get that. But we're here because Sanctuary is different. One of the most important reasons you're special is because of your conservative residents. I would hate to ignore that part of what makes this town unique. Even if we could get someone in the background. Just so we could see how they're dressed. No faces. We'll hear them but won't see them."

Reuben shook his head slowly. "Maybe."

I cleared my throat, trying not to look as nervous as I felt. "What about that boy . . . what was his name? Uh, Elijah? Do you think he might be willing to help us?"

"I don't know. Maybe, if he won't actually appear on camera. I'll ask his parents. They've been in Sanctuary a long time. Nothing to hide that I know of." He smiled. "Guess I make it sound like we're a den of spies. I hope you don't get the wrong idea."

I shook my head. "No. After thinking about it, I realize that a lot of people move to small towns because they're trying to get away from something." I took a sip of my iced tea and noticed my hand shook slightly. "You said Elijah's family had been here a long time. Was Elijah born here?"

"No. I've been in Sanctuary six years. They'd only been here a couple of years before I came. They used to live in Jamesport, an Amish town. Have you heard of it?"

"Yeah. Our station did a special on the Amish a couple months ago. Because of that, I can't include them in this piece."

"Too bad. They would have welcomed you with open arms. They cater heavily to tourists."

"So the Amish town would welcome us, but the more progressive Mennonite town doesn't want us here? That's a little confusing."

He shrugged. "Different towns have different spirits, Wynter. Sanctuary is a wonderful town full of incredible people. We just—"

I grinned. "I know. Have secrets."

Reuben laughed. "No matter how you say that, it doesn't sound right."

"So the Fishers were Amish?"

He shook his head. "No, they've always been Mennonite. There are quite a few Mennonite families in Jamesport."

"Can you tell me a little bit more about Elijah and his family?"

He rubbed his chin, which sported a day's worth of stubble. Normally, I liked a clean-shaven face, but for some reason, on Reuben, the unshaven look worked.

"Well, Elijah's father, Nathan, is a farmer. They have a beautiful farm not far from town. His mother, Anna, is a very sweet woman. They're leaders in the church."

"Which church? I noticed two when we came into town."

Reuben nodded. "That's right. Sanctuary Mennonite is the more conservative church. That's where the Fishers attend. The other church is Agape Fellowship. We have Mennonite roots, but it's much more liberal."

"How liberal?"

Reuben grinned. "Not that liberal. We're nondenominational—similar to other mainstream churches, but we haven't completely shaken off our Mennonite roots. We still believe in simplicity, but only as a choice we make—not as a directive from the church."

"How do the two churches get along?"

"Great. We support and respect each other. We have dinners

and activities together. Sanctuary Mennonite is just a place where our conservative residents feel more comfortable. Some of them were brought up in strict Old Order or Amish homes. Although they've moved beyond a lot of the restrictions, they aren't willing to discard all the traditions they were raised with." He shrugged. "Frankly, I agree with many of the doctrines they endorse. I just don't choose to live as starkly as they do."

"So the Fishers are very involved in the church?"

"Yes. Nathan is an elder."

"And who is the pastor?"

Someone called out Reuben's name, and he waved to an elderly man sitting on a bench across the street. "Jacob Troyer is their pastor. And you met the pastor of Agape yesterday."

I frowned at him.

"Jonathon Wiese."

"Wow, he seems pretty young to hold a position like that."

"He's a little older than he looks, but he's younger than some, I guess. He went through seminary, so he's fully qualified. He's a great pastor."

"I think it's wonderful the two churches work together so well. Not sure that happens much in other towns."

"We all work hard to keep the peace."

"And then some woman from a television station waltzes in and turns everything upside down?"

"That's about it." He chuckled. "Don't worry. We've weathered worse storms than you. You're only a minor squall."

"Gee, thanks. No one ever called me that before."

Reuben laughed. "I'll call the Fishers and see if they'd be willing to talk to you."

"That would be great. I'd really like to meet them. Even if

they don't want to be on camera, I'd love to ask them a few questions."

He shrugged. "We'll have to see. I wouldn't get your hopes up though." His eyebrows suddenly shot up as he looked at something over my shoulder. "Good timing. There's Elijah. Would you like me to introduce you?"

I tried to stay calm, but turning around and seeing Elijah walk toward us startled me. I tried to say yes, but somehow I choked on the word. All I could do was nod.

Reuben looked at me with concern. "Are you all right? Maybe this isn't a good time."

I waved my hand at him. "No, I'm fine." My voice came out in a whisper. I took a deep breath and nodded. "Really, I'm okay. Just a tickle in my throat."

"Okay." He still looked a little alarmed, but he called out Elijah's name.

I don't know what I expected. That somehow we'd look at each other, and I'd instantly know the truth. But it didn't happen that way. As Reuben introduced the young man, I studied him closely. The resemblance to Ryan was startling—but there were differences. Elijah's hair was darker. Almost black. Ryan's had been light-brown. Of course, aging could explain that. My father's hair darkened as he grew older. Elijah's jaw was stronger. Not unusual for a boy on the verge of becoming a man.

"Elijah, this is Wynter Evans. She works at a television station in St. Louis."

"Yes, I heard you were here."

The young man's voice didn't ring any bells. Of course, I hadn't heard my brother speak in nine years, and I couldn't remember what he sounded like. Besides, his voice would have deepened by now.

"I'm glad to meet you, Elijah." I searched his face for any sign of recognition. I'd changed since my teenage years, but probably not so much my brother couldn't make the connection. There was nothing abnormal in Elijah's reaction. Yet somehow I felt . . . something.

"Wynter is doing a story about Sanctuary," Reuben said. "She wondered if she might be able to interview you for it. Off camera. She wants to know more about your conservative lifestyle. Would you be willing to do that?"

Elijah was silent for a moment but finally shrugged. "I don't know. I'll have to check with my parents."

"Thank you, Elijah," I said. "Reuben says you've lived in Sanctuary about seven or eight years?"

He nodded. "Before that, we lived in Jamesport. My father inherited some farmland outside of town from one of his brothers, so we moved here."

I cleared my throat, partially because it still felt odd after my choking experience but also because I was nervous. "And how long did you live in Jamesport, Elijah?"

"I was born there."

If what he said was true, he couldn't be my brother. When he spoke, I noticed his pupils dilated slightly, and he looked away. I'd read a book once about how to tell if someone was lying. I figured it might come in handy during interviews. Reporters were frequently pulled into fantastic tales by people who just wanted to be on TV. Being able to differentiate between those who were dishonest and those who told the truth was critical. If I believed the signs I'd learned from that book, Elijah Fisher had just lied to me.

"Why don't you talk to your parents and let Wynter know about the interview?" Reuben said. "If they have any questions,

tell them to talk to me. I can assure them you won't be filmed."
He looked over at me. "You don't have to use his name either,
do you?"

"No. Not if his parents are uncomfortable about it."

Reuben swung his gaze back to Elijah. "How does that
sound?"

"It sounds all right to me, but like I said, my parents will have
to make the final decision. I'll talk to them and let you know."
He nodded at me. "It was very nice to meet you, Miss Evans."

"It was nice to meet you too, Elijah. I hope to talk to you
soon."

I watched as he walked away. The entire time we talked, he'd
seemed nervous and distracted. I hadn't spent much time around
teenage boys. Maybe I was reading too much into his manner-
isms.

Or maybe Elijah Fisher had recognized me.

CHAPTER

NINE

By the time I got back to Esther's, Zac had caught up on my brother's case. He ushered me into his room and shut the door.

"I don't think we should do this very often," I said, once the door was closed. "I don't want Esther to think something's going on."

Zac snorted. "You're not really my type."

"Thanks. But not the point."

"I get it."

"I met some people in town. Got permission to do a couple of interviews. Have some ideas about what we can film. It's still not enough. Reuben's going to set up some other interviews for us. Hopefully, we can start filming soon."

"Sounds good," Zac said. He sounded distracted, and it worried me. Although my priority for being here was to find my brother, we still needed to work on the story. Ed wasn't going to be happy to find I'd ignored his directive to avoid this town. Our only way around incurring his wrath was to do an exceptional job on the Sanctuary piece. All I could do was hope it would be enough to save our jobs.

Zac went over to his laptop, which he'd put on the bed. He'd pulled a stool up next to it to create a makeshift workspace. "I've found a lot of information, but I wish we could talk to someone official. It would really help."

I pushed away my concerns about our story and switched my focus to what Zac was saying. "I have a contact in the St. Louis police department, but I hesitate to call him. We use him for news stories. If I get in touch with him, he might tell someone at the station."

"It's possible he couldn't help us much anyway. The case is pretty cold."

"I know. Besides, I've spent the last few years doing all the research I can. I even talked to one of the detectives that worked on Ryan's case. I don't think speaking to someone who had nothing to do with the original investigation would uncover anything I don't already know." I sighed. "It would help if Harland Burroughs, the serial killer suspected of taking Ryan, hadn't been killed in prison."

"Did he ever admit to kidnapping your brother?"

"No. According to the detective, Burroughs talked in length about the boys whose bodies were found. Like he was proud of what he'd done. But anytime he was asked about Ryan, he clammed up. Wouldn't say anything. The authorities were so intent on finding my brother, they decided to offer Burroughs a deal. Life in prison instead of the death penalty. Not something they wanted to do. But in an effort to find Ryan, they were willing to try anything. Unfortunately, Burroughs was murdered by an inmate before they had the chance."

"Why was he killed?"

I shrugged. "I guess even criminals have a code of honor. Child killers and abusers are targeted in prisons. The police suspect a guard purposely left him vulnerable, but it was never proven."

"Well, even without talking to the police or Burroughs, it didn't take long for me to notice something odd about your brother's case."

I peered over his shoulder and looked at the information he'd pulled up on his computer. "There are a lot of strange things about his abduction."

Zac stared up at me, his hazel eyes full of concern. "Harland Burroughs killed eleven boys. Every single body was discovered. He didn't try to hide them. As you said, he was proud of himself. So why wasn't Ryan found? It doesn't make sense." He pulled up a different screen. "Here is Burroughs's kill zone. You know that killers have an area of comfort. All the other boys were taken from this ten-mile radius. But Ryan was way out of this zone." His eyes narrowed as he stared at me. "Also, Ryan had brown hair. Every other boy was blond. Ryan was seven. All the other boys were between twelve and fifteen. No matter how you look at it, Ryan doesn't fit Burroughs's profile."

"These are the same things I found, and the inconsistencies bothered me too."

"Did anyone else bring this up with the police at the time?"

"I asked the detective that question. They were convinced the similarities outweighed the differences."

"What about your parents? Did they have problems with the way things were handled?"

"I have no idea. I was just a kid when Ryan went missing. My parents tried to shield me from the details. I didn't even know about Burroughs until I saw something on TV. My father and I didn't talk about what happened until I was almost twenty."

"And what did he say?"

"Not much. Just the basics. I asked him if Ryan might still be alive, but he didn't believe it. He said Ryan would have tried to contact us."

Zac was quiet as he considered this. "Did Ryan know his address and phone number?"

I shrugged. "I honestly don't know. Our home wasn't normal before he was taken. I get the impression most kids would be taught to memorize that kind of information, but I don't remember anyone sitting us down and teaching us much of anything."

Zac frowned. "What do you mean?"

I sat down in the chair across from the bed. "My father started drinking a couple of years before Ryan disappeared. Most of my mother's attention went to him. My brother and I got what was left over. After Ryan went missing, my father stopped drinking . . . for a while. I think he was trying to be strong for my mother. Then he started up again and eventually left. My mother lost her son and her husband in the span of a few years. No one should have to go through that."

"Maybe Ryan wanted to contact you but didn't know how."

"All he had to do was ask someone for help. His story was all over the media."

Zac sighed. "Burroughs was a hot topic. The media highlighted all the boys he abducted, not just Ryan. I think your brother was lumped together with the other cases. There aren't many stories just about Ryan. I hate to say it, but the enormity of Burroughs's crimes may have helped to cover up your brother's case."

"I hadn't thought about it like that," I said slowly, "but I see what you mean. Maybe someone saw him, but no one really remembered one boy's face from the long list of pictures in the paper." I thought a moment. "But that doesn't explain why Ryan didn't tell someone he needed help."

"What about Elizabeth Smart? She was fourteen. Twice Ryan's age. She didn't try to get away, and by all accounts she came from a very happy family. Then there's Jaycee Dugard and Shawn Hornbeck."

"You're talking about Stockholm syndrome," I said. I took a deep breath. "All of those children were—"

Zac held up his hand. "I know that, Wynter. But not all cases of Stockholm syndrome include physical or sexual abuse. Emotional manipulation makes kids easy targets. And with problems at home—"

"Ryan would have been a perfect candidate for a kidnapper."

"Almost makes you wonder if the kidnapper knew that."

"I doubt it," I said. "He just happened to pick a vulnerable kid. Who knows? Ryan might not have been his first attempt that day."

Zac nodded. "Any reports of other children being approached?"

I shrugged. "Not that I know of. No one ever mentioned it to me."

"So, if Ryan's alive, and he was kidnapped, how in the world could he end up in a Mennonite town with a family that loves him?"

"I have no idea. Before they came here they lived in Jamesport."

"The Amish town? So they were Amish?"

"No. According to Reuben, they were always Mennonite. Jamesport has Amish and Mennonite families."

"Correct me if I'm wrong, but I'd guess most kidnappers aren't Amish or Mennonite. Kind of hard to make a getaway in a horse and buggy." Zac stared at his computer screen for a moment. Then he snapped his fingers. "Wait a minute. We're missing something important here. What better place to hide out than in an Amish or Mennonite town? Limited media access. Not much connection to the outside world." He looked up at me, his eyes wide. "It makes a strange kind of sense, doesn't it?"

I frowned back at him. "Yes. But I just can't see conservative Mennonite people kidnapping a young boy. Doesn't fit with their religion."

He snorted. "Religion. A lot of evil things have been done in the name of religion."

I exhaled sharply, "And a lot of good has been done as well."

He shook his head. "Let's stay focused." He closed his eyes for a moment, obviously thinking. Suddenly his eyes snapped open. "What if the person who took Ryan wasn't Mennonite? What if he gave him or sold him to a Mennonite family?"

This time I couldn't hold back a laugh. "You mean like the Amish Mafia?"

"No, Wynter. I'm not joking. What if the family didn't know he was abducted? What if they thought they were just giving him a home? The kidnapper could tell them the boy was an orphan. Maybe even set it up like an adoption."

I stood up and walked over to the window. As I stared out at the town of Sanctuary, I tried to make sense of his question. "Why in the world would someone kidnap a child and set up a phony adoption with a Mennonite family? I don't think most Mennonite people would have large sums of money. Couldn't have been very profitable."

"I know the premise is a little confusing. But you have to admit that hiding someone in a town like Sanctuary would be a great way to keep a kidnapped kid from the prying eyes of the world."

"I . . . I guess it would, but I still think someone trying to profit from stealing a child would approach a family with lots of money. Not a simple Mennonite family."

Zac started to say something else, but I turned and raised my hand to stop him.

"It's almost three o'clock, and I promised Esther we'd talk." I walked over and patted him on the back. "Look, I appreciate everything you're doing. A lot of what you say is logical. Especially about Burroughs. Frankly, I'm beginning to think you picked the wrong side of the news. You could be a great investigative reporter."

He smiled, but I could see the intensity in his eyes. "Maybe the money side of the adoption scenario doesn't make sense, but the rest of it does. It's possible there's something else behind this besides money."

"Thank you, Zac. I feel . . . I don't know . . . better, I guess, having someone else to talk to. Someone who doesn't treat me like I'm crazy for thinking my brother might still be alive." I was shocked to feel tears form in my eyes. I quickly turned away, but I wasn't fast enough.

"I don't think you're crazy," he said gently. "If he's out there, we'll find him, Wynter."

I nodded and left the room. Being vulnerable made me uncomfortable, but at the same time, I felt a huge sense of relief. As if the weight I'd carried around for so many years had lightened a bit because someone else was helping me carry it. Zac's comments rolled around in my head. There certainly were secrets in Sanctuary. Could my brother be one of them?

I found Esther in the kitchen, taking cookies out of the oven.

"Wow, those smell great."

She smiled. "These are sugar drop cookies. My mother used

to make them. I think you'll enjoy them." She put the cookie sheet down on top of the stove. "How about some coffee?"

"Sounds wonderful."

"You go sit in the living room. I'll bring our cookies and coffee out there."

I headed toward her large living room. It was a room that had been lived in. Whispers from the past created pictures in my head of children running across the floor, calling out to each other. The carved oak furniture was old and beautiful, but small scratches and scuff marks from little shoes proved it was a room where life had been lived with enthusiasm. The sheer curtains covering Esther's windows moved gently in a light breeze like ghosts from the past dancing on wisps of memories.

I thought about my childhood home. Before my father started drinking, Ryan and I had been joyful, rambunctious. I could still hear my mother yelling at us to settle down and quit running in the house, but there wasn't anger in her voice. Just the sound of a family sharing one another's lives. Then little by little darkness began to push out the light. Our house grew quiet, and all of us became captive to my father's mood swings. Mom's attempts to oblige him made her grow old right in front of our eyes.

Then one day everything was gone. First my brother. Then my father. And finally, my mother. She was alive, but only in shadows. After my father sold our home, Mother and I moved to a small tract house. No running. No laughter. Everything kept clean and in order as if a perfect environment could mend our broken hearts.

It didn't.

Smelling moisture in the air, I went to the front door to look outside. Sure enough, dark clouds slowly rolled toward us, full of the promise of rain. As if confirming an incoming storm, a gust of wind picked up gravel and whisked it down the road in front of Esther's house.

Standing on the porch, looking out across the small town, I felt a sense of peace. As if the problems of the world waited somewhere outside the boundaries of Sanctuary. I remembered one of my favorite Scriptures as a child: *He will cover you with his feathers, and under his wings you will find refuge; his faithfulness will be your shield and rampart. You will not fear the terror of night, nor the arrow that flies by day.* That's just how it felt, as if God himself had created this place of safety. I stood there for a few minutes, allowing the tranquility to surround me. Although Zac's comments confused me, there was something about standing on that porch that soothed my jumbled emotions.

As my eyes swept the empty street, I was startled to see August, the cook from The Oil Lamp Restaurant, leaning against a lamppost, smoking a cigarette. His intense expression appeared almost menacing. Could he have been outside my room last night? I still wasn't convinced anyone had actually been there, but seeing him now made me wonder.

Feeling uneasy, I turned to go back inside, but as I reached for the front doorknob, I noticed the lid to Esther's mailbox hanging open. Several pieces of mail dangled precariously. Afraid the wind might blow them away, I pulled everything out and closed the lid.

I was juggling them together when I noticed the top piece of mail was a large envelope with my name scrawled on it. There was no postmark. Obviously someone had stuck it in the box with all the other mail. A chill ran through me. I swung around, wondering if August had left it for me. He was gone. I looked down the street, but he was nowhere to be seen. Even though I could no longer see him, I couldn't shake an eerie feeling of being watched. "Get a grip, Wynter," I mumbled to myself. I glanced down at the envelope again. Could it be another threat?

I'd just closed the door behind me when Esther came into the living room with two cups of coffee.

"I brought in your mail."

"Oh, thank you, dear. Would you put it on the table by the door?"

I put all the other envelopes on the table but held on to the one with my name on it. "I found something in your mailbox for me."

"I asked Martha to print up some information about Sanctuary and send it over," Esther said. "That must be it."

"Oh, great. Thank you." Breathing a sigh of relief, I put the envelope on the coffee table.

Esther and I spent the next hour talking. She was a wealth of information about the town, although a lot of what she said echoed what Reuben had already told me.

Once she'd exhausted her knowledge about Sanctuary, I directed my questions toward the Mennonite Church and its beliefs. "Esther, I notice you wear a prayer covering all the time. Can you tell me why?"

"Some Mennonites wear one because it's a tradition. Covering a woman's head was a custom in the early church. It isn't one now and shouldn't be something done for the wrong reasons. I'm afraid some in our church have made it a source of pride, as if wearing a covering makes us more spiritual than others. For me, personally, I wear a prayer covering to remind myself that Christ is my head. That my life, my mind, my entire personality, is covered with His love and grace. That He is the one who covers me." She smiled. "Does that answer your question?"

I nodded. "That's beautiful. I have to admit I've wondered if your church judges those who don't believe the same way."

"Oh, honey. Churches aren't judgmental. People are. Unfortunately, even in Sanctuary, I hear these kinds of blanket judgments. This church is wrong, this teacher is wrong, on and on and on. I go to only one church, and the Word of God is my teacher. I don't throw around my opinions about others. I believe we'll all have to give an account of our careless words someday, and I don't want to have to explain to God why I was bad-mouthing a preacher I don't know or a church I've never attended. How silly is that?"

As if emphasizing her words, the storm outside finally broke, and the sound of rain hit the roof. It was a relaxing sound. I suddenly wished I had a book to curl up with in my comfortable room.

"I hear the same thing," I said. "I think it's one of the reasons I haven't been to church for so long. At work, I see enough backstabbing and gossip. Listening to it from Christians turns me off."

"And that's the worst part, isn't it?" Esther said sadly. "It's not a very good witness to the world."

"No, it's not." Even though Reuben had answered my questions about the Fishers, I decided to broach the subject with Esther. "I met a teenager in town. Elijah Fisher? His family is conservative Mennonite?"

She nodded. "A wonderful young man. He's a blessing to this town, and to me. Always willing to help anyone who needs it."

"I found him interesting. You know, a teenager living such a simple life. What do you know about him? Was he raised Mennonite?"

"I don't actually know. His family moved here when he was

young. Maybe ten years ago. I'm not sure. His parents are dear friends of mine." She looked at me through narrowed eyes. "There are other conservative Mennonite young people in Sanctuary. Is there something about him that troubles you?"

I smiled. "No, not at all. Just curious." Not wanting to raise her suspicions, I decided to back off. It was clear I needed to find out more about Elijah before he came to Sanctuary. "Well, thank you for talking to me, Esther. I really appreciate your help."

"I'm not sure what you have planned for tomorrow, but you might have a hard time talking to folks on Sunday. It's the Lord's Day in Sanctuary."

"That's fine. Zac and I have a couple of other places to visit. If we can get some interviews set up for Monday and Tuesday, that would be great."

"I don't think you'll have any problems." Esther took a bite of her cookie. "What time will you leave tomorrow?"

"After lunch. These other towns are close-by."

"Oh, good. Then you will be able to attend church in the morning. If you want to understand Sanctuary, you must include our faith. It is the foundation of who we are." She smiled. "Sanctuary Mennonite starts at nine, and Agape Fellowship begins their services at nine-thirty. I realize you can't attend both churches at the same time. And although I'm sure you will be able to interview some people at Agape, it won't be allowed at Sanctuary Mennonite."

I nodded slowly. "Actually, I'd like to attend both, but why don't I start with Agape?" Esther looked a little disappointed. I wanted to go to her church, especially because the Fishers attended, but I needed some film. I thought for a moment. "Esther, does your church have any other services?"

"Tomorrow night at six o'clock."

I frowned and shook my head. "I'm afraid we won't be back by then."

"We do have two Wednesday meetings a month, but our next meeting isn't until next week."

"We have other places to visit, and even after we get back to St. Louis, everything we've filmed will spend time in editing. There's still plenty of time. How's this? I'll try to make it to your church next Sunday. If I can't do that, we'll be back here for your Wednesday service."

Esther's face lit up with a huge smile. "Oh, that would be wonderful."

"Do we need permission to attend?"

"No," she said with a light laugh. "We're a church. We do encourage people to attend, Wynter."

"Do I have to . . . I mean, should I . . ."

This time she chuckled heartily, her face wrinkling in amusement. "No, you don't have to dress like we do. Just dress modestly. You'll be fine."

"Wonderful. Thank you, Esther."

She nodded. "I'm so glad I can help you."

I stood up. "I can't thank you enough for your hospitality."

"You are very welcome, dear. It's so nice to have company. This house has been too quiet." She handed me the plate of cookies. "Why don't you take these upstairs for Zac? And tell him there's coffee on the stove and fresh lemonade in the refrigerator. You two help yourself to anything you want."

I smiled. "It's going to be hard to say good-bye. You're spoiling us, Esther. You're an amazing hostess."

She shook her head. "You've truly given me much more than I have given you. I'm so thankful to have new friends."

"We are too."

She sniffed a few times and dabbed at her eyes. "Dinner will be at six. Reuben said he would join us tonight."

"Sounds wonderful. I have a little work to do before then."

"You go right ahead. I plan to take a nap. When you're my age, a nap becomes a requirement."

I grabbed the envelope I'd put on the table and headed upstairs. Frances, a beautiful calico cat, ran past me, probably on the way to my room. I stopped to listen at Zac's door and could hear him clicking away on his keyboard. I knocked softly and after a few seconds, he swung it open. I handed him the plate of cookies.

"From Esther. She said to tell you there is coffee on the stove and lemonade in the fridge."

"Thanks. She made me a huge sandwich for lunch. I'm not sure I can eat anything else."

"Wait until you taste these. If you don't finish every last one, I'll eat the plate."

"I'm gonna weigh five hundred pounds by the time we leave this place."

"Wouldn't hurt you to put some meat on your bones."

"Thanks." He pointed at his camera bag. "Ready to get something on film?"

"I don't think so. Let's wait for Reuben to set up a few more interviews. I think I'd rather knock most of it off at once instead of bothering these people in bits and pieces. I get the feeling that will go over better. The more they see us, the more they won't want to see us. Does that make sense?"

He nodded. "I guess so. I feel like I'm not accomplishing much."

"Well, tomorrow we'll get some good stuff in a couple of other nearby towns. At least we'll be moving forward. I'm going to work on our schedule and go over some historical information Martha sent me. Oh, and we eat again at six."

"Great. I might need help rolling down the stairs, so wait for me, okay? We'll go down together."

I laughed and said good-bye as he closed his door. By the time I got to my room, I was actually feeling a bit sleepy. Had to be the slow, small-town atmosphere getting to me and the sound of rain on the roof.

I kicked off my shoes, got the little stool, and after moving Frances over a bit, climbed up on top of the quilt. I pulled my laptop next to me but decided to look over Martha's information first. However, after I opened the envelope and looked at the pages inside, I almost fell out of the bed—which could have had dire consequences since I was so far from the ground. The pages didn't contain the history of Sanctuary. They were clippings from newspapers. All of them about babies kidnapped from Missouri hospitals.

CHAPTER

TEN

"What does this mean?" Zac looked through all the pages I'd found in the envelope. He looked as mystified as I felt.

I plopped down in the chair. "Obviously, someone in Sanctuary wants us to look into this. Maybe they think the person who committed these kidnappings lives here."

"But where's the cryptic note with the clue we need to find the kidnapper?"

I grinned at him. "Why does the note always have to be cryptic? Why can't it just say, 'Here is the name of the person who took these babies, and here is the address where you can find him or her'?"

"Because it's never that easy. Not in any of the books I read anyway."

"Well, it should be." I rubbed my temples, trying to massage away the beginnings of a headache. News stations were always getting "stories" from tipsters whose imaginations were much more active than their common sense. "I'm happy to look into this but not right now. Finding out the truth about Elijah comes first. Besides, we have to get something on tape for our report.

This could be nothing more than someone's vivid imagination. That cook from the restaurant was standing across the street when I found the envelope. Maybe he put it there."

Zac gulped. "Oh, great. So if we don't investigate, he'll poison our food? I'm not eating in that restaurant."

I smiled at him. "Now who's paranoid?"

He stared down at one of the pages. "You don't think this could be connected to your brother in some way, do you?"

"How could it be? Ryan wasn't a baby."

Zac's eyes narrowed. "But he went missing. Just like these children."

"All of those incidents happened in Missouri. Ryan was taken in Illinois."

"It's not that far away, Wynter. Just over the bridge. And perhaps you're forgetting that if Elijah is Ryan, you found him in Missouri."

"I don't know." I took the pages from him, folded them, and put them back in the envelope. "I'll look this over later."

Zac shook his head. "There's definitely something going on in this town, and I intend to find out what it is."

"Or maybe we're just chasing shadows," I said with a sigh. "I'd hate to lose my job over a wild-goose chase."

Zac frowned up at me. "You're not getting cold feet, are you?"

I leaned against the closed door. "I don't know. Maybe I'm just tired. Or maybe it's bringing all this up again. Feels over-whelming."

Zac studied me carefully. "I guess it would be. Sorry. I don't mean to be insensitive."

"You're not. Sharing my situation with you has been cathartic. But walking back into this darkness is difficult. My emotions are out of control."

He nodded. "We'll talk more tomorrow on the road. By the way, where are we going? To Jamesport?"

"No, it's too far. Would take us over ten hours. Besides, I can't use it for our report. But somehow I need to find out about the time the Fishers spent there."

Zac flipped over to another screen on his laptop. "I have a friend in St. Joe who works for a local newspaper. He's done some investigating. Jamesport is only about an hour away from St. Joe. Why don't I ask him to pop over and ask around a bit?"

"I don't know. Telling you about my past has been hard enough, and I don't know your friend."

"I won't tell him about Ryan. I'll just ask him to nose around. Get what information he can about the Fishers. He doesn't need to know why."

I turned the idea over in my mind. Obviously, if Elijah had been born in Jamesport, I was wasting my time. But if we caught Elijah in a lie, things would certainly become much more interesting. "Okay," I said finally, "but tell your friend to be careful. I don't want the Fishers to find out we were asking questions about them."

"I'll tell him it's background information for a possible story and that he needs to fly under the radar. I'll also offer to reimburse him for his lunch." Zac grinned. "This guy would drive anywhere for a good meal."

"Thanks, Zac."

"No problem. By the way, you never told me where we're going tomorrow."

"We'll head to Bonne Terre and visit the mines. If we have

time, we'll go to the Black Madonna Shrine and Grottos near Eureka."

Zac's eyebrows shot up. "The what near where?"

"A place that will fit right in with Ed's desire to find spots most Missourians haven't heard of. It's really pretty cool." I grinned at him. "I've heard miracles happen there."

He blew out a quick breath. "Well, we could certainly use one, huh?"

"You've got that right."

"What time are we leaving?"

"After lunch. And . . . after church."

His eyes widened, and he gave me a thin smile. "Whoa. You let me know when you're out. I'll be waiting here."

"No, I want you there. We'll need some film."

"I thought Mennonites—"

"We're going to the other church. I'm thinking we'll get some great shots and a few short interviews."

He stared at his computer screen as if it could offer him a way of escape. "Can I wait outside?"

"No, Zac. Part of the job."

I wasn't being completely honest with him. Since coming to Sanctuary, my lack of church attendance had started to bother me. Not sure why, but for the first time since Ryan's disappearance, I felt the desire to go back. The idea frightened me a little, and I didn't want to go alone. Besides, maybe it would do Zac some good. I had no idea why he hated everything spiritual, but if he enjoyed himself tomorrow, perhaps it would help him. At least that's what I told myself. I wasn't ready to admit to anyone that it might help me too.

Zac shook his head. "Okay, but I'm doing this under duress."

I grinned. "Whatever it takes to get you in church." I looked down at my watch. "It's a little after four-thirty. I'll meet you outside your door at five 'til six."

"You're really just trying to pay me back for what I did to you, right? Making me go to church." He sighed deeply. "Boy, try to sabotage someone one time, and they never forget it."

I couldn't hold back a giggle. "You're too much, Zac. Really."

As I turned to leave, I saw him smile. I was really starting to like Zac. What a difference a day made.

My headache had gotten worse, so I took an aspirin and lay down. After a few minutes, I nodded off. Even though I'd only seen it in pictures, I dreamt about the Black Madonna Shrine. I was standing in front of it when the face moved. Out of the lips came my brother's voice calling my name. "Emily, please find me. Don't give up. Help me." Startled, I sat straight up in bed, and put my hand over my mouth. A loud noise echoed in my head. Had I actually screamed or had I been dreaming? I wiped the back of my hand against my forehead. It was covered with sweat. Shaking, I got out of the bed, using my little stool to help me down. I'd taken my clothes off and was in my underwear when a knock came at the door. "Just a minute," I said loudly. I quickly pulled on my dress pants and shirt. When I opened the door, Zac stood there, his eyes wide with alarm.

"Are you okay?"

I nodded. "Did . . . did I yell?"

"I wouldn't call it yelling. More like a bloodcurdling scream. Almost scared me to death." He pushed past me, looking over the room. "I thought you were being murdered."

I lowered myself down onto the couch, my body still trembling. "No. Just another dream about my brother." I pushed the hair out of my face. "Do you think Esther heard me?"

"I doubt it. I noticed she wears a hearing aid. Besides, I believe she's sleeping. I went down a few minutes ago to get some lemonade, and she wasn't around. The door to her room was closed."

"Good."

Zac studied me carefully. "You didn't tell me these dreams of yours were so scary."

I shrugged. "Sometimes they're not. But there have been some doozies. This was one of them."

"I'm sorry, Wynter. I really am." He started to leave but stopped with his hand on the doorknob. "You're not alone, you know. Thanks for telling me the truth about Ryan. You won't be sorry. I intend to do everything I can to help you."

"Thank you, Zac."

I locked the door behind him, though I wasn't certain why. The dream made me feel weak and frightened. I checked the time. Thirty minutes until dinner. I grabbed some fresh clothes and hurried to the bathroom. A short, cool shower helped. I dried my hair and quickly braided it. By the time I left the bathroom, I felt a lot better. After putting my dirty clothes back in my room, I hurried out to the hall and found Zac waiting for me. When we reached the bottom of the stairs, we were greeted by the aroma of something wonderful. My stomach churned with anticipation.

"Oh no," Zac mumbled. "Here we go again."

As we entered the dining room, we found Reuben already waiting.

"Good evening," he said with a smile. "Hope you're hungry. Esther's been cooking up a storm."

His rugged good looks were accented by a black sweater and jeans. My breath caught when I saw him. I tried to cover up my reaction by coughing lightly.

"I wasn't hungry until I smelled dinner cooking," Zac said. "What are we having?"

Reuben shook his head. "A Mennonite dish, Zac. Not sure you'll like it."

Zac plopped down at the table. "Since we got here, I've eaten enough for four people. And liked every single thing."

Esther came into the room carrying a plate. "Reuben King, just what are you telling Zac? Shame on you." She sat the dish down on the table. "We're having fried chicken and mashed potatoes. Nothing to fear."

Zac grinned. "I'm not afraid of your food, Esther. My only fear is not being able to get into my clothes. Usually I don't eat much. Fruit, yogurt, granola bars—whatever's handy." He let out a long sigh. "When I get home, I may have to learn to cook. Don't think I can go back to the way things were."

I patted him on the back. "Women love a man who can cook. You'll be a catch."

Zac frowned. "I'll have you know I don't have any problem getting dates. So far, no one's questioned my culinary skills."

I laughed. "Esther, let me help you."

"Thank you, Wynter," she said with a smile. "If you would carry in a few things, I would appreciate it."

"I'll help too," Reuben said, standing to his feet.

Esther waved her hand at him. "You sit down. Wynter and I can get it."

"Are you sure?"

She nodded, and I followed her into the kitchen. For someone who lived a simple life, Esther's kitchen was pretty modern, except for the old gas stove across from the kitchen sink. I'd seen pictures of those ancient appliances. Huge, with two doors below and a large cooktop. Esther caught me looking at it.

"That stove belonged to my grandmother, and then my mother. Now it's mine." She smiled. "I wouldn't use anything else. In my opinion it does a much better job than any modern appliance available today."

"I believe it. You know, my mom used to be a good cook too."

Esther put a large platter of fried chicken into my hands. "Did you tell me she'd passed?"

"No. She's still alive. She just doesn't cook much anymore."

"Oh?"

Esther studied my face as if waiting for an explanation I couldn't come up with anything except a lie—or the truth—and I wasn't willing to share either.

"I-I'll take this in and come back," I said quickly. When I walked into the dining room, Reuben jumped up and took the huge platter from my hands and set it on the table. "I'll be back," I said. When I whirled around, I almost knocked Esther down.

"Just a couple more things," Esther said, "and we'll be ready to eat."

"Are you sure Zac and I can't help?" Reuben asked.

Esther smiled at him. "Thank you, Reuben, but we're fine. Maybe you and Zac can clear the table later." She sat a big bowl of mashed potatoes down on the corner of the table. "You know, I was taught that women should serve the meals without help from the men."

"Do you still believe that?" I asked, slightly horrified by her statement.

She shook her head. "No, but I love preparing and serving food for my friends. I have more trouble with some of the other traditions that were taught to me as a child."

"Like what?" Zac asked.

108

"Like excommunicating members of the church for disobe-
dience."

"I thought Mennonites didn't shun people," I said.

"We don't," Esther answered. "Shunning means a member
is not only expelled from church but also rejected by his family
and friends. Mennonites don't do that, but the church used to be
harsher when I was young. Now we try to work with members
who are struggling. And we pray." She shook her head. "I have
to be careful though. Some of those old judgments find their
way into my mind sometimes. I fight them, because more than
anything, I want to please God. I know now that God desires
mercy and not judgment, so I try hard to be merciful. Some of
my friends have a tougher time changing their old habits. They
stay in comfortable patterns instilled in them many years ago.
But I want God to challenge me. To reveal truth to me. The more
I seek His wisdom, the more I know Him. And to me, knowing
Him is everything."

Her voice softened to a whisper by the end of her statement,
and I found myself both touched and bothered by her words.
I remembered being passionate about God when I was young,
but it had been a long time since I'd felt that kind of devotion.
Ever since Ryan was abducted.

Esther and I went back to the kitchen and retrieved two more
dishes. Then we joined Zac and Reuben at the table.

"Reuben, will you say grace?" Esther asked.

He nodded and bowed his head. Zac and I did the same. While
Reuben prayed, I opened one eye and snuck a peek at Zac. This
time he actually had his eyes closed and his head bowed. Was
this town getting to him too?

After Reuben said, "Amen," we began to help ourselves to the
wonderful dinner Esther had prepared. The fried chicken almost

melted in my mouth, and the mashed potatoes were rich with butter and cream. Zac, who'd been complaining about eating too much, had three helpings of everything.

Reuben was telling us about some of the people he'd lined up to speak to us when I asked whether Elijah's parents had okayed his interview.

He shook his head. "I'm sorry, but Elijah and his family are gone."

I dropped my fork, and it clanged against my plate. "What? What do you mean *gone?*" I couldn't keep a note of hysteria out of my voice.

His eyes widened with surprise. "I mean they left town for a while."

"Do you know where they went?"

Reuben put his fork down and stared at me. "Wynter, why are this boy and his family so important to you? Ever since you got to town, you keep bringing them up. We have several other people who've agreed to be part of your feature. Why does Elijah matter so much?"

"He . . . he doesn't. I just wanted an interview with someone more conservative. I thought a young person's point of view would be interesting."

He sighed and leaned back in his chair. "I'm not stupid, you know. You're not being completely honest with me. I've felt it ever since you arrived in Sanctuary. If you won't tell me the truth, I don't think I can help you anymore. It's not that I think you mean us any harm, but until I understand your hidden agenda, I can't take any chances."

Zac caught my eye and gave me a warning look. My out-of-control emotions were going to cost me everything if I didn't rein them in. I took a deep breath and forced myself to calm down.

"I'm sorry, Reuben. We're here for a limited time, and this feature is really important to my career. So far, we don't have anything on tape."

"Important to your career?" he said. "What do you mean?"

I told him about the new station owners and how I might be in line for the anchor chair. "You see, if this doesn't go well, it could cost me a promotion that means a lot to my future." As I talked, I assuaged my guilty conscience by reminding myself that everything I was saying was true, even if it wasn't the complete story. I was relieved to see the tension in Reuben's face lessen.

"Thank you for being honest with me. You know, there's nothing wrong with ambition—as long as it's kept in perspective and your priorities are in order. But using other people to get ahead is wrong."

"I know that. I promised we wouldn't jeopardize anyone in Sanctuary. Nothing's changed."

"Reuben King, you need to trust this young woman," Esther said firmly. "And no more arguing at the table. Josiah and I had a firm rule: Manners were required during meals. He's been gone almost thirty years now, but I swear I can still hear his voice sometimes." She blushed and shook her head. "You probably think that's silly. The fancies of an old woman."

"No, I don't," I said. "The people we love never really leave us."

"You know, Wynter," Esther said slowly, "I realize I'm not young, but I'll let you interview me if it would help."

"Wouldn't that get you in trouble with the people in your church?"

Esther chuckled. "It wouldn't be the first time I've bent the rules, and it won't be the last. I'll run it by our pastor, but I don't think he'll mind. He's a lot more progressive than people give him credit for."

"Thank you, Esther. That would be wonderful. And we can always blur your face if it helps."

She smiled. "I don't know how much it would help me, but it might make your viewers happier."

We all laughed at her self-deprecating humor.

"Are you sure you want to do this?" Reuben asked. "I know you don't like TV."

While Esther and Reuben discussed the merits and downfalls of television, I tried to listen, but the knowledge that Elijah was gone had shaken me to the core. How would I find the truth if he wasn't here? Why had the Fishers left? Were they hiding something? Were they trying to keep Elijah away from me?

The television debate continued through the meal and into dessert. Over coffee Reuben brought up some interviews he'd arranged. He mentioned several names I didn't know, and a few I did. I was happy to hear that Martha was still willing to talk to us. And Jonathon Wiese, the pastor of Agape Fellowship, had agreed to be on camera as well.

"What about Rae—what was her name? Buettner?" I asked. "Might be interesting to have her input as an outsider."

"She's not an outsider," Esther said. "She's one of us."

"I meant that she doesn't go to church. Since this is such a religious town, I thought maybe talking to someone who doesn't fit the mold might add another perspective. Besides, she's certainly colorful."

"I can tell you right now that Rae won't do it," Reuben said. "She's a very private person. I once wrote an article for the paper in Fredericktown about how she saved my dog. Thankfully, I showed it to her before I mailed it. I thought she was going to have a stroke. Refused to let me send it."

"She saved your dog?" I asked. "How did that happen?"

"A couple of years ago, Abner Ingalls, who runs the hardware store next to Randi's café, was visiting family in Bonne Terre. They were at a local park, fishing and cooking out, when they saw someone throw a bag into the lake. Abner heard a sound coming from the bag and ran over to where it had been tossed. He dove in, found the bag, which was already under water, and swam to shore. Inside was a small golden Lab puppy, almost dead. He got the puppy breathing and brought it back to Sanctuary so Rae could take a look at it. She X-rayed the puppy and actually found a bullet in his chest."

"Oh, my goodness," I said, unable to stop the tears that sprang into my eyes. "Who in the world would do something like that?"

Reuben shook his head. "I can't explain it, Wynter. Some people have ways of looking at things that I can't begin to understand. Anyway, Rae operated on the puppy, removed the bullet, and treated him. Then she called me. I'd just lost my old black Lab, Buford. At first I said no, but Rae brought the puppy over and sat it down in front of me. 'This dog needs a home, Reuben King,' she said, 'and you need a dog. That's all there is to it.' Then she walked away and that was that. I named him Lazarus—"

"Because he was raised from the dead," I finished for him. "Great story."

"Yeah, I thought so, but like I said, Rae wouldn't let me tell it. She does so many good things, but she shuns attention and thanks."

"Sounds like a humble person," Zac said.

Reuben laughed. "Maybe. But when it comes to her work, she doesn't have much humility. Martha's son, Fred, took his cat, Gabe, to a vet in Cape Girardeau when they were on vacation, and Rae had a fit. Told him he should have brought Gabe back to Sanctuary so she could treat him. Rae thinks our animals belong to her—and to her alone."

"Sounds committed."

Reuben grinned. "She is. I'm afraid to take Lazarus anywhere else. And I mean that literally."

"Okay, I won't ask her," I said. "Thanks to you and Esther, we have plenty of people to interview. But I would still like to have a young conservative Mennonite person to talk to. Off camera is fine. If you think of anyone else, let me know."

Reuben's eyebrows met together in a deep frown. "You know, I've been thinking about that. You're not doing an exposé, Wynter. From what you told me, this is supposed to be an informational piece. So why is it important to interview someone like Elijah? Are you trying to find something negative? If so, you won't find that here. No one lives in Sanctuary because they have to."

"It's not that. I just wanted this to be something more than a puff piece."

"But that's what it is, isn't it?"

I couldn't answer his question because he was right. Thankfully, Zac took up the slack and saved me from having to cover my true intentions.

"Why did the Fishers leave town?" Zac asked. "Was it because we wanted to talk to their son?"

Reuben shook his head. "No, not at all. Nathan has a brother who lives outside of Fredericktown. He goes there frequently to help him with his farm. His brother, Samuel, does the same for Nathan."

We finished dinner, Reuben left, and Zac and I headed upstairs. As I lay in bed, Clyde cuddled up next to me while I stared at the ceiling and wondered about Elijah's departure. Were the Fishers really at Samuel's, or were they in hiding? I tossed and turned for a while before falling into a troubled sleep.

CHAPTER
ELEVEN

The next morning, Zac made it through the entire church service without any outward signs of trauma. He stood off to the side and filmed Jonathon as he preached. We had gotten permission to film, but the elders and Jonathon had requested that we try not to disrupt the service. Zac did a great job. I doubted that most of the people in the sanctuary even noticed him.

The praise service was enthusiastic and moving. We sang songs that were new to me, but there was something about them that felt personal, as if those singing them really knew God. I glanced at Zac a couple of times, and although he remained stoic, it was obvious from his expression the worship touched him.

For a young man, Jonathon exhibited a confident presence in the pulpit. I noticed that some of the women in the church seemed to be interested in more than just the sermon. Jonathon had startling blue eyes and thick black hair that framed an interesting face. His looks weren't cookie-cutter handsome, but he was certainly appealing.

The sermon focused on Philippians chapter three, verses

thirteen and fourteen. Jonathon encouraged his parishioners to follow the apostle Paul's commitment to forget the past and concentrate on the future.

"Too many people are changed by one or two events in their lives. Something that colors their perceptions and alters the course of their existence on this earth. Usually the event is traumatic, something painful. But our lives are made up of many moments—good and bad. One incident should never define us, because God has already defined us. He calls us His beloved children. Victors—not victims. He calls us *overcomers* not *overcome*. We are new creations."

I felt like God was speaking directly to me. I thought about the changes that occurred in my family after Ryan went missing. All of us were altered by his disappearance. Not only in our emotions, but also in the way we reacted to one another. I couldn't help but wonder why we hadn't pulled together instead of allowing ourselves to be torn apart. What was it in us that had driven us to become weaker instead of stronger?

Jonathon went on to say that no one ever won a race by running backward. Instead, we need to keep our eyes forward if we ever hope to find the destiny that God has for us. His words struck a chord in me, and I knew I would remember them for a long time.

Outside the church, I talked to several people about Sanctuary and actually interviewed a couple of them for our report. Jonathon was happy to talk to us and was very articulate about the town's strong spiritual foundation.

After a quick lunch at Esther's, Zac and I took off. Before we left, I made a phone call I didn't want to make. I needed help and there was only one person I knew who might be able to provide it. Jonathon's sermon had given me the courage I needed to take a step of faith.

Zac and I took the tour of the Bonne Terre mine. When we walked down the stairs into the mine, I felt as if I'd entered another world. The boat trip on the below-ground lake was eerie and silent, and somewhere in my mind I could hear the echoes of chisels and tools carving out the huge passages we drifted through. Rather than being claustrophobic, it was peaceful. I felt protected from the confusing world above me. I watched as the heads of divers popped up around us, causing the still water to ripple. It was a surreal experience.

Ed had approved the mine tour in Bonne Terre, even though everyone in Missouri knew about it. Surprisingly, a large number of Missourians had never taken the tour, in spite of it being a big tourist attraction. Missouri was rife with abandoned mines and littered with caves. Maybe the appeal of the tour wasn't strong enough for people so used to the incredible natural and man-made features that made Missouri so special. We interviewed our guide after the tour and caught the reaction of a few of the visitors.

Afterward, we headed to a little Italian restaurant not far from the mine. Angelo's had a reputation for great pizza and calzones. Small and cozy, it was the kind of place where patrons dusted off their chairs before sitting down and ignored the stickiness of the plastic green- or red-checkered tablecloths. From the moment we stepped inside, the incredible smells made my stomach rumble with hunger and my mouth salivate with anticipation. Faded murals celebrating Italy decorated the walls. Grapevines covered porticos of Italian piazzas drenched in sunlight.

My eyes swept the room. I spotted him sitting at a corner table, already looking uncomfortable. I walked toward him, Zac on my heels.

"Hi, Dad."

My father stood up, a throwback to the old-fashioned manners of his youth.

"Hello, Emily."

He stuck his hand out toward a surprised Zac. I should have told him I'd called my father, but for some strange reason, I hadn't been able to find the words.

"I'm Lyndon Erwin," he said.

Zac took his hand while shooting me a look designed to let me know he didn't appreciate the ambush.

"Zac Weikal," he said. "Glad to meet you."

I was pretty sure he wasn't.

Dad waved his hand toward the chairs across from him. "Have a seat. I waited on you to order. Their stromboli is incredible, but it's huge. Anyone want to split one?"

"Not me," I said. "I want pizza."

Dad raised an eyebrow. "You still eat those weird pizzas?"

I studied him for a moment. Although his hair was grayer, he was still a handsome man. My mother had always said he reminded her of James Garner from *The Rockford Files*, her favorite television show in the seventies. Now Dad looked like Jim Rockford in his fifties, still handsome, still dashing.

"Yeah, Dad. Still eating those weird pizzas."

He shrugged and turned his attention to Zac. "How about you, Zac? Feel like splitting a stromboli?"

Zac nodded. "Sounds good to me."

Dad turned to look for the waitress, who was already on her way over to us. When she got to the table, Dad turned on the charm. It was like a switch he could flip on and off at the drop of a hat. Most people seemed to find it appealing, but it embarrassed me. I still hadn't recovered from his attempt to captivate my college friends with his overblown charisma. In the end, I'd dissuaded him from visiting me on campus. Seeing him a couple of times a year at a neutral location had been more than enough contact for me.

I refused to drop in on his new family. Ditching Mom for a woman with two kids hurt. I met his new wife once and took an immediate dislike to her. She was everything Mom wasn't—overdone makeup, bleached hair, and eyes as dead as a shark's. It was immediately clear to me that my father's money was the main attraction. I felt sorry for her children, who looked like they were only biding time until they could make their escape.

Dad ordered a stromboli for himself and Zac and then looked at me. "What do you want, Emily?"

"I'll take a small pizza with cheese, green pepper, and pineapple," I said to the waitress, whom Dad had just referred to as "sweetie."

She nodded.

"What kind of a pizza is that?" Dad asked, shaking his head. "Pizza should have meat," he said to the waitress, whose name tag said *Sally*. "Isn't that right, Sally?"

She smiled. "I like my pizza with mushrooms and pineapple."

Dad colored slightly. "Guess you and I are the only ones who understand Italian food, Zac," he said loudly. "Women just don't get it, do they?"

Zac shrugged. "Guess everyone's tastes are different."

I thanked Sally for taking our order, giving her an out so she could scurry away.

"I asked you here today because I need help, Dad," I said, trying to get right to the point.

"I'm glad I was available, Emily. I've been out on the road for two weeks and just wrapped up my business in St. Louis last night. I head back to Chicago tomorrow."

"What kind of work do you do?" Zac asked.

I nudged him under the table. Once my dad started talking business, he could go on for at least an hour. He used to regale everyone he met with stories about his mortgage banking company. After he sold out and went into insurance, the long-winded diatribes began to diminish in length, but the boasting continued.

"Insurance," he said. "I run my own agency."

Surprisingly, that was it. Caught off guard, it took me a moment to gather my thoughts and jump in before Dad came up with something else work related.

Briefly, I explained my assignment. Then I said, "Dad, I want to show you a picture." I took the file folder of photos out of my tote bag, pulled out the shot of Elijah, and pushed it across the table. "This boy. He . . . he looks like Ryan. I came out here to find out if it could possibly be him."

My father's face went pale as he stared at the photo. "Ryan's dead, Emily. How could you possibly think—?"

"But what if he's not? What if someone took him? Kept him? I've got to know, Dad. I won't walk away until I know for certain this isn't him."

My father hadn't taken his eyes off the picture since I'd shoved it in front of him. "But it can't be him. If Ryan was alive, he would have contacted us."

Briefly, I explained all the reasons that assumption might be wrong. Everything Zac and I had discussed.

"So you see, it *is* possible. Ryan was only seven when he was taken. His abductors could have told him anything." I paused to take a deep breath. "Look, Dad. I went to Sanctuary half expecting to look this teenager in the face and know he wasn't Ryan. I wondered if the picture I saw was a fluke. Just an odd-angled shot of someone who happened to look like my brother. But the young man I met looks like the picture that caught my eye. The one that made me wonder if it could be him. And now he's disappeared. I can't help but think that someone might be trying to hide him. You're the only one who has the answers I'm looking for. The only one who can help me."

My father finally broke his gaze away from the photograph and looked up at me. I was surprised to see tears in his eyes. "If you think this is Ryan, why haven't you called the police? You have no business taking this on by yourself."

"Before the authorities descend on Sanctuary, I want to know I'm not starting something that will blow up in my face and cause trouble for innocent people. That's why I need your help. You can identify Ryan better than I can. You know things about him that I don't. Like birthmarks, scars, physical markers I can't remember clearly. If you'll help me, if you'll see this young man for yourself—"

My father jumped to his feet. "You should have left this alone, Emily. You really should have left this alone."

With that, he walked out the front door. I heard his car door slam, his engine start, and his tires squeal as he drove away.

Zac's mouth was open. "What just happened?" he asked finally. "Is he coming back?"

"No. He's gone." Anger coursed through me, tasting like sour bile in my throat. "That's my father. Running out when his family needs him. I should have known."

Just then, Sally came to the table with our food. She frowned at my father's empty chair. "Is he coming back? Should I keep his food warm?"

"If you don't mind, just put his half of the stromboli in a box. We'll take it with us."

As she walked away, Zac leaned back in his chair and studied me carefully. "So now what?"

I picked up a piece of pizza. "Now we eat. Then we figure out our next move."

I should have enjoyed Angelo's great pizza, but at that moment, it tasted like ashes in my mouth.

TWELVE

Our visit to the grotto was interesting. The guide told us the story of the shrine, which turned out to be a real testament to dedication and hard work. The shrine had been rebuilt after a devastating fire in the fifties. Vandals had attacked it more than once, but the Franciscan Brothers who cared for it restored it time after time. I tried to stay focused on its fascinating history, but I had a hard time concentrating. My father's actions back at the restaurant had opened old wounds that were now bleeding.

We got back to Sanctuary around six o'clock. Zac had eaten my dad's half of the stromboli in the car, but I was hungry. Esther wasn't home when we arrived, and I assumed she was attending evening church services.

Zac went upstairs to unpack his gear while I raided the refrigerator. Cold chicken, potato salad, and a delicious fruit relish made for a quick dinner that I ate in the kitchen. After I cleaned everything up, I fixed myself a second glass of tea and took it upstairs. The door to Zac's room was open. We hadn't talked much on the way home. I'd been too upset, and Zac had wisely kept quiet while I dealt with my bruised feelings. I stopped by his door and leaned against the frame. He was sitting on the bed, obviously waiting for me.

"What's our next move?" he asked.

"I've been thinking about that. I know Ed will expect an update tomorrow. I can't lie to him, Zac. Either I tell him we're still in Sanctuary and why, or we leave and call him from somewhere else."

"You need to be careful."

"Trust me. I'm aware of that. Did you call your friend in St. Joe?"

He nodded. "Talked to him last night. He planned to visit Jamesport today. He should be calling anytime now."

"I need to think," I said. "I'm going for a walk. Maybe by the time I get back, you'll have heard from him. Then we'll decide what to do. If Elijah's family is on the run, we've got to move quickly. I can't take a chance on losing my brother a second time."

"It's your decision, Wynter. Not mine."

"You're wrong. We're friends. We'll decide together."

Zac's smile was genuine. "Thanks. I'm glad you see me as your friend."

"Well, you are. Be back in a bit."

When I went into my room I found Clyde and Frances sleeping on my bed. They both opened their eyes and looked at me with disinterest before going back to sleep. I almost stepped on a tail sticking out from under the bed. I bent down and found Sam curled up in a ball on the floor. Obviously his older joints hadn't allowed him to jump up onto the high bed. I would have picked him up and put him next to his kitty friends, but I was concerned he'd have trouble getting down again. I took a minute to pet each one of them, and then changed my clothes.

It felt great to slide on jeans and a comfortable shirt. I exchanged my heels for sneakers and pulled my hair back in a ponytail. I'd just put my clothes away when I noticed a small box on the dresser. When I opened it, I found several pieces of fudge. That's when I noticed a note that had been placed under the box. It simply said "Welcome!" Although I appreciated Esther's gesture, I wasn't hungry and dropped the box off with Zac on my way out. He was only too happy to accept it.

As I walked down the stairs, they creaked beneath my feet. It was a comforting sound and once again reminded me of my grandmother's house. I heard her voice in my head. *"Without God, nothing makes sense, honey. More than anything else, seek Him. Keep Him close. He's always nearby, never farther away than a whispered prayer."*

I stopped at Esther's front door, my hand on the knob. "Are you still there, God?" I asked quietly. "I have no right to ask for your help, but if you could show me what to do, I certainly would appreciate it."

I stepped out onto the front porch and breathed in the soft spring air. There weren't many people out. Most of them were probably in church. As I walked, I looked more closely at the buildings that made up downtown Sanctuary. There were only a few houses on Main Street, including Esther's and Janet's. The business district was four blocks long and contained the two restaurants, the hardware store, a small general store, two buildings without names on the outside, a quilt shop, a clothing store, a secondhand store, and a redbrick building divided into three businesses. The building housed Sanctuary Christian School, Sanctuary Library, and Sanctuary Post Office. The ancient buildings were painted, clean, and cared for. Sanctuary was the epitome of homespun charm. A town caught in time, seemingly untouched by modernism, disinterest, or lack of respect. The idea of graffiti felt like heresy, and littering seemed like a crime worthy of imprisonment.

On the far side of Sanctuary sat Agape Fellowship. Its white spire was the tallest point in town. Sanctuary Mennonite was just two blocks away. The plain structure didn't have a spire or a cross. In fact, unless you were close enough to read the sign above the entrance, you could mistake it for a commercial building. However, it seemed completely appropriate for the plain people who worshiped there.

There were more homes on neighboring blocks, but almost everything was within walking distance. Reuben had told me that quite a few residents owned farms outside of town, but they were still part of Sanctuary.

I headed toward Randi's café, hoping to get a cup of coffee. Before I reached the restaurant, I made a decision. Something I'd been toying with since yesterday. As if God was confirming my conclusion, I looked down the street and saw Reuben walking toward me.

"Church out?" I asked.

"Yeah, just dismissed."

"Hey, I wanted to talk to you if you have some time," I said. "I'm headed to Randi's for coffee."

"Sounds great." He waited for me to catch up and then walked next to me toward the diner.

"I'm surprised she's open on Sunday," I said. "Figured almost everything would be closed on the Sabbath."

Reuben grinned. "You're right, but Randi does a great business on Sunday. After church her café is packed."

As we strolled down the street, we were passed by several

buggies. Obviously the Mennonite church had completed services too. Reuben called out to most of the people who rode past us. He seemed to be friends with almost everyone in town. A woman coming toward us called out his name, and he stopped.

"Wynter, this is Sarah Miller," he said as she approached. "She teaches at our small private school."

I reached out and took her hand. "I'm glad to meet you. I was surprised to learn that a town this small had its own school."

Sarah, a tall, thin woman with red hair in a bun and a smattering of freckles across her face, smiled. "It's supported by the churches. There are some parents in our town who don't want their children to attend public school."

I smiled at her. "How interesting. I wonder if you'd allow me to interview you. I'd love to find out more."

"You're the lady from the news station in St. Louis?"

"Yes. It wouldn't take long, Sarah. What do you say?"

I noticed Reuben and Sarah exchange quick glances.

"I . . . I don't know," she said slowly, dragging the last word out. "You can't film the children. Many of them come from conservative Mennonite homes. Their parents won't allow them to be on camera."

"That's fine. I'd just be talking to you."

Another look at Reuben. What now? Was everyone in Sanctuary keeping secrets?

"I . . . I guess it would be all right," she said finally. "Maybe you could come by the school tomorrow?"

"Sounds great. I'll see you then."

She nodded and walked away without saying good-bye.

"Okay, what gives?" I asked. "Another person with a deep, dark past?"

He smiled. "Let's get some coffee, and I'll tell you about Sarah."

Once we got to the café, Reuben ordered coffee and urged me to try Randi's coconut macaroon pie. A nut for coconut, I had to say yes. One bite put me into coconut heaven.

"Randi could make a go of it anywhere," I said after swallowing the first delicious bite. "I'd ask why she lives here, but I'm afraid to."

He laughed. "Randi isn't in witness protection or anything, if that's what you mean. She just loves Sanctuary. Her mother owned a restaurant in Columbia. When she died, Randi decided to carry on the family tradition, but she didn't want to deal with the stress of running a large establishment. She stumbled upon Sanctuary when she came to see a friend who lives in Farmington. This place was empty and she asked permission to move here. She was welcomed with open arms."

"So there's at least one person in Sanctuary who isn't living a surreptitious existence?"

Reuben shook his finger at me. "Now you're just making fun of us."

"Kind of." I put another bite of pie on my fork. "Now tell me about Sarah."

The joviality in his expression disappeared. "Sarah's parents were murdered when she was only six. The men who broke into her house missed her and her older sister because they hid in a small storage closet under the stairs." He frowned. "Her hesitation in talking to you comes from not wanting to be associated with such an awful crime from her past. She doesn't want it to become her identity. Can you understand that?"

I put my fork down. Although I tried to blink back the tears that filled my eyes, I couldn't stop them.

Reuben looked alarmed. "I'm sorry, Wynter. Have I said something to upset you?"

I grabbed a napkin from the table and dabbed at my eyes. I glanced back toward the kitchen. August wasn't there, and I breathed a quick sigh of relief. For some odd reason, I didn't want him to see me cry.

"I completely understand how Sarah feels, Reuben. You see, I'm in the same situation. I have something I need to tell you." My voice shook, and I took a deep breath, trying to calm myself. "I . . . I haven't been completely honest with you. Not since we got into town." Our eyes met, and the concern I saw there made me feel even guiltier.

"You're not really doing a story about towns in Missouri?" he asked, looking a little confused.

"No. I mean, yes." I picked up my coffee and drank slowly, trying to gather my thoughts. I put my cup down and tried again. "We *are* doing a story, but I came to Sanctuary because I saw a picture. A picture of Elijah Fisher."

"Elijah?" He shook his head. "I'm sorry, Wynter. I don't understand."

Taking one more deep breath, I launched into the entire story. My brother's disappearance, the reason we came to Sanctuary, and everything that had happened since we'd arrived.

"I've been hiding the truth from you," I said, keeping my voice low so no one else could hear us. "All I can say in my defense is that I had no reason to trust you. Maybe now you can understand why I got so upset when you told me Elijah and his family had left town."

Reuben just stared at me. I couldn't tell if he was in shock, or if he was trying to process what I'd told him.

"Say something," I said finally. "I'm praying you'll understand. That you won't hate me."

"I don't hate you," he said softly. "But I have to admit I'm not happy about all the lies and secrecy."

"I know, and I feel terrible about it. I hope you can see why I couldn't just waltz into town and start claiming my kidnapped brother was living here under a different name."

"Do you really believe Elijah is your brother?"

"That's the problem. I don't know. And I'm not sure how to find out. I have no desire to cause trouble in Sanctuary. Especially since finding out there are people counting on their continued anonymity. I don't want to do something I can't take back. That's why I wanted to talk to Elijah. I'd hoped I could find out the truth before—"

"You called the authorities?"

I nodded. "But then you told me Elijah and his family were gone, and I'm wondering if I made a mistake."

Reuben was quiet as he studied me. "So what is it you want me to do?" he said finally.

"I want your help, Reuben. Not just to find the truth, but to handle this situation in a way that won't harm anyone. I've—" My nose started to run, and I quickly dabbed at it. "I've started to care about this place. There are good people here. People I don't want to hurt. Telling you the truth is scary. Until this trip, my boss in St. Louis was the only person I'd ever shared my story with. I had to tell Zac, and now I've told you. I don't trust people easily."

"Well, I'm glad you decided to confide in me." He ran his hand over his face. "I need time to think. Can we meet for breakfast and talk again? After I have a chance to process this a little bit?"

I nodded. "But please don't ask me to leave, Reuben. I can't do it."

He reached out and took my hand. "I won't. My problem is finding a way to balance my responsibilities to Sanctuary against my feelings for you."

"You have feelings for me?" A strong rush of emotion flowed through me, taking me by surprise.

Reuben's serious expression lifted a little. "Yes, they started the first moment we met, and they've only grown stronger the more I've been around you. I'd like the chance to get to know you better. Unless you have no interest . . ."

"I-I'd like to get to know you better too," I said softly. "But I have to warn you that I have a hard time—"

"Trusting people. So you said."

I nodded. "Ever since I was a kid."

He smiled. "Well, I like a challenge."

I returned his smile but couldn't help wondering if he really could get past the barriers I'd built around my life. As I looked at him, I knew I wanted to find out.

"I'll do whatever I can to help you, Wynter. But no more lies, okay?"

"No lies. I promise."

He let go of my hand and nodded. "All right. First of all, we need to know if Nathan really took his family to his brother's place. You let me take care of that, okay?"

"But you can't tell him the truth. If Elijah's my brother, Nathan could move his family far away, and we might never be able to find them."

"I can't believe Nathan Fisher would be involved in kidnapping a child. He's a good person. And so is Anna."

"I believe you. It's possible they have no idea who Elijah really is."

Reuben stared at me, his expression solemn. "Thank you for trusting me. It means a lot."

I hesitated a moment before saying what I knew had to be said. "Before we go any further, you know a relationship between us probably won't work, don't you? I live in St. Louis and you live here. It may not be *that* far away, but I have no plans to move, and I assume you don't either. I don't want you to help me because you think we have a future together. It wouldn't be right."

He smiled slowly. "Why don't we let God work that out? If we're supposed to be together, the details will fall into place."

"So you still like me? Even though I lied to you?"

He laughed lightly. "Yes, I still like you. In the end, you told me the truth. I know it wasn't easy for you."

"You know, Jonathon hit the nail on the head during his sermon this morning. The day my brother disappeared, my life ground to a halt. I quit trusting people. Stopped trusting God. I can see now that almost every decision I've made since had something to do with what happened to Ryan." I shook my head. "Want to hear something funny? I love being a reporter, but when I was a kid, I really wanted to be a writer. Thought I'd write novels someday." I shrugged. "Eventually I realized I couldn't do it."

"I don't understand. Why would your brother's disappearance keep you from writing?"

I stared down at the table, searching for the right words. "I don't know if I can explain it, but writers exist in their stories and characters. Their lives pour through their words. Every time

I sat down to write, the hurt I carried inside tumbled out onto the paper. My characters were searching for answers—just like I was. Not the same answers, but their motivations and mine were too tightly intertwined. I couldn't handle it. Couldn't face it."

"'Writing is easy. You just open a vein and bleed.'"

I smiled. "You know that old Red Smith quote?"

He nodded. "My sister Maggie writes."

"Really? Has she been published?"

"Not yet. But she keeps trying. I guess it's pretty hard to get a foot in the door."

"So I've heard."

Reuben drank the rest of his coffee. His eyes searched the room, looking for Randi. When she came out of the back, he motioned to her for more coffee.

"You'll be up all night," I said.

"I'll probably be up anyway. This situation with your brother is unsettling, to say the least."

"Look, I know this is way off the subject, but I want to ask you something totally unrelated to Ryan."

"Shoot."

"Do you know anything about babies being stolen from hospitals in Missouri? This happened over a five-year period. I think the last one was a few years ago."

He looked surprised. "As a matter of fact, I do. I have a friend who is a Madison County sheriff's deputy. He told me about it once. It's been a while though. He was very concerned about it at the time. I have no idea if they ever caught the person responsible." He frowned at me. "Why are you asking?"

I told him about the newspaper clippings someone had left for me.

"I don't understand," he said when I finished. "Why would

anyone in Sanctuary save those stories? And why give them to you?"

I shrugged. "I have no idea, but my guess is this person thinks they know something about the kidnappings and wants me to look into it. News stations get all kinds of weird stuff sent to them. It's not really all that unusual."

"Does any of it ever pan out?"

"Once in a great while. But for the most part, these tips come from people who spend too much time alone."

"Still, it concerns me that this package originated from someone in Sanctuary."

"I wouldn't worry about it yet. Might be nothing. When you have time, I'd like to show you the stories. Maybe you can remember something your friend told you that's not in the articles."

"Sure, but I really don't know much." He glanced at his watch. "It's getting late, and you have a busy day scheduled for tomorrow. I'll walk you back to Esther's."

"Sounds good."

At that moment, Randi walked up to the table with a carafe of coffee. Reuben put his hand over his mug.

"Changed my mind, Randi. We're heading out."

"Sorry to take so long. August didn't come into work, and I've been trying to cover the place by myself."

"Doesn't sound like August," Reuben said. "He's always here."

"I know. I tried calling him, but there wasn't any answer. I plan to stop by his place after I close. Make sure he's okay."

"Did you check with Rae?"

She nodded. "She was as surprised as I am. She hasn't heard from him since yesterday."

"Do you want me to go by his apartment?"

"No. I'll do it." She gave Reuben a quick smile, a gesture she hadn't granted me yet. "But thanks." Ignoring me completely, she walked away.

"I've known August Metzger for a long time," Reuben said thoughtfully. "Never known him not to show up for work."

"You mentioned Rae. Are they friends?"

"More than friends. They've been together for a couple of years now. Unfortunately, Rae isn't interested in marriage. I think that bothers August. He'd like to make their relationship permanent."

I shook my head. "Hard for me to envision them as a couple. He gives me the creeps. Always watching me."

"What do you mean?"

I told him about the way August stared at me the first time I visited the restaurant. "And then I saw him across from Esther's. He seemed to be watching the house." I shrugged. "Maybe it doesn't mean anything, but it was enough to give me the heebie-jeebies. To be honest, I've had the feeling of being watched ever since I got to town. Even the first night here, I was certain I saw someone across the street, staring up at my bedroom window."

"August is an odd duck, but he's harmless. I wouldn't worry about him." Reuben looked around the room. Almost everyone was gone, and the only other couple left was paying their tab. "Well, Randi's about to close up. Let's get you home."

"Where's your truck?"

"Parked at the church. I'd rather walk awhile, if you don't mind. I can get my truck after I leave you at Esther's. Something about walking outside after a rain. I love it."

"I'm game if you are."

He put some money on the table, said good-bye to Randi,

and we left. Reuben was right. The storm from the night before had baptized Sanctuary with the scent of rain. A light breeze carried the fragrance on its wings. It felt fresh and invigorating. I realized this unusual town had captured a piece of my heart. Leaving it behind would be difficult.

"We'll miss you when you leave," Reuben said suddenly, as if he'd been reading my mind.

"I was just thinking how much I'll miss Sanctuary. This is a special place. Even if I don't find Ryan, I'm glad I came."

Reuben stopped walking and gazed intently at me. "And if you do find him?"

"I don't know," I answered truthfully. I frowned at him. "You realize that if Elijah is my brother, I'm afraid I won't be able to keep Sanctuary out of the news. It would be a huge story."

"Does it have to be?"

I took a step back. "I don't know what you mean."

He sighed and stared down at the ground. "I'm not convinced Elijah is Ryan, but if he is, and if Nathan and Anna adopted him, thinking it was legal, why stir up a hornet's nest? The authorities think your brother is dead, right? Why not just reestablish a connection and let Elijah make his own decision about what happens next in his life?"

"Someone did this," I said firmly. "And they need to be punished. My family has lost so much."

Reuben nodded. "You're right. And if that person is still alive, I agree. He should be brought to justice. Sorry, I guess I hadn't thought it all the way through." He came closer to me and took my hand. "Discovering the truth and restoring your family is the most important thing. Whatever it takes, I'll walk through this with you."

Before I had a chance to utter a response, he leaned in and

kissed me lightly. Then he smiled. "Looks like it might rain again. We'd better hurry."

We walked the rest of the way in silence. When we reached Esther's porch, I started to say good night, but the door suddenly flung open. Esther stood there, her eyes wide.

"It's Zac. Something's wrong. You'd better come quick."

THIRTEEN

Reuben and I rushed up the stairs to Zac's room. He was lying on the bed, his face stark white, dark circles under his eyes. He looked awful.

"What's wrong?" I asked Esther.

"I'm not sure, child," she said. "But it looks like food poisoning. What did you eat today?"

"We . . . we ate Italian food in Bonne Terre, but I don't think it could have been that."

"Well, I gave him ipecac syrup. It's what I used to give my children. His stomach was certainly full of something."

"Wait a minute. We kept part of a stromboli in the car all afternoon, and Zac ate it on the way home."

Reuben frowned. "That's probably it. Something with meat and cheese should be refrigerated."

I felt Zac's forehead. It wasn't hot, which seemed to confirm Esther's original diagnosis.

"You can quit talking about me like I'm dead," Zac mumbled. "And quit feeling me, Wynter. I'm not a child."

"Stop looking like a corpse, and I'll stop touching you. How are you feeling?"

Zac pulled himself up into a sitting position. My original evaluation of his color changed from white to pale green.

"Like a big truck ran over me, backed up several times, and tried to finish the job." He shuddered. "I will never eat Italian food again. Never ever. Nor will even one more drop of ipecac syrup ever make it past my lips in this lifetime. Not as long as I have breath in my body."

Although I was still concerned for him, I had to smile. No one could combine physical illness with affronted emotions the way Zac could.

"Maybe it isn't Italian food you need to avoid. Eating food that's been sitting in a hot car all afternoon isn't the smartest thing you ever did."

Esther leaned over and wiped his face with a damp cloth. "I think he's doing better." She smiled at Zac. "I know you hated my remedy, but it seems to have done the trick."

"I don't think many people use ipecac now, Esther," I said. "Maybe we should call the hospital and ask them what to do."

"*Pshaw,*" she said. "Modern medicine doesn't have all the answers. Zac will be a little tired for a couple of days, but he'll be up and around soon. My children went through this."

Zac's eyebrows shot up. "You gave your kids food poisoning?"

Esther patted his shoulder. "Not to worry. It happened at church picnics. Potato salad and tuna salad that sat out too long in the sun. I never cooked anything that made them ill."

Zac looked relieved. "Wynter," he whispered through pale, dry lips. "This is just what we needed. Call Ed and tell him I'm sick. That we'll need a few more days."

"I . . . I don't know," I said. "It's not really honest . . ."

"You won't be lying," Zac said weakly. "I've never felt so bad in my entire life." He pointed at me. "Just don't tell Ed where we are."

"Okay. I'll try. It would be helpful to get a little more time."

"I'm happy to sacrifice myself for the cause," Zac said dramatically, falling back on his pillow.

I patted him on the head. "You're my hero. Now why don't you get some sleep? I'm right down the hall. I'll check on you later."

"I'm going to sit with him awhile," Esther said. She picked something up from the nightstand. "Brought this from downstairs." She rang a little ceramic bell. "Used this when my children were sick." She wiped Zac's forehead again. "After I leave, if you want anything, you just ring it," she told him. "Wynter will hear it and come." She nodded at me. "Sorry to put you out, but I'm afraid I won't hear the bell all the way downstairs. You wake me if you need me though, and I'll get up."

"Thanks, Esther, but I think he'll be fine."

"If he hasn't improved by morning, we can ask Rae to come by and take a look at him."

Zac's eyes widened. "You . . . you mean the veterinarian? What am I, a dog?"

"*Shh,*" Esther said. "She knows about people too. The closest doctor is in Fredericktown. Rae's always willing to help, and she's good at it."

Zac sighed. "Wow. Ipecac and a veterinarian for a doctor. The charm of this small town is wearing thin."

Reuben laughed. "Small-town living can certainly be a challenge. You were lucky to get sick at Esther's. She's pretty smart."

"We're going," I said as Zac's eyelids began to flutter. "You get some sleep."

"Okay." He drew out the word, and then his voice dropped off completely. It was replaced by snoring.

"Are you sure you want to sit with him, Esther?" I asked. "I don't mind . . ."

She waved her hand at me. "Not at all. Makes me feel useful again. Like when I took care of Benjamin and Rebecca."

The catch in her voice got my attention, and I looked at Reuben. He gave me a slight nod. "Why don't you walk me to the door, Wynter?" he said.

I touched Esther's shoulder. "I'll be right back."

"That's fine, honey. You take your time. He'll probably sleep for quite a while. He's pretty worn out."

I slipped out the door, and Reuben followed me. When we got down the stairs, I grabbed his arm and pulled him aside.

"Look, I don't want to be nosy, but is everything all right with Esther's children? Their rooms seem like shrines, and she hasn't mentioned seeing them recently."

Reuben took my hand and led me over to the front door. Then he pushed it open and we stepped out onto the porch. The wind had picked up, and there was a definite chill in the air, although the rain Reuben had predicted wasn't here yet. Spring in Missouri was mercurial. I could dress warmly in the morning and be sweating by the afternoon. Today the reverse was true.

"After Josiah died, Esther was both mother and father to those kids. Of course, the community helped her quite a bit. That's Sanctuary. We see ourselves as one big family." He grinned. "Not in a creepy way. No one here believes we own other people's children, but when one of us needs help, all of us pitch in."

"You all get together for a good old-fashioned barn raisin'?" I asked with an exaggerated twang.

He laughed. "Actually, that happened once. But usually, no.

It's more like when someone's sick, people bring food, and when a mother loses her husband, the church makes sure she has plenty of help."

He leaned against one of the posts that held up the porch's roof. "Most of the kids in Sanctuary go to public school in Barnes. It's only about ten miles from here. The school's a good one now, but it was kind of a mess when Ben and Becky went there many years ago. They got involved with some bad kids. Esther did her best to keep an eye on them, but it wasn't enough. Ben took off when he was eighteen. He's been in trouble ever since. I'm not sure when Esther last heard from him. And that might be a good thing. When he does call, he wants money. Once he realized Esther didn't have any more to give him, he quit contacting her."

"What about Rebecca? Esther said she was married and living in Springfield."

Reuben nodded. "She is. After a rough start, she straightened herself out. But she always says she's too busy to visit her mother. Esther doesn't drive, so she never gets to see her grandchildren. To be honest, I think Becky's too embarrassed to let her rich husband see where she came from."

I pulled myself up and sat on the railing. "Man, I can't believe it. Esther's one of the nicest people I've ever met. Someday she'll be gone. I wonder how her kids will feel then."

"I don't know." Reuben shook his head. "I actually called Becky once and tried to talk to her about her mother. That didn't go well."

"I suppose you had the perfect life. You and your family are close?"

"Yes, we're very close. We lost my dad about seven years ago. My mom lives in Jefferson City, and Maggie lives in Kansas.

No childhood trauma to report." As soon as the words left his mouth, his face fell. "Wynter, I'm so sorry. I wasn't thinking."

"Please, Reuben. Don't worry about it. I don't want anyone to walk on eggshells because of me." I gazed out at the silent streets. "So why do you live here instead of near your family?"

He smiled. "My parents owned a farm just outside of town. After my dad died, I inherited the farm, lock, stock, and barrel. Maggie didn't want it, and I did."

"So you're a mayor slash farmer?"

He laughed. "Add another slash. I do a little writing too. Guess it runs in the family."

"Wow. I'm impressed."

"Don't be. I write copy for farm equipment catalogs. Not very exciting. I won't be popping up on the *New York Times* Best Seller list anytime soon."

"Still, it's . . . cool."

Reuben's eyebrows arched in surprise. "You're the first person to think describing a spark plug for a John Deere tractor is cool."

"Well, I do. You know, I don't tell many people that I like to write. They tend to look at me like I just announced I was running for Miss America. I told my mother about it after I enrolled in college. She thought I was delusional. I changed my major from creative writing to broadcast journalism."

"Well, I don't think you're delusional. You should follow your passion."

"I am. I enjoy my job."

"That didn't sound very convincing."

I smiled. "I may not be *passionate* about it, but I am content. Perhaps that's enough."

"So what are you doing tomorrow?" he asked.

"Well, I can't do actual interviews without my photog, but I can work on questions and decide where to shoot. With your help, we have several good candidates for the piece. I'll talk to those I think will work well for our story and narrow it down to four or five. Then when Zac feels better, all we'll have to do is film the final interviews and get our background shots."

"I'll stop by in the morning and check on Zac," he said. "If he's doing okay, I'll take you to breakfast. Maybe I'll tag along while you work, if it's okay."

"I'd like that. I'm sure people will feel more comfortable if you're with me. Thanks, Reuben."

"Wynter . . ." Reuben hesitated.

"Yes?"

"Promise me you'll be careful."

The seriousness of his tone made my stomach do flip-flops. "What do you mean?"

"I don't know. The note stuck on your windshield. The newspaper clippings. Zac getting sick. Individually, none of them are ominous. But all of them together? It makes me nervous."

"I'll admit the note was a little scary, but as far as the rest of it . . . I don't see any connection. Zac got sick because he ate food that wasn't refrigerated. It might have been dumb, but I don't think it's anything to be concerned about."

"I know, but it's still disturbing. All these things happening at the same time." He stepped up closer to me and put his hand under my chin. "Promise me you'll be cautious, okay? Don't take any chances."

I put my hand on his. "I'll be careful. I promise."

I knew he was going to kiss me, and I was right. Even though I couldn't see a future for us, my feelings seemed to have a mind of their own.

I gently pushed him away. "I'd better get inside. See you to-morrow."

"See you tomorrow."

I watched him until he turned the corner. Then I went inside. Before going to my room, I stopped to check on Zac. He was still sleeping. Esther sat in the chair knitting. She smiled and nodded, letting me know she wasn't quite ready to leave.

When I opened my door, weariness washed over me. I kicked off my shoes and collapsed on the couch. Reuben's concerns for my safety made me feel disquieted. Ever since I'd come to Sanctuary, I'd concentrated on finding out the truth about my brother. Being concerned for my own safety hadn't really occurred to me. But what if Elijah *was* Ryan? And what if his kidnapper was living in Sanctuary? Of course, it was possible the Fishers weren't what they seemed to be. But it was much more likely they'd been duped by someone else. Could that person be watching me? Afraid I might get too close?

These questions rolled around in my mind for a while, but they were like feathers in the wind, blowing every which way without any discernible pattern. Finally I forced myself to get ready for bed. I'd just changed into my pajamas when someone knocked on my door. I opened it and found Esther standing there.

"I'm headed to bed, Wynter," she said. "Zac is sleeping peace-fully. I left his door open so you could hear him if he needs help. Might be best if you left yours open as well. Mind you, the cats will probably find their way in."

As if on cue, Maizie came running in and jumped up onto the bed.

I laughed. "I don't mind one bit. I love having them around, and so does Zac."

148

Esther looked pleased. "They've certainly taken a shine to both of you. And don't worry about Zac. I doubt he'll wake up. Best thing he can do is get some rest."

"Thank you, Esther. I'm so glad you were here to take care of him." I reached out and hugged the small woman.

"I certainly love having you here," she said when I released her.

"Zac and I are very grateful. We both feel at home."

She reached up and patted my cheek. "You get some sleep too. Come on down in the morning when you feel like it. I'll wait on breakfast until you're up and around."

"Thanks, but please don't go to any trouble. I'm good with toast and coffee."

"Whatever you want. Good night."

As she walked away, I suddenly remembered something. "Oh, and thank you for the fudge."

Esther turned around and gave me an odd look. "Fudge? I'm not sure what you mean."

"The box of fudge you put in my room."

"Must have been someone else. It wasn't me. But if you want something sweet there's pie and cookies in the kitchen."

I assured her I wasn't hungry and said good night. The reality of her response made my skin crawl. I quietly walked down the hall to Zac's room. His gentle snoring was the only sound I could hear. Clyde and Frances watched me from Zac's bed as I searched everywhere for the box of fudge. Even in the trash can.

It had disappeared.

FOURTEEN

"Contacting the police is a big step," Reuben said.

I'd called him first thing after I got up. He came over and had breakfast with Esther and me. Now we sat out on the front porch in Esther's white rocking chairs, drinking coffee.

"Someone put that fudge in my room," I said in a low voice. "Someone besides Esther. I gave it to Zac, and he got really sick."

"But it could have been the stromboli."

"Yes, that's true. But where did the fudge come from? And why would someone take the box?"

He took a sip of coffee. I could tell he was turning the situation over in his mind. "You've got to ask Zac about it."

"I did, but he was still groggy. He doesn't remember eating the fudge. In fact, he doesn't remember much at all about last night."

"Maybe you should ask him again when he's feeling better."

"I will. So what do I do now?"

He shook his head. "I honestly don't know. All we have are suspicions, coincidences, and innuendos. Nothing solid. Nothing we could turn over to anyone in an official capacity."

"I know. I'd mark all of this down as my overactive imagination if it wasn't for the box of fudge. That box didn't grow legs and walk out of Zac's room."

"Maybe Esther forgot she gave them to you. She's getting older. Elderly people forget things."

I snorted. "I'm sorry. You've met Esther. I wish I was that sharp."

Reuben sighed. "You're right. I'm just trying to make sense of all this. I'm having trouble believing someone snuck into Esther's and left poisoned fudge in your room. They'd be taking a huge chance of getting caught. How could they be sure you'd eat it? And to be honest, I can't think of one single person in Sanctuary capable of such an act."

"People aren't always who they seem to be, you know. I've interviewed a lot of people who were sure their friend could never murder anyone or their employee wouldn't steal from them. People hide behind masks."

"I know that. But Sanctuary is . . . different."

I wasn't going to argue with him. Frankly, I understood how he felt. But towns were made up of human beings, and I knew from experience that most human beings have secrets.

"I called Randi this morning," Reuben said. "August is gone."

I frowned at him. "What do you mean . . . gone?"

"Gone. Randi checked out his apartment. His clothes are missing. He packed up and left."

"Does he have a car?"

"He used to have a truck, but I think he got rid of it. The Greyhound bus stops in Barnes. All he had to do was find a way to get there. He could be anywhere by now."

I stood up. "This gets crazier all the time."

"You think August put that fudge in your room, don't you?"

"It's the only thing that makes sense. I'm pretty sure he sent me those articles, and it's possible he also wrote the threatening note Zac found the first night we arrived. His behavior toward me has been strange ever since I got here."

"He would have had to sneak into Esther's, find your room, and leave the fudge without being seen. How would he know which room was yours?"

I shrugged. "It wouldn't be hard to figure out. A quick look around would make it clear which room was mine."

"Still, it's just so risky."

"I know. You said that earlier. But you people don't believe in locked doors. He could have easily done it while we were gone yesterday. And even if Esther was home, she doesn't hear very well. She could have been taking a nap."

"That's true." He got up from his rocker and stood next to me. "But I have to wonder why he'd do that, Wynter. Why would he send you those articles, wanting you to investigate the kidnappings, and then try to harm you? And even if he did leave the fudge, for some reason I can't fathom, why skip town before he knows if his plan worked? It doesn't make sense. I don't think August is responsible for this. He might have sent the clippings, but that's it."

"Maybe he wanted me to check into the kidnappings from St. Louis, not here. Perhaps the fudge was supposed to make me sick so I'd go home."

"I don't know. Still doesn't sound right. Besides, it appears that he left early yesterday. You found the box last night."

"He could have put the fudge in my room while we were in church."

"You went back to Esther's to change clothes after the service. Did you notice the box then?"

"No, but it could have been there. Maybe I missed it. I was in a hurry."

"Maybe." He drained the rest of the coffee. "Look, why don't you put off talking to people this morning about your story? You can easily do it later today or tomorrow. Zac's going to be out of action for at least a couple of days. Why don't we drive over to Samuel's farm and see if the Fishers are there?"

"You can't call them?"

"I thought about it, but I couldn't come up with a reason that wouldn't spook them. The last thing we want is for them to leave. For now, I think it would be best if we just drove out there. They probably won't like us showing up unannounced, but we need to find out if Nathan and his family are there without tipping them off."

"What excuse are you going to give them for our visit? I mean, if the Fishers aren't there?"

Reuben shrugged. "I have no idea. Maybe I'll tell them the truth."

"But wouldn't they contact Nathan and tell him? We might lose them for good."

Reuben shook his head. "We're going to have to wing it, Wynter. I guess if I have to, I can tell them we had car trouble and need to use their phone."

"Okay, but let me see how Zac's doing first. And I need to call my boss. I'm hoping I can get us more time without tipping him off as to where we are."

Reuben held out his hand. "Hand me your cup. I'll give it to Esther while you take care of these other things."

I'd just given him my coffee cup when I noticed a familiar car coming down the street. It took a moment for me to accept what I was seeing. My father drove up in front of Esther's house and parked.

"Do you know this guy?" Reuben asked.

"It's my father. I can't imagine what he's doing here."

We stared at each other through his windshield as if we were locked in some kind of weird battle of wills. Finally Dad opened his car door and stepped out.

"What are you doing here?" I asked.

As he came up to the porch, I was shocked by the pallor of his skin and the circles under his eyes. He looked almost exactly the way Zac had last night.

"I've got to talk to you, Emily." He looked at Reuben and frowned. "Alone. And right now."

"I don't understand. Why—?"

"I'm not going to stand outside and discuss this," he retorted. "Where can we go so we can be alone?"

"Is Mom okay?" As soon as the words left my mouth, I realized my father wouldn't have any idea about my mother's welfare. It was just a knee-jerk reaction. "What's this about, Dad?"

For a moment, my father seemed to sway as if he were on the verge of fainting. His appearance and attitude caused my chest to tighten with fear. Could it have something to do with Ryan? Had he been found? Was he dead?

"You and your father talk inside," Reuben said. "I'll wait for you at the café. We'll leave when you're done."

"I don't know . . ."

Reuben took my arm. "This seems important, Wynter."

"Okay, but I want you to stay."

"No," my dad said with force. "This is family business. Between you and me."

Anger rose inside me. "You have *family* business, Dad? I find that funny, since family doesn't seem to mean much to you."

"Please, Emily . . ."

"No. Reuben is my friend. He knows all about Ryan, and I want him with me. I feel closer to him than I do to you."

"If it makes any difference, sir," Reuben said, "nothing you say will be repeated to anyone else. Nor will I interfere in any way with your discussion."

My father looked as if he wanted to argue, but suddenly the fight seemed to go out of him. "Whatever. I don't care anymore."

"Why don't we go inside?" Reuben said, holding open the front door.

My father walked slowly up the porch stairs and followed Reuben into Esther's living room. She came out of the kitchen and looked surprised to see someone else with us.

I quickly introduced her to my father and then asked if we could have some time alone.

"Of course, dear," she said. "I was on my way up to see how Zac's feeling today. You take your time. I'll stay upstairs until you're finished." She offered us a sweet smile. "Can I get anyone something to drink or eat?"

"Thanks, Esther. If we need anything, we'll get it," Reuben said.

She nodded. "Coffee's still on. Just took some turnovers out of the oven. You all help yourself."

I noticed my father staring at her, taking in her simple clothing. As far as I knew, he'd never known any Amish or Mennonite people.

"Thank you, Mrs. Lapp," he said. "I'm sorry to put you out."

"No trouble at all. Wynter is such a blessing to me. And please, call me Esther."

"Thank you, Esther."

My dad's charm was still intact, but he'd toned it down. I was grateful. His phony persona would have been especially embarrassing in front of the elderly Mennonite woman.

We waited until Esther disappeared up the stairs. Then I sat down on the couch with Reuben. Dad sat in the rocking chair next to us. He looked as if he'd aged ten years in the last twenty-four hours. I'd had so much hope that I'd finally found Ryan. If Dad was here to tell me they'd discovered his body, it would crush me. I was grateful Reuben was by my side.

"What's wrong with Zac?" Dad asked.

I explained that he was ill and it was probably food poisoning.

"I'm sorry to hear that."

"I don't think you're here to talk about Zac."

"You're right." He took a deep breath. "This . . . this is very difficult for me to say."

"Does it have something to do with Ryan?" My voice shook, but I didn't care.

He shrugged. "I don't know. That's the problem. All these years, I've been certain that what happened to your brother had nothing to do with what I did. But now . . ." He stared at me with tears in his eyes. "Where is this boy who looks so much like my son?"

"We're not sure. Reuben and I were on our way to find him when you got here. His family suddenly left town."

Dad ran his hand through his hair. "You . . . you can't let them get away. It's possible this young man could be your brother."

"But you always said he was dead."

"And I was convinced of that. Until last night."

"What are you talking about?"

My father stood up and paced back and forth in front of me. Reuben and I waited in silence until he sat down again.

"I had no plans to ever tell you this, and I certainly never wanted your mother to know. But the picture of that boy—"

"Dad, you're scaring me. What's going on?"

He stared down at the floor for several seconds, and then took a deep breath. When he finally looked up, I was shocked by his expression. My father was afraid. Reuben reached over and took my hand, as if he knew something awful was coming. I felt it too.

"As you know, the night you were born, your mother and I couldn't make it to the hospital in St. Louis because of a major winter storm. We only got as far as a small rural hospital about two miles from our house."

"I don't understand. What does this have to do with Ryan?"

"Please, Emily. Don't interrupt me. This is hard enough." His eyes darted toward the front door, and for a moment, I wondered if he planned to suddenly run out like he had at the restaurant.

"When we got to the hospital, there were only a few people there. Just one nurse in obstetrics. The storm had closed roads all around, and no one could make it through." He took another deep breath and blew it out slowly. "We were worried at first, but the nurse assured us that she could deliver our baby without any problem. There was another expectant mother there. She and her boyfriend had made it to the hospital minutes before the storm hit."

I turned to stare at Reuben. Had my father lost his mind? Why were we talking about something that happened years before Ryan was even born?

"Your mother had a terrible time, Emily. It wasn't the nurse's fault. She did everything she could. When our baby was born, she was blue and not breathing. The nurse rushed her into another room to try to help her breathe."

"What do you mean?" My voice came out in a whisper, but I couldn't seem to speak any louder. I wasn't certain anyone could hear me.

"Our baby died, Emily. But the other baby, also a little girl, was born healthy. The nurse told me the parents didn't plan to keep her. They were going to put her up for adoption. That's when we . . . we came up with a plan. At the time it seemed so right. So perfect. We would take the healthy baby, and your mother would never know the truth. She wasn't emotionally strong, you know. There had been . . . problems. I was afraid of what would happen to her if she knew her baby had died." He turned to look at me, his face void of emotion. "We were doing well financially. My company was growing. So I talked to the parents, offered them fifty thousand dollars for their child, which they snapped up. I also gave the nurse a large sum of money, although she didn't ask for it. We took the other baby to your mother's room and told her she was doing just fine. When the doctor finally arrived, the nurse told him about the baby who died and presented the living baby as ours. The doctor didn't question it."

I would have stood up, but I couldn't actually feel my legs. "Are you telling me . . . ? Are you saying . . . ?"

"You're not our biological child, Emily." Tears ran down his face. "It never mattered one bit, you know. You're my daughter. You were mine from the moment I held you in my arms."

"I can't . . . I can't believe it."

"I know this is hard, but you've got to let me finish. I need to tell you why this might have something to do with Ryan's disappearance." He clasped his hands together as if preparing to pray. "Everything seemed fine. Everyone was happy. Even though my heart was broken by the loss of our little girl, we had you. You were everything any parent could ever want. Eventually, I began to feel as if my baby hadn't really died, and the feelings of grief lessened. Your mother's mental health improved, and over the years, I lost any regrets about my decision that night. Our lives went on, and six years later we had Ryan. He was perfectly healthy. We had a happy family."

"What about my birth mother and father?" I asked. "Did they ever contact you? Didn't they want to see me?" I felt such a deep wound in my soul, yet these were people I'd never met. Never known.

"No, I'm sorry. I did keep track of them though. They were both killed in a motorcycle accident when you were five."

I nodded, feeling numb and stupid, as if I couldn't completely understand what my father was saying. My mind grasped the words, but somewhere inside, they didn't make sense. I couldn't seem to process them.

"When you were ten and Ryan was almost four, I got a call. It was a man who called himself Mac. He told me he knew the nurse who'd helped us. She'd recently died of cancer. But on her deathbed, she admitted to him what happened that night. She felt guilty about hiding the truth, even though she still believed she'd done the right thing. This man began to blackmail me. Threatened to call the authorities and tell them what we did. The results could have been devastating. You could have been taken away from us, and your mother . . . well, I knew she couldn't stand the strain. It would have destroyed her. So I paid. About a year later, he called again. And I paid again. For the first time, I began to wonder if what we did was wrong. Then

I'd look at you—you were so beautiful and so special—and I'd know, down deep inside, that you were always supposed to be ours."

"Then you could have adopted me, Dad. Legally. None of this had to happen."

"You're wrong," he said sadly. "Before you were born, your mother was hospitalized for a while due to severe depression. Thankfully, after you were born, she started getting better. But any attempt at adoption would have revealed the past, and we would have been denied."

"So you kept paying this man? For how long?"

"Until I couldn't pay him anymore. Until there wasn't any more money. Basically, I'd given him everything I had. Even though I didn't want to do it, I finally told him it was over. If he wanted to go the police, he'd just have to do it. But I warned him that they'd probably charge him with blackmail. The problem was, I had no idea who he was or how to find him. The only information I had was that he'd known the nurse who'd delivered you. Not much to go on." He shook his head. "No matter what the consequences, I simply couldn't take the strain anymore financially or emotionally. I'd started drinking, just trying to get through the day. Every morning I woke up with the fear that this might be the day I lost you—and your mother." He rubbed his eyes. "I know there's a hell, because I lived in it during those years."

"That's why you changed," I said, more to myself than to anyone else.

"Yes, I was so stressed, I couldn't keep it together. My drinking was supposed to numb the panic I faced every day, but it only made everything worse. In trying to protect my family, I failed you. The hurt I wanted to protect you from came anyway, and

I was the instigator of it." He met my gaze. "I'm sorry, Emily. Truly sorry."

At that moment, I couldn't deal with his apology. Nor could I sort through his story. I was bombarded with emotions, feelings, and thoughts that were too overwhelming to sort through. I struggled to find the one thing that mattered most. "What does this have to do with Ryan?"

He wiped his face on his sleeve. "After I refused to make any more payments, the phone calls stopped. He went away. Even though I kept waiting for the other shoe to drop, it didn't. I came to the conclusion that my threat had worked. Bringing my sins to light would also illuminate his. He was afraid and that fear had driven him away. I'd just started to believe my nightmare was over when Ryan was abducted."

"Could this man have been behind Ryan's disappearance? Could this be revenge for refusing to pay him?"

"That certainly crossed my mind. I'd decided to tell the police everything and let the chips fall where they may when they told me about Harland Burroughs. They were convinced he'd taken Ryan. Their evidence was so compelling, I believed them. In the end, I decided not to say anything about the blackmailer. Your mother was distraught. Her doctor told me she was close to having a complete mental breakdown. Since it seemed the man who blackmailed me had nothing to do with your brother's kidnapping, I couldn't add to her emotional instability."

"But there were all kinds of discrepancies between the other children Burroughs took and Ryan. What if you were wrong?"

"Going through that, it was like my mind was frozen. I had some questions, things that didn't make sense, but the police explained every one of them away. I went along with them because I couldn't think. Couldn't process what had happened. I was trying to take care of you and your mother, and that took all my energy."

"If you cared so much about us," I retorted, "why did you leave us? And why did you sell our home out from under us?"

The tortured look in his eyes almost took my breath away. "I sold the house because we couldn't afford to keep it, Emily. Our money was gone, and I'd spent so much time away from my company, I lost it."

"I thought you sold it and made a lot of money."

He shook his head. "I didn't make a penny. In fact, the company was in debt. I turned it over to my vice-president before we were completely ruined. He was able to turn things around and save it. I didn't have the energy or the will to do it. Losing Ryan took every spark of ambition out of me. I went into insurance just to keep food on the table. I make enough to get by, but I don't have the kind of money we used to have." He ran his hand over his face. I could see the weariness in his expression.

"And I didn't leave you, Emily. Your mother is the one who filed for divorce. It wasn't my idea. I tried to change her mind, but she wouldn't listen. I finally left because she told me she couldn't stand to look at me anymore. I reminded her of Ryan. She blamed me for his kidnapping."

I was stunned. "I don't understand. Why would she blame you?"

A tear snaked down the side of his face. "That morning . . . that awful morning, I yelled at your brother about something so . . . so trivial. I tripped over his bike when I went out to get the paper. I'd told him time and again to put his bike up in the garage at night. But he'd forget and leave it out." He shook his head. "I was under so much pressure. Stressed out about how I was going to keep us all afloat. I said something terrible to him. I didn't mean it the way it came out, but the look on his face—"

"What did you say?"

"I said my life would be a lot easier if I didn't have kids." He covered his face with his hands, as if trying to hide from Reuben and me. When he took them down, I saw the guilt etched sharply into his features. "I know how that sounds. I'd just gotten off the phone with a client, and we'd been talking about the differences in our lives. He didn't have children. My remark was in reference to him and said out of frustration. But after Ryan walked out the door, I realized how awful it was. Like—"

"You didn't want him."

"Yes. I planned to apologize when he got back. But he . . ."

He didn't need to finish the sentence. Ryan never came home.

"But Ryan wasn't taken because of something you said, D-Dad." Suddenly, the word *Dad* felt foreign in my mouth. Like a word I didn't understand and didn't have the right to use.

"I know that, but your mother blamed me. She believed Ryan was gone because he thought we didn't want him."

"That's crazy."

"It might not be true, Emily, but it felt true. It still feels true. Those words echo in my mind every day. They've never left me. They probably never will."

"Surely she realizes now that it wasn't your fault."

"I think she does. But we don't talk anymore. I have no idea if she still blames me."

The daughter inside me wanted to reassure him. Comfort him. But another part of me—the confused and hurt part—couldn't do it. Couldn't reach out. I looked sideways at Reuben, who had remained silent throughout my dad's revelation. I could see the compassion in his eyes, but he didn't say anything.

I swung my attention back to my dad. "Why are you telling me this now?"

"After talking to you yesterday, I began to wonder if Ryan might actually be alive. Maybe this boy really is Ryan."

"What changed your mind? The picture I showed you?"

"The picture and . . . this. It was sent over a week ago, but I was out of town. I just opened it last night."

He reached into his jacket pocket and pulled out an envelope. He handed it to me, and I took out the folded piece of yellow, lined, notepad paper inside. I unfolded it. In rather awkward handwriting were the words: *Your son is alive and your daughter is in terrible danger. There's no time to lose.*

FIFTEEN

I left my father downstairs with Reuben. Although I needed time to deal with the truth about my birth, finding Ryan had to come first for now.

I knocked on Zac's door. It was opened by Esther.

"Everything okay, honey?" she asked.

I nodded. "Fine. I wonder if I could have a moment with Zac?"

"Of course. I think he's tired of my company anyway. Old women's stories aren't very interesting."

"I'm sure that's not true," I said, trying to paste a smile on my face. "I'll be downstairs in a few minutes."

After Esther closed the door behind her, I went over and stood next to Zac's bed. He was sitting up, Clyde curled next to him. I was pleased to see that Zac's color was much improved.

"I have to ask you a couple of questions," I said, keeping my voice low.

"You look like you've seen a ghost," he said. "I thought I was the sick one."

"I can't get into everything now, but this has been quite a day, and it's barely begun. You picked a really bad time to get sick."

"Sorry. Next time I'll try to pick a more convenient time to almost die."

"I'm glad you're okay, Zac. Now shut up and listen."

His eyes widened, but he didn't say anything.

"First of all, did you hear from your friend last night?"

He shook his head. "Wow. I forgot all about that. I seem to remember hearing my phone ring, but I was too sick to answer it." He gazed around the room. Then he pointed at the dresser. "There it is. Hand it to me."

I grabbed the phone and took it back to the bed. "Before you check your messages, tell me something. The fudge I gave you last night. Do you remember it now? You didn't earlier."

At first Zac look confused. Then awareness changed his expression. "Oh yeah. The fudge. I do remember. I ate a couple of pieces, but it wasn't very good. I threw the rest of it away."

"I looked in your trash. The box wasn't there."

"I emptied my trash can before I went to bed. It was overflowing, so I took it downstairs. Tossed everything in the big metal trash bin on the side of the house."

"Okay. I'll have to look out there."

"Why in the world . . ." Realization dawned. "You think the fudge made me sick?"

"I have no idea, but when I asked Esther about it, she said she didn't put that box in my room. There was a note too that said, 'Welcome.' I threw that away. Wish I'd kept it now."

"Wow. That's interesting."

"Yes, and a bit scary."

Zac nodded. "I'll be checking out everything I put in my mouth from now on." He frowned. "What else did you want to ask me?"

I pointed at his phone. "It was about your friend. Check your messages."

Zac punched several options on his phone and then looked up. "No message, but he did call. I'll call him back now." He immediately pressed a button, put the phone to his ear, and then waited. After a moment, he shook his head. "It's going to voice mail." I listened while he left a message and then hung up. "Sorry. We'll just have to wait for him to call back. What's going on?"

Trying hard to keep my emotions in check, I quickly told him about my father's revelations and about the note stating Ryan was still alive.

"Wow, Wynter," he said when I finished. "I can't believe it. Are you okay?"

I shook my head. "No, but I've got to think about Ryan now. That note makes me think that Elijah really is Ryan."

"Maybe, but it only said your brother was alive. It didn't say he was Elijah."

I sat down on the edge of Zac's bed. "You're right. The one thing I don't understand—"

"You mean there's only one?"

Even though I didn't feel like it, I smiled involuntarily. "No, you're right. There's a list of things I don't get, but one point really bothers me."

"And what is that?"

"If the person who sent the note knows what's going on—I mean, if he knows where Ryan is—why doesn't he just tell us?"

Zac sat up a little straighter in bed. "Good point. It's like he's playing a game."

"Or like he wants to help us but yet he doesn't."

Zac fell back against his pillows. "It's too much for me to

figure out. I'm too weak. My brain is barely functioning." He frowned at me. "Did you call Ed?"

"Yes, and we have some extra time."

"I'm sure he wasn't happy about it."

"No, but what could he say?"

"I guess my near-death experience isn't all negative."

"Funny." I pulled my legs up and clasped them with my hands. "I've got to get back downstairs. I have no idea what to say to my father."

Zac sighed. "Look, Wynter, I'm the last person to give advice on family. My father took off when I was a kid and never came back. There's a man downstairs who went through a lot to be your father. And he's still trying. I know all this has been a shock, but if he didn't love you—and your brother—he wouldn't be here now, right? And he certainly wouldn't have told you the truth about what he did."

"Maybe. I don't know. At least I understand some things now that I didn't before."

"Like why everyone else in your family has dark hair?"

"No, but good point. I was thinking about why my father changed so much. Why he sold our house. But—"

"But what?"

I turned to look directly at him. "He said my mother asked for the divorce. It's the first time I ever heard that. Why didn't she tell me the truth?"

He shrugged. "Sometimes it's easier to blame others for what we do. Maybe she holds him accountable for what happened."

"That makes sense. I guess he yelled at Ryan that last morning, before Ryan got on his bike. My mother blames him because my brother never came home."

"But it wasn't his fault, Wynter. The real blame lies at the feet of the person who took him."

"I know that."

Zac reached over and put his hand on my arm. "Maybe you should point that out to your dad. It might help him."

"He doesn't feel like my dad right now."

Zac pulled his hand back and shrugged. "Then who is? The man who sold you?"

His comment felt like a slap in the face. I couldn't form a response. Instead, I started to cry.

"Oh, man. I'm sorry." He struggled to sit up again. "I'm such a jerk. I didn't mean to be so blunt."

"No, it's not you," I said between sobs. "It's just such a shock. Feels like my life has been turned upside down."

"I understand."

"I know you're right, Zac. It's all just too much to handle right now. But I need to focus on Ryan, not me." Suddenly, a horrifying thought popped into my mind. "I'm not really Ryan's sister." The words came out in a whisper.

Zac grabbed my hand. "Wynter, look at me." When I did, I saw determination in his face. "Answer this question without thinking first. Without pausing. Will you do that?"

I nodded slowly.

"Is Ryan your brother?"

I started to hesitate, but Zac shook his head. "No hesitation. Is Ryan your brother?"

"Yes," I blurted out. "He's my brother. He always will be."

"Then doesn't that make you his sister?"

I squeezed his hand. "How does a smart aleck like you get to be so intelligent?"

He shrugged. "I like to keep my super intellect a secret."

I smiled at him. "I don't think that will be a problem." I tried to pull my hand away. "You can let go of me now. I'm okay."

He released me. "All right, but if you need me, you know where to find me."

"Yes, I do. In bed, milking all the attention you can get."

"Hey, as you said, I'm no dummy."

I looked into his eyes. "No, you're not a dummy; you're a good friend. I doubt anyone else on this planet could get me to smile right now—except you."

"Thank you for that. I know I don't really deserve to be your friend. I was ready to betray you, but you understood and forgave me. That's a rare quality."

I knew he was hinting about my father, but I didn't say anything. I hadn't moved anywhere close to forgiveness yet. It was too soon. "Just let me know when you hear from your friend. I'd really like to know if Elijah was born in Jamesport before we go any further with this."

He nodded. I turned to go, but he called my name.

"Yes?"

"Hang in there, Wynter. You'll get through this. I just know it."

"Better be careful. You're starting to sound like one of those religious nuts you hate so much."

He traced a pattern on his quilt with his index finger. "Maybe they're not all as nutty as I thought."

Not knowing what to say, I just nodded, closed the door behind me, and headed downstairs. Instead of going into the living room, I cut through to the kitchen and went out the back door. I found Esther's large metal trash bin next to the house, but it was empty. The trash had been picked up, probably earlier this morning. Now there was no way to find out if the fudge was responsible for making Zac sick.

When I went inside I found my dad pacing back and forth across the living room floor. I heard Reuben's voice, but he became silent when I walked into the room.

"Don't stop talking on my account."

"It can wait," Reuben said. "How's Zac?"

"Doing good. He sent a friend of his to Jamesport to check out Elijah's story, but we haven't heard from him yet."

"What story?" Dad asked.

"Supposedly Elijah was born there. If that's true, obviously he can't be Ryan."

"I would be shocked if he's not," Reuben said. "You've apparently stirred up something."

I sat down in the rocking chair. "I guess you're right. So at what point do we call the police?"

"I don't know," Reuben said, shaking his head. "We don't really have anything to give them yet."

"Even if this friend of Zac's says Elijah wasn't born in Jamesport, it doesn't necessarily mean it's true," Dad said. "Unless his information is something more than hearsay, it can't be trusted."

I sighed. "You're right. I hadn't thought of that." I frowned at Reuben. "Maybe we need to go there ourselves. Now that I've got a little extra time—"

"No," Dad said. "I'll go."

I started to protest.

"Emily, I need to help. Please. This is my son. Let me be involved."

Before I could respond, someone started pounding on Esther's door. I went over to open it and found a woman standing there. "I'm Janet Dowell, a friend of Esther's. Is . . . is Reuben King here?" She was younger than I'd imagined, with sandy-blond hair and blue eyes that were wide and full of tears.

Reuben stepped up behind me. "Hi, Janet. What's going on?"

"It's August."

"What about him? Has he come back?"

She shook her head as tears spilled down her cheeks. "No, Mayor. They found him in a field outside of town. He's . . . he's dead."

CHAPTER

SIXTEEN

Reuben left with Janet, and I went to find Esther. She was in the laundry room at the back of the house. I told her about August."

"Land sakes," she said. "What in the world happened?"

"I don't know. Janet said they found him in a field outside of town."

She took her apron off and flung it on top of the washer. "If you don't mind, I'd like to walk over to the church and see if they know anything more. Will you keep an eye on Zac?"

"Of course, I will. He's doing much better though. I think you can quit worrying about him."

"Oh, honey. I don't worry anyway. I just pray and trust God. Zac will be fine." She leaned in close to me. "God has His hand on Zac. You know that, don't you?"

Startled, I nodded even though I had no idea what she was talking about. She turned to leave but stopped and came back, linking her arm through mine. "You know, Wynter, most people try to trust God based on His Word. And that's the way it should be. Every promise of God is true, and we can be confident that even if every man lies, God does not." Her light-blue eyes peered into mine. "But believing someone's words, whether it's a person in our lives or God himself, only comes second to knowing their heart. If you understand someone's heart, you can believe what they say. Do you understand what I mean?"

Again I nodded dumbly. She hugged me and toddled off. I stood there, thinking about her comments. Since arriving in Sanctuary, a lot of Scriptures had been coming to me. Scriptures I told myself I believed, yet they weren't really alive to me. Was it because I hadn't taken time to know the author of those words?

I started back toward the living room. The man I called Dad was waiting for me. Was I thinking about *what* he told me, or was I concentrating on *who* he was? My head pounded with confusion. Everything had changed. Not only about the way I'd come into my family, but also what I'd believed about my father. He hadn't left us. What did that mean to me? My world had just been turned upside down, and I had no idea how to get it right side up again.

On my way to the living room, I discovered Zac coming down the stairs, dressed, and with his hair combed.

"Hey, you're supposed to be in bed," I said sternly.

"I'm determined to join the world of the living, if you don't mind."

"I don't mind at all." I linked my arm through his, and together we joined my father in the living room.

"Zac," Dad said. "How are you feeling?"

"Much better, thank you. I thought I heard Reuben earlier," Zac said as he sat down on the couch.

"You did," I said. "He went into town. August Metzger, the cook from Randi's café, was found dead a little while ago."

"What?" Zac frowned at me. "What happened?"

"They don't know. Esther went to the church to see if she could get more information."

"That's too bad." He shook his head. "The main reason I came down was to tell you I heard from my friend Mark. The guy I sent to Jamesport."

"What did he say?"

Zac glanced over at my father and then at me.

"It's okay," I said. "He knows all about it."

"I'm afraid the news isn't as helpful as we'd hoped. Mark nosed around as much as he could without appearing suspicious. Several people remembered the Fishers. They lived there all right before coming to Sanctuary. But as far as Elijah goes, one guy said he *thought* Elijah was born there, but another woman couldn't remember Elijah at all."

I sighed with exasperation. "So where does that leave us?"

"Back to my original idea," Dad said. "I'm driving to Jamesport."

"Are you sure, Dad?"

"Yes. You need to stay here in case Elijah comes back."

"Okay, but please keep in touch. And don't tip anyone off. The Fishers might have friends that still live there. We don't want them to find out someone's asking questions. They might run so far away we'll never find them."

"I understand, Emily."

I glanced at the clock. It was almost eleven. "When will you leave?"

"Now. We need this information as soon as possible."

"Do you want me to make you something to eat first?"

"Thanks, but I'll pick up something on the way. It looks like a storm's moving in, and I'd like to stay in front of it."

"Okay, Dad. Please be careful."

He nodded. "I will." He reached into his pocket and took out the note he'd shown us earlier. "Why don't you keep this? I'd feel better knowing it's here where I can't lose it."

"Okay." I reached out and took it from him.

He stared at me for a moment before turning toward the front door.

"Don't you need to call Angela and tell her where you'll be?" Even saying his new wife's name made me sick to my stomach.

Dad stood for a moment with his hand on the doorknob, not looking at me. "Angela left me two years ago, Emily. We're divorced."

Without saying another word, he walked out, closing the door behind him.

I turned to Zac, my mouth hanging open. "I can't believe I'm only finding out now. He could have told me."

"Could he?" Zac asked.

"What are you saying?" I snapped. "Are you trying to make me feel sorry for a man who's been lying to me my whole life?"

"Look, Wynter, the last thing I want to do is upset you, but it seems to me that man *gave* you your entire life. I mean, who knows where you might have ended up if he hadn't taken you home from that hospital? He raised you, spent almost all his money protecting you—"

"You mean protecting himself."

Zac scowled at me. "He paid a blackmailer because he didn't want to lose you. And he didn't want you to lose your parents. Can't you see that?"

I plopped down on the couch next to him. "Why are you defending him?"

"I'm not defending him, but I think you need to sit back and take another look at this situation. Your father took you home from the hospital because he loved your mother so much he didn't want her to know her baby died. Then he raised you, loved you, and did everything in his power to protect you."

"If he'd wanted me so badly he could have—"

"Adopted you? How? By telling your mother her daughter died? By possibly pushing her over the edge? And what about her past? I think he's right in saying that most adoption agencies would have turned down their application."

I shook my head. "I hear what you're saying, Zac, but that doesn't make it right. Look at all the trouble his actions caused."

Zac sighed. "I know. But you need to look past his actions and consider his heart."

I felt as if I'd been punched in the face. Were Esther's words coming back to haunt me? "You . . . you don't know what you're talking about," I mumbled, hoping he'd back off.

"Maybe I don't. But I know what it's like to let something negative affect your entire life. I did it, and I don't want you to make the same mistake."

"What are you talking about?"

"My parents were married for five years before I was born. After I arrived, my father decided he didn't like competing for my mother's attention. He demanded that either I be put up for adoption or he would leave. Mom refused to give me away, and he took off. Left my mother with nothing. No money. No job and no training. She'd married right out of high school, and my dad hadn't allowed her to work. She struggled for several years. Started off on welfare, and then finally got a job in a restaurant. She worked as hard as she could, even taking extra shifts so she could earn more money. Still, we barely scraped by. Eventually, she was diagnosed with rheumatoid arthritis, and it got harder and harder for her to work. Finally, she lost her job because she couldn't keep up.

"We'd been going to the same church for years, and sometimes they'd help us with food. It wasn't much, but we were grateful for it. My mom considered these people family. Things got worse and worse until finally, desperate to take care of me, she officially filed for divorce from my father and asked for child support. He'd never given us a penny. Never checked up on me. Never called. Never visited. By this time he owned a large car lot and was making good money. When the elders in our church found out, they kicked her out, telling her it was a sin to divorce her husband. I was only eight when it happened, and I can still remember the look on her face when they called her out in a service, in front of the entire congregation. She was in complete shock. They gave her the chance to repent. To call off the divorce. She tried to explain. Tried to make them understand, but when she refused to repent for her supposed sins, two elders came over, took us by the arms, and led us out of the building."

"Oh, Zac. I can't believe it."

"Well, believe it. When the door slammed behind us, my mother sank to her knees on the sidewalk. I was crying, trying to help her up. I couldn't understand what had happened. Then I looked over at the sanctuary windows and noticed a woman who had been Mom's best friend sitting there, watching us. She looked upset, and for a moment I thought she was going to come out and help us. But finally she just turned her face away. After a few minutes, my mother got up, took my hand, and led me back to the car. We drove away from that church and never went back."

"I'm so sorry." I moved closer and took his hand. "Surely you realize most churches don't act like that. My family went to church for years, and they never treated anyone so . . . so shamefully."

He squeezed my hand. "The service here was great. Full of love and joy. As I sat there listening to Jonathon, I realized my attitudes about life were colored by that one terrible experience. Everything has been tainted by it. And it was a mistake. Our lives are more than one or two bad incidents."

Too choked up to speak, I just nodded.

"A couple of years later, my mother found another church. She kept asking me to go with her, but I wouldn't. I was angry at religion and angry with her for getting sucked back in. But the person I was the angriest with was God."

"What those people did had nothing to do with God."

"I know. But I was trapped by my rage. Couldn't open my heart to Him or to any Christian, even after my mother found the right kind of church—one where people loved her, accepted her, and treated her like true family."

"Does she still go there?"

"Yes. Going on twelve years now." He smiled. "After we get back, I'll take some time off and visit her. I think it's time we went to church together."

I smiled at him. "I'm sure that will make her very happy."

"I should have done it years ago. I've lost valuable time with my mother because I couldn't move past that terrible incident."

"Are you trying to tell me I'm doing the same thing?"

"Your treatment of your father revolves around what happened to your brother, doesn't it? Everything is tied to Ryan's abduction."

"My father drank before Ryan disappeared."

"True, but he was under incredible pressure. In time, I think your family could have recovered. But when Ryan was taken, it all spiraled out of control. There was no going back. No chance to start again."

I squeezed his hand one more time and then let it go. "I hear what you're saying, but I need some time."

"I know. It will take a while. But do it *with* your father. The two of you will get better faster if you have each other. It's what I should have done with my mother."

"Zac, one thing terrifies me."

"What's that?"

"At some point Mom will have to be told the truth. About me. About Ryan."

"You can face that later. Just concentrate on what's happening now. Not what might happen later. When the time comes, if you and your father can present a united front, you can both help her through it."

I started to tell him I wasn't sure my mother would listen to anything my father said, when the front door opened and Reuben came in. His expression was grim.

"It was definitely August?" I asked.

He nodded. "Someone bashed his head in."

I heard Zac's quick intake of breath. "He was murdered?"

"Yes. Someone killed him and left his body near the road outside of town. We know he packed at least one suitcase, but it wasn't there. Who in the world would kill someone for a bunch of stuff that wasn't worth anything? It's crazy." He shook his head. "Things like this aren't supposed to happen in Sanctuary."

"I'm sorry, Reuben," I said. "I know August was your friend."

He sank down in a chair across from us. "We weren't really all that close. August was hard to get to know, but he was one of us. That makes it tough."

"Have you talked to Rae?"

"Yeah, she was at the restaurant. As you can imagine, she's very upset."

"So what happens now?" I asked.

He sighed. "Well, we called the sheriff. He and his deputies are out there now securing the area." He offered me a weak smile. "You may have another excuse to stay in Sanctuary. No one is supposed to leave town right now."

Zac and I exchanged looks. "I still want to go to Nathan's brother's house. Will we be able to do that?"

"I don't know. Let me talk to my deputy sheriff friend, Paul Gleason."

"Thanks. I'm praying Elijah's really at his uncle's."

"And if he is?" Zac said. "What will you do?"

"We'll turn around and come back. Until we have more answers, I don't want to make them suspicious."

Reuben scanned the room. "Where's your dad?"

I explained to him about the call from Zac's friend and my father's decision to go to Jamesport. I was glad he'd left before the sheriff shut down the roads out of town.

"Okay. I'll talk to Paul. Find out when we can get out of here. I promised Rae I'd take her over to the church to see Jonathon. We need to plan a service for August as soon as they release his body. He didn't have any family, so we're it."

I nodded. "Fine. I've got to call Ed . . . again." An idea popped into my head. "If I tell him we're near Sanctuary and there's been a murder, he may actually tell me to check it out."

"You take care of that, and I'll come back when I have more information. If Paul says we can't leave, there's nothing I can do about it, Wynter."

"Please try to convince him. We can't let the Fishers get away."

"I understand." He reached over and grabbed my hand. "I'll do my best. I promise."

He left just as Esther returned. She came in the door, her usual smile missing.

"Are you all right?" Zac asked.

She nodded. "Losing a friend is sad."

"I didn't know you and August were close," I said.

She went over to the chair where Reuben had been just moments before and sat down. "When August came here, years ago, he'd been through a bad divorce. He loved his wife, but she found another man. August's heart was broken. Randi knew him from a restaurant in Festus. She was just getting ready to open her café and still didn't have a cook. She offered him the job, and he accepted. August liked to keep to himself, but he was still part of our community. He came to our church dinners and took part in other social activities—always alone.

"Then he and Rae found each other. Rae's personality made up for his quiet spirit. I think August felt complete around her because she allowed him to be himself. She did the socializing, and he enjoyed the benefits without having to say much. It was a perfect match." Esther smiled sadly. "Rae will miss him. More than most people could understand."

"Janet was really upset."

Esther sighed. "I think Janet and August were kindred spirits. Both of them kept to themselves, and they shared painful pasts." She stood up. "Have you had lunch?"

I shook my head.

"I'll prepare something."

"Let me help," I said.

"Thank you, Wynter, but if you don't mind, I need a little time alone in my kitchen to pray. I hope you understand."

"Yes, of course."

Zac and I were silent until she was out of sight.

"So do you still think August was stalking you?" Zac asked.

I sighed deeply. "I don't know. I feel like I'm missing something. Like there's a common thread that links everything together, but I just can't find it."

"Is August's death part of the pattern?"

I studied him. "I don't know. What do you think?"

"Well, the timing is certainly odd."

"If August was the one who sent me those newspaper clippings, and now he's dead—"

"Maybe those clippings are more important than we realize. Could they be connected somehow?"

I stared at him for a moment. "It's possible," I said slowly, my mind trying to sort through all the information from the past several days. "After lunch I'm going through those articles again. Could be I missed something important."

Zac nodded. "Might be a good idea."

I noticed how tired he looked. "Are you sure you're doing okay? Do you need to rest awhile?"

"I think I do," he said, sounding reluctant. "I feel like such a wimp."

"You have nothing to feel bad about. I'm just happy you're getting stronger."

"Me too."

Esther called us and we went into the dining room for lunch. After we'd eaten, I followed Zac up the stairs to his room.

"Take it easy," I told him as he sat down on his bed. "You'll be back to your ornery self anytime now."

He snorted. "Trust me. I'm too afraid to stay sick. If Esther comes after me with that nasty stuff again, I'll jump out the window."

"Well, the front porch roof is only a few feet below us. The worst damage you can do is to cause yourself a lot of embarrassment."

"Anything's better than Esther's remedy for food poisoning."

"Poor baby."

He smiled wryly at me. "I detect a note of sarcasm in your tone."

"Oh? I'm sorry. I meant that comment to be dripping with it."

He wrinkled his nose. "Have you considered leaving the news behind and going into comedy?"

"Maybe tomorrow. I need time to work on my routine." I smiled at him. "You get some sleep. I'll check on you before dinner."

"If Reuben gets permission for you to leave town, let me know before you go, okay?"

"I will."

I closed the door and went to my own room. For the life of me, I couldn't figure out how the kidnapping of babies in Missouri could be connected to the abduction of a young boy in Illinois, but I had to take a look. Someone in Sanctuary sent those clippings because they felt they were important. Was it just a coincidence, or was something more going on?

I closed my door and went to the drawer where I'd put the envelope.

It wasn't there.

SEVENTEEN

I stood staring into my drawer for a while. Frankly, I couldn't believe my eyes. First the fudge. Now the newspaper articles. Hoping Zac had taken the envelope, I went back to his room. Unfortunately, he had no idea where it was.

Hurrying back to my room, I turned on my laptop. It didn't take me long to find the original stories. In the last seven years there had been eight abductions from Missouri hospitals, the last one occurring a little over three years ago. In six of the cases, no one noticed anybody taking the baby. In one instance, a witness saw a woman near the nursery with a large bag. Police wondered if it was used to carry the baby out of the hospital. In another abduction, a new mother noticed a nurse come into the nursery and wheel a baby out, but she wasn't sure which baby was removed. She assumed the nurse was taking the baby to its mother. Surveillance cameras didn't help much. Many people came in and out of the nurseries, but no one appeared suspicious. And cameras near the entrances and exits just showed people carrying suitcases and bags in and out, making it impossible to tell if anyone was hiding a baby.

I sat back and pondered the information. How could seven babies be whisked away from different hospitals without anyone realizing something was wrong? Surely it wasn't that easy. Although I read each story carefully, I couldn't see any connection to my brother's kidnapping. I took the note my father had given me out of my pocket and read it again.

Your son is alive and your daughter is in terrible danger. There's no time to lose.

It was handwritten and nondescript except for the first letter *t* on the words *terrible, There's, time,* and *to.* The top line was extra long, drawn out almost to the end of the word. But unless we could match the handwriting to someone, it wouldn't help us. It was possible police could take fingerprints from the note or the envelope. Of course, that would mean calling them in, and we weren't ready to do that yet.

I slapped the note down in frustration. Our entire case seemed to be hiding in the shadows. Shadowy clues that didn't make sense. Incidents that seemed ominous. But trying to drag them into the light wasn't working. We had no solid leads. No real evidence.

I looked at the envelope the note had come in. It had been mailed to my father a week before Zac and I arrived in Sanctuary. Whoever sent it knew we were coming. A new and frightening thought popped into my head, making it hard to catch my breath.

A sudden knock on the door startled me. I got up and opened it. Reuben stood there.

"We've been given permission to leave town, as long as we return by this evening," he said.

"Great." I motioned him inside and shut the door. "Reuben,

whoever sent this note to my dad mailed it about a week before we got here."

He frowned. "You contacted Martha two weeks before you left St. Louis. She obviously spread the word all over town."

"But, Reuben, how would this person know about my dad? To find him they'd not only have to know about *my* past, they'd also have to know my real name. I've gone to great lengths to hide it. How could anyone in Sanctuary have that kind of information?"

The stunned look on his face revealed his understanding of the implications. "You're right."

"Unless the weird things that have been happening aren't about Sanctuary at all. They're about me—and my brother."

He stared at the letter in my hand. "We shouldn't jump to conclusions."

I sighed heavily. "But that's all we have. Unsubstantiated conclusions. I think we need to focus on Elijah. He may be the key to everything."

Reuben shrugged. "I don't know."

"Look, I know you love this town, but you have to face the facts. Something's not right here."

"Do you think Ryan's kidnapper lives in Sanctuary?"

"I'm beginning to wonder about that. But who sent me those clippings? The kidnapper wouldn't do it. He doesn't want to draw attention to himself." I rubbed my forehead. "And how are those kidnappings connected to Ryan?"

"Look, although I can't prove it, I'm certain Nathan and Anna Fisher had nothing to do with taking Ryan. They would never kidnap a child."

"You might be right. From what Zac's detective friend says, the Fishers were living in Jamesport when Ryan was taken. If that's true, they couldn't have done it. I have to wonder if they know who did, though." I sighed. "Let's get going. We're just spinning our wheels. If Elijah is the key, we need to find out the truth about him." I jumped up, grabbed the letter, and slid it back into the envelope. "We're taking this with us."

"Why?"

"Because I'm not letting it out of my sight. The clippings are gone."

Reuben's mouth dropped open. "Gone, as in someone took them?"

"I'm sure I put them in the dresser drawer. When I came upstairs to my room, they were missing." I picked up a light jacket, since a quick look out the window showed more clouds moving in. Springtime in Missouri was volatile, to say the least.

"If Elijah's not at his uncle's—"

"We'll have a talk with your friend Paul." I put my hand on his arm. "I don't want to put anyone at risk, Reuben. A man's dead. It might not have anything to do with what's going on, but if it does and we don't say anything . . ."

"I know, and I agree." Reuben put his hand over mine. "We'll find the truth, Wynter. I want you to know you're not alone."

"I do know that. You and Zac have been so helpful. I don't know what I'd do without you."

"Zac is a good friend," he said, his voice husky. "But I hope I'm becoming more than a friend."

"I know chasing after my brother hasn't given us time to explore our feelings. I'm sorry."

He put his finger on my lips. "Don't apologize. Your commitment to your brother is one of the things I love about you."

He took his finger from my lips and gently brushed away a strand of hair that had escaped from my braid. "Please don't push me away, Wynter. No matter what happens. I know you've been hurt."

"I'm trying, Reuben. I really am."

He took my hand off his arm and kissed my fingers. "Good. Now, Samuel's farm isn't far away, but we should get on the road. Depending on what we find, we might want to spend a little time there."

I nodded. "Let's go."

I stopped by Zac's room. He was sound asleep. We told Esther we were leaving and headed out of town. Reuben's truck was nicer inside than I'd expected. When we got out on the main road, the storm Dad had been concerned about hit us with its full force. I was grateful we hadn't taken my little Prius. Reuben's huge vehicle was up to the challenge of heavy rain and gusty winds.

We didn't talk much on the way to Samuel's house. Trying to be heard above the sound of the rain, the wind, and the windshield wipers seemed to take too much effort. I appreciated having time to think about what might happen at Samuel Fisher's house. If Elijah was there, the plan was to leave. We'd know where he was and that his parents weren't trying to hide him. If he wasn't there, we'd contact Paul Gleason, tell him our story, and ask for his help.

Gradually, over the sound of the rain, another noise grew in intensity. I checked the side mirror and saw a truck coming toward us faster than anyone should be driving in these kinds of conditions.

"That guy's going too fast," I said loudly, trying to be heard above the noise. "You'd better slow down or pull over."

Reuben glanced in his rearview mirror. "Some people shouldn't be allowed to drive." He let up on the gas pedal, rolled down his window, and motioned for the other driver to pass. But instead of going around us, he drew up closer. Reuben motioned once again, his arm getting soaked by rain. No response. He pulled his arm inside and closed the window. "What's wrong with this guy?"

Without any warning, the truck rammed us.

"Hold on," Reuben yelled.

I looked over toward the side of the road. After a line of trees, the ground dropped sharply. Missouri was full of hills, and we were driving next to a dangerous slope. Before I could warn Reuben, the black truck pulled up next to us, sideswiping us. I tried to see the driver, but the windows were tinted, and I couldn't see inside the cab.

Reuben's face was white as his truck began to spin out of control, getting closer and closer to the edge of the ravine. As we headed toward certain disaster, the other truck sped up and took off, leaving only a trail of water and gravel from the road. Before we went flying off the edge and down into the ravine, Reuben suddenly turned the steering wheel the other way, bringing us to a stop just inches from the edge.

"Are you okay?" he asked shakily.

"I-I'm fine. That guy tried to run us off the road." I shook my head in disbelief. "He did that on purpose."

"Yes, he did. Wait here."

Reuben got out of the truck and walked around his vehicle. I noticed his door creaked when he opened it. I watched him, trembling with emotion.

"We could have been killed," I said when he got back in the truck.

"Maybe that was the idea." He pulled on his door. It closed but didn't appear to latch securely. "The truck's banged up, but I can still drive it."

"Why would someone do that?"

Reuben shook his head, and his hands clasped the steering wheel with so much pressure, his knuckles were white. "I have no idea."

"Did you see his license plate?"

"No. I was too busy trying to stay alive."

We sat in silence for several moments, just listening to the sound of the rain on the truck's roof.

"We have to assume it had nothing to do with—"

He snorted. "Yes, I know. Just add it to the list of things that have nothing to do with anything else." He turned toward me, his expression taut, his eyes narrowed. "After we leave Samuel's, we're definitely talking to Paul. We could have been badly hurt, Wynter. Or worse."

I nodded. A tear of frustration fell from my eye, and I quickly wiped it away.

"Don't worry. Paul's not an idiot. I'm confident he won't let the Fishers take Elijah away where we can't find him. I should have insisted we contact Paul before now."

"With what? Conjecture? Innuendo?"

"Well, I hope our trip to Samuel's will finally change that." He leaned toward me and put his hand on my cheek. "I'm so grateful you're okay. If anything had happened to you . . ."

"I know. I feel the same way about you, Reuben."

"Good." He took his hand back, put the truck in gear, and started driving.

It took us about forty-five minutes to reach Samuel's farm. Reuben pulled over to the side of the road as soon as the farmhouse came into view. The house was large, white, and old. There was a barn and several outbuildings on the property. A modern tractor sat next to several other pieces of machinery. Two black buggies without horses were parked a few yards away. I assumed the horses were inside the barn, out of the rain.

"Modern equipment *and* buggies?" I said.

"Many conservative Mennonites have modern farm equipment," Reuben said. "They need it to take care of their crops. This situation is a little different though. Naomi Fisher is conservative, but Samuel left the church several years ago after a disagreement with Pastor Troyer. Nathan is worried about his brother. Believes he's backslidden."

"Just because he doesn't go to church?"

"I'm not sure. Nathan seems genuinely concerned though."

"Does one of those buggies belong to Nathan?"

"No. I'm sorry, Wynter."

"How can you tell?" I asked, unable to keep the disappointment out of my voice.

"The top of Nathan's buggy is gray. Those are black."

I grabbed his arm. "We need to get closer. Maybe Nathan parked on the other side of the house."

Reuben didn't answer, but he put the truck back in gear and began driving slowly up the dirt road. I kept my eyes peeled, hoping to see a buggy with a gray top, but as we passed the other side of the house, no other buggy was visible.

"Maybe it's parked behind the house," I said, letting go of his arm. "Can we—"

"If we get any closer, they could see us," Reuben said. "I don't want to alert them. If Samuel warns his brother . . ."

The rain began to pound harder on the roof of the truck. Frustration overwhelmed me. "I don't care anymore," I said.

We were so close. I just couldn't go back without some answers.

"Wynter, we can't . . ."

The rest of Reuben's words were lost behind the sound of
thunder as I opened the door of the truck and began to run
toward the farmhouse.

EIGHTEEN

The downpour made it hard to see, but I kept going. I knew Reuben would follow me, but I had no intention of being stopped. I had to have some answers, and I was tired of being patient. Tired of waiting for the right moment and worrying about what *might* happen. Ryan's voice was growing louder in my head. I had to know the truth. If someone knew where he was, I intended to find him—no matter the cost. I fell down twice but didn't pay any attention to my wet, dirty jeans or my mud-caked sneakers. As I ran, I realized that what Zac had tried to tell me was true. Ryan *was* my brother. Blood ties or not, we were joined and always would be.

Behind me, I could hear the roar of Reuben's truck, so I ran off the road, through a culvert, and pushed myself between the fence rails that surrounded the property. As I wiggled through the small opening, I thought I felt a sharp pain but decided to ignore it. I glanced to my left and noticed a gate guarding the long driveway. Reuben would have to get out of his truck and open it if he wanted to follow me all the way to the house.

That gave me just enough time to make it to the porch before he could stop me.

Although it seemed as if I'd been running forever, in truth, it only took a few minutes to reach the front of the house and fling myself at the door. I started knocking loudly, and a few seconds later, the door was opened by a startled woman, who appeared frightened by my presence on her front porch. Before I had a chance to say anything, a tall, thin man came up behind her.

"Are you in trouble, young lady?" he asked, his tone gruff.

"No . . . I mean, yes." I wiped my face with my hand. It was impossible to tell the rain from my tears. "Are you Samuel Fisher?"

He nodded. "Yes, I'm Samuel. Who are you?"

"Please," I sobbed. "Please talk to me. I'm Wynter . . . I mean, Emily Erwin. Ryan Erwin is my brother. I think you know him as Elijah. I've got to find him. Talk to him. You may be the only people who can tell me where he is."

Samuel didn't respond; he just stared at me. I heard Reuben's truck pull up behind me. His door creaked open and then closed. His footsteps pounded up the steps and onto the porch.

"Samuel. It's me. Reuben King."

"Reuben, what's the meaning of this?"

For a moment, I thought Reuben might grab me and try to drag me back to the truck. But instead, he put his arm around me.

"Samuel, Wynter needs to talk to you. She also needs to get warm. Will you let us in?"

"Oh, Samuel," the woman said, compassion on her face. "This poor woman is soaked to the skin." Her eyes widened as she stared at me. "And she's bleeding. We must help."

I looked down and was shocked to see a growing red stain on the front of my shirt.

Although it appeared to be done out of reluctance, Samuel reached over and unlatched the door.

"Come in," he said, standing to one side.

Reuben gently guided me into the house. We entered a simple but cozy living room. A fire burned in the fireplace, and a wonderful aroma permeated the air.

"You come with me, young lady," the woman said. "I'm Naomi Fisher. I will tend to your wound and get you out of those wet clothes. Then you can warm up in front of the fire."

I started to walk toward her, but she motioned for me to stop. "I think we need to take your shoes off first."

To my horror, I realized I'd tracked mud into her house. "I'm so sorry. I didn't realize . . ."

"It doesn't matter. My husband almost always forgets to wipe his feet before coming inside. I am used to cleaning up after him."

She gave me a warm smile, which made me feel even worse about my negligence. I slid off my shoes and handed them to her. She carried them back to the front door and set them out on the porch.

After a quick glance at Reuben, I followed the woman out of the living room and up the stairs. She led me to a bedroom with a huge carved bed and matching dresser.

"Will you remove your shirt? I will get antiseptic and bandages."

I nodded and slipped off my shirt. There was a long scratch across my abdomen. Probably caused by a nail on the fence poles I'd pushed myself through. Although the wound wasn't serious, there was a lot of blood. I felt light-headed and wanted to sit down, but I was too dirty and didn't want to get mud on the quilt that covered the bed.

Naomi came back into the room with something in her hands. "Oh, my dear. You look pale. You should sit down."

"I . . . I don't want to ruin your quilt."

"It can be washed. Please. Sit down before you faint."

I sank down on the bed, grateful to get off my feet before I passed out. Naomi quickly cleaned the scratch and then covered it with gauze and tape. "You should have that looked at by a doctor when you get home," she said.

"I will. Thank you."

"I am glad to help." She put her supplies on the dresser. "I only have simple dresses for you to change into. One of them will have to do."

"That's fine," I said. "I appreciate it."

She removed a cornflower-blue dress with small white flowers from her closet. Then she pulled a heavy slip out of a dresser drawer. "I'm about your size. I think this will fit you. Take those wet things off. All of them. This will keep you warm until I can wash and dry your clothes."

I started to tell her that tossing them in the dryer was enough, but when I looked down, I realized how filthy I really was.

"I'm sorry to cause you so much trouble."

"You seem to be on an important quest," she said quietly. "I have no reason to turn you away."

She put the dress and the slip on the bed. "You must also have something for your feet." She went back to the dresser and pulled out a pair of thick socks. "This should help. I will wash off your shoes and dry them as well." She took a small blanket out of another drawer and put it down on the floor. "Put your wet things on this. I will wait outside the door while you change. Let me know when you are finished."

"I will."

She nodded and left the room, closing the door quietly behind her. I quickly undressed and pulled on the slip and dress. There was no mirror in the room, but with the light from a lamp behind me, I could see my reflection in the window. The woman looking back at me certainly didn't look like Wynter Evans, the reporter. With the simple dress and my braided hair, I almost looked the part of a Mennonite farmer's wife. I checked my hair in the window. Although it was wet, it was still tightly braided and had survived my mad dash in the rain. I pulled on the socks Naomi had given me. My feet felt like ice, and the warm socks felt wonderful.

"I'm finished," I called out.

The door swung open, and Naomi came back into the room. She nodded her approval when she saw me. "The dress looks better on you than it ever did on me."

Under her prayer covering, Naomi wore her dark hair in a bun. Although her features were somewhat plain, she had a nice trim figure.

I smiled. "I'm sure it doesn't, but that's very kind of you."

She bent down, pulled the edges of the blanket together with my rain-soaked clothes in the middle, and picked everything up.

"You go on downstairs and sit in front of the fire. I'll get this in the washer and join you in a few minutes. I think some hot coffee and a piece of warm rhubarb pie will help you feel better." She tipped her head toward me and left.

I'd wanted to ask her about Elijah and his parents but decided to wait until we were downstairs. I needed to confront both of them. I was determined to get answers before I left this house and had no intention of waiting any longer to learn the truth.

As I came down the stairs, I could hear Samuel and Reuben talking. Had Reuben broached the subject without me? But as I neared the living room, I realized they were talking about crops. I frequently found myself forgetting that Reuben was a farmer. Having never seen his farm, it was hard to form an image of him working in his fields, planting crops, and bringing in a harvest.

The men stopped speaking when I came into the room. Reuben looked at me with concern. "Are you all right?"

I nodded. "Just a scratch. I'm fine."

"Please sit here," Samuel said, rising from his chair and pointing toward a small love seat near the fireplace. "You need to warm up." He took a large quilt off the back of the couch where Reuben sat. "And put this around you. You must be cold."

As if agreeing with his assessment, my body shivered involuntarily. "Thank you. I appreciate it." I took the quilt, sat down on the soft love seat, and pulled the quilt over my shoulders. The warmth from the fire and the coziness of the room helped me to relax a bit. But then the incident on the road and the reason for our visit pushed their way back into my mind.

Naomi peeked from around the corner. "Samuel, help me bring some coffee and pie to our guests."

He stood up and left the room, leaving Reuben and me alone.

"Did you say anything?" I whispered.

He shook his head. "Not yet. Please don't jump on them. We need to ease into this."

"Ease into it?" I said, recognizing a note of hysteria in my voice. "I'm not interested in protecting their social sensibilities. I want to know where my brother is. I'm tired of waiting until everything is just right."

"I thought you didn't want to spook them. Didn't want them to let Nathan know we were asking questions about Elijah," he said darkly. "This isn't really the way to accomplish that, is it?"

"I know, I know. But I just can't wait anymore. I'm frightened. It's like I can feel Ryan slipping away."

"I understand that, Wynter. But alienating the Fishers won't help us. We need to present our concerns to them as if we consider them to be partners in finding the answers we need. If you make them feel we're on opposing sides, they'll get defensive."

I sighed. "Whatever. But I don't intend to dance around this. I'm not leaving here without the truth."

At that moment, Naomi and Samuel came back into the room. She carried a tray with cups and a coffee carafe. He held two plates in his hands.

"I have sugar and cream in case you use them in your coffee," Naomi said as she put the tray down on the large coffee table. "And pie for both of you."

"Won't you have some?" I asked.

Samuel smiled and patted his lean stomach. "I'll save my pie for after dinner. It's a treat I enjoy before bed."

"We feel bad eating in front of you," Reuben said.

"Please don't," Naomi said. "I love to watch people enjoying my food."

Naomi prepared my coffee the way I asked. Then she got a small wooden tray from behind the couch and put it next to me, since the coffee table was too far away for me to reach it comfortably.

"Thank you so much." I took a bite of the warm pie and was greeted with an explosion of tart rhubarb combined with sugar and cinnamon. "This is wonderful. I've had rhubarb pie only once before, and it was kind of sour."

Samuel smiled. "Naomi is one of the best cooks in Madison County. She has a drawer full of blue ribbons from the state fair to prove it."

"I can believe it," I said, taking another bite and washing it down with coffee.

"Now," Samuel said, his thick black eyebrows knit together in a frown, "what is this you want to know about Elijah?"

Reuben swallowed a bite of pie and put his plate down. "Wynter . . . I mean, Emily, lost her brother when she was young. He was abducted. We have reason to believe he might be in this area. Basically, we're looking for information. Any young men around the age of seventeen who might have been adopted." He cleared his throat. "You see, we think he may have been illegally adopted—by people who had no idea there was anything wrong with the adoption process."

Reuben was softening the situation, making it easier for the Fishers to tell us what we needed to know.

Samuel and Naomi looked at each other with puzzled expressions. Then Samuel turned his attention back to us. "I'm sorry, Reuben, but we know of no boy that age who could be the person you're searching for."

He directed his gaze at me. "On the front porch, you mentioned Elijah. Surely you don't think he is your missing brother?"

"I . . . I don't know," I said truthfully. "I came here because I saw a picture of him when he was younger. He looked exactly like my brother, Ryan."

"A picture," Naomi said with a frown. "Nathan would never allow his family to pose for pictures. Where did you see this?"

"It was a candid shot. Taken by the mother of a friend of mine. Elijah was out on the road in a buggy when she snapped the photo."

"Have you met him in person?" she asked.

I nodded. "Yes, once. Then he and his parents left town. We hoped he was with you. That way we could talk to him."

Samuel was silent for a moment. "If I prove to you that Elijah is not your brother, will you leave my family alone?"

"Well, of course. I don't want to bother them if there's no reason to."

Samuel nodded at his wife. "Naomi, will you get the box of papers I keep in the spare room?"

She got up immediately and left the room.

"Nathan and his family are visiting Anna's sister near Ironton. She just had a baby."

"Samuel," Reuben said, "is there *any* possibility that Elijah could be Ryan Erwin? Was he adopted?"

"I think it would be best to answer your question by showing you something that will bring an end to your concerns."

Naomi came into the room, carrying a metal box. "Is this the one you mean?" she asked her husband.

He nodded and held out his hands. After she gave him the box, he opened the lid and riffled through it. About a minute later, he pulled out a folded piece of rather yellowed paper. He opened it and perused it carefully.

"Yes, this is it." He handed the paper to Reuben. "We have this because Nathan and Anna were given several extra copies. They gave one to us for safekeeping, just in case anything happened to the original."

Reuben looked it over and his face fell. Then he handed it to me. It was a Certificate of Live Birth issued from Missouri seventeen years ago. A baby boy was born to Anna and Nathan Fisher. His name was listed as Elijah.

NINETEEN

"I . . . I can't believe it." I didn't want to cry in front of Samuel and Naomi, but I couldn't help it. "I was so sure," I whispered.

Naomi got up from her seat and came over to the love seat. She sat down and wrapped her arms around me. "Oh, my dear, I am so sorry. You must miss your brother very much."

I nodded but couldn't respond. So everything that had happened was nothing more than a series of random events? Had I wanted so badly to believe I'd found Ryan that I'd twisted innocent coincidences into something sinister?

"I'm sorry we caused you so much trouble."

"Nonsense," Naomi said, still holding me. "You did the right thing. You needed answers. I hope we have given that to you." She let me go and looked into my face. "Now you can go on with your life. Perhaps your search for your brother will continue, or perhaps it will stop now. You must decide. But God has set a path before you. I pray you will find it."

"Th-thank you."

She gave me one last hug, then went back to her chair. "I am glad we were here to help you."

"You've been wonderful," Reuben said. "As soon as Wynter's clothes are ready, we'll get out of your way."

Samuel frowned. "You have called her *Wynter* several times, yet she calls herself *Emily*. I don't understand."

I explained the difference between my real name and the name I used at the station. I wasn't sure they understood, since television didn't seem to be a part of their lives. I didn't see one anywhere in the room. However, they seemed interested in the special I was working on and suggested a couple of other towns that might make good additions to our list.

Before long, my clothes were dry. I went upstairs to change, laying the dress and slip on the bed. For just a moment, I sat on the bed and looked around the room. Once again I thought of my grandmother. With my mother's delicate emotional health and my father's drinking, visiting her had been my salvation. I felt safe in her house. I could still remember Sundays after church. She'd invite her brother and sisters over for fried chicken and conversation. All four elderly siblings, gathered around the table, talking about their lives when they were young, making each other laugh. They always treated me like one of the group. Great-Aunt Edna, Great-Aunt Minnie, and Great-Uncle Charlie. I missed them all so much. I gazed out the window to the fields of wheat and thought about the pain of saying good-bye to Ryan. Was it finally time?

Feeling a sense of almost overwhelming sadness, I walked out of Naomi's room, giving it one last look. Then I closed the door and went to find Reuben.

"Again, thank you," Reuben said to Samuel and Naomi as I came into the room. "We appreciate your hospitality."

"It's no problem," Samuel said. "I am grateful we were able to send you in the proper direction."

Naomi gave me a quick hug. "You will be in our prayers."

"Thank you," I whispered.

Reuben and I left the house and got in the truck. The Fishers stood on the front porch and waved to us as we left. I watched them in the side mirror. Once they stopped waving, they turned to face each other. Naomi looked upset, flinging her hands around. Then she went into the house. Samuel waited a moment, looking down at the porch floor for a few seconds before going inside.

Their actions seemed a bit odd. Maybe we weren't quite as welcome as we'd thought. Frankly, I didn't care what they'd said to each other. No more theories for me. All I wanted was to finish my interviews in Sanctuary, get out on the road, and complete the report. I missed Mr. Henderson. Except for a week's vacation I'd taken between jobs, I'd never been away from him this long. I was certain Megan was taking good care of him, but I missed his soft nose touching my cheek in the morning—his way of telling me it was time to get up and feed him. Esther's cats were certainly filling the gap, but as much as I adored them, they weren't Mr. Henderson.

I should have been missing my apartment as well, but since this trip, I'd started to wonder if the modern touches I'd so carefully surrounded myself with really expressed my true personality. Maybe when I got back, I'd start looking for a house. Something old, with character.

"You're being very quiet."

I jumped at the sound of Reuben's voice. "Just thinking."

"I know you're disappointed."

"Yes, I am. I thought I'd finally found Ryan."

"I don't think you should give up. Who knows? He may still be out there somewhere."

"I'm not sure about that anymore." I grunted. "Seems my father spilled his guts for nothing. I doubt he'll be too happy to find that out."

"Well, at least you have the truth now. Maybe that will give you what you need to build a relationship with trust." He looked over at me. "He loves you, Wynter."

"Maybe. I guess so. I wish he'd told me the truth a long time ago though. I could have handled it."

"Maybe. Maybe not. But he did what he thought was best for you and your mom."

I shrugged. "I don't feel like talking about my dad."

"Okay. What do you want to talk about?"

I stared out at the rain-soaked fields as we drove past. The showers were lighter now but remained steady. "All the weird things that have happened since I got to Sanctuary. Once I began to wonder if someone was trying to keep me away from Elijah, things started to make a strange kind of sense. But now . . ."

"Nothing makes sense."

I stared at him and nodded. "Who sent that note to Dad and why? And what do those clippings mean?"

"I can't explain the note," Reuben said slowly. "But as far as the newspaper stories, maybe someone is simply trying to point you toward the person or persons behind the kidnapping of those babies. Maybe the whole situation with Ryan clouded the truth. The real story."

I sat up straighter in my seat. "You might have something there. I guess I need to take Ryan out of the equation." Saying those words hurt, and my voice broke. But I was determined not to cry again, so I cleared my throat and continued. "When

I get back to St. Louis, I intend to do some digging and see if I can find some additional information about these cases."

"When you get back to St. Louis?"

"Well, yes. I've got to finish the interviews in Sanctuary, wrap up this story, and get back to work." I studied him for a moment. "You know I have to leave. Right?"

"Yes, I know. I just . . . I don't know, I hoped . . ."

"Reuben, I have feelings for you. I told you that. But I have to go home. My life is there. We'll see each other. I promise."

"Of course we will," he said quietly. "Maybe for a while, but eventually we'll realize how different we are. That we aren't looking for the same things in life."

"What did you think? That I'd quit my job and move to Sanctuary? And do what? Maybe it's just me, but I didn't see a television station anywhere. Or, for that fact, a television."

He shrugged. "Maybe you could write. Isn't that what you said you really wanted to do?"

"Do you know how few people ever get published? It's a long shot at best."

"I know you can do it." He turned his head to look at me. I was touched by the sincerity in his expression. "I happen to believe you can do anything."

"Oh, Reuben. Can you really see me in Sanctuary, writing suspense and mystery novels? Doesn't really fit the ambience of your town, does it?"

He smiled. "Maybe you could use a Mennonite town as a backdrop."

I couldn't suppress a giggle. "Mennonite suspense. I can't see it."

"Maybe that's a dumb idea. But following your passion isn't dumb."

"You could move to St. Louis."

He shook his head. "Hard to run a farm from St. Louis."

"You could do something else, you know."

He was quiet for a moment. "On the way back to town, I'd like to show you my farm."

I started to protest, but he held up his hand. "Ten minutes. That's all I ask. It won't put you behind that much on your schedule."

"Okay. But only ten minutes."

We drove on silently, the rain pinging off the roof and windshield. Somehow I felt disconnected. The whole reason for my trip to Sanctuary had been to find Ryan. Now that I knew he wasn't here, it was as if I'd already begun to distance myself from the town and everyone in it. I didn't belong anymore. There was no reason for me to stay once my story was complete.

As we neared the road to Sanctuary, Reuben turned off on a road leading the other way. After a few minutes, a house came into view. An old Victorian, painted grayish-blue with white trim. Behind the house was a huge red barn. As we got closer, I saw horses grazing in a large fenced field. They were beautiful. Long faces and huge eyes. Arabians. I'd collected horse figurines as a child, always hoping that someday I'd own one.

Reuben turned into a long driveway, surrounded on both sides by fields, their burgeoning crops glistening with rain. He pulled up in front of the old house and parked.

"This is it," he said.

I could hear the pride in his voice.

"This farm has been in my family for three generations. I grew up here and so did my father. Someday I hope to pass it along to my children."

"Is Maggie your only sibling?"

"Yes," he said, nodding. "But she never loved the farm the way I do."

Reuben got out of the truck and came around to my side. He opened my door and helped me out. I winced as I stepped down."

"You sure you're okay?"

I nodded. "I'm sore, but the bleeding's stopped. I'll be fine."

I looked at our surroundings. "This is incredible, Reuben."

"Something about this place captured my soul when I was a boy. I can't imagine living anywhere else. This is . . . home."

The sound of barking came from somewhere, and suddenly a beautiful golden retriever came running around the side of the house. He jumped up on Reuben, getting mud on his jeans. He didn't seem to mind.

"I take it this is Lazarus?"

Reuben laughed as he hugged the excited dog. "Yes, this is Lazarus." When he told the dog to get down, Lazarus obeyed immediately and sat down at his master's feet, his mouth in a wide grin.

Reuben motioned for me to come closer. "Lazarus, this is Wynter."

I knelt down in front of him. "I'm very pleased to meet you, Lazarus."

The retriever put his paw out. I shook it, even though it was muddy. "You're a very handsome fellow."

Lazarus wiggled up closer to me, and I put my arms around him.

"He really likes you," Reuben said.

"I have the feeling he likes everyone, but thank you."

"You stay out here," Reuben told him. "You're too muddy. I'll give you a bath tonight."

The dog seemed to understand. He followed us up the steps and onto the front porch, lying down on a rug near the door.

"This is a wraparound porch," I said. "My grandmother's house in Springfield had one. Don't see too many of them anymore."

As he reached into his pocket and took out a ring of keys, he smiled. "Maggie and I used to play on this porch. We'd run around on it until my mother couldn't take it anymore. 'You kids settle down right now,' she'd yell. 'Or I'll give you something to run from.'" He chuckled. "Never could figure out what that meant. When I was older, I asked her about it. She just laughed and admitted that she had no idea. As long as it put the fear of God in us, she'd accomplished her goal."

"Does your mother live alone in Jefferson City?"

He slid the key into the doorknob. "No, she lives with my aunt. She's doing fine. As feisty as ever." He opened the door and waved me inside. "I've tried to get her to move back in with me, but she won't do it. She wants me to get married and thinks she'd be in the way. She's very stubborn."

"So that's where you get it."

He laughed. "I guess so."

He ushered me into a large room with incredibly high ceilings. A huge staircase with wooden railings led to the upper floors.

"Let's go this way," he said.

I followed him into another room with a magnificent wood-burning fireplace. Floor-to-ceiling oak shelves lined with books sat on either side. The windows in the room were huge. They began a few feet from the floor and stretched up at least nine feet. I'd never seen anything like them before.

"What room is this?" I asked.

"I use it as a library. I'll show you the living room and the kitchen in a minute." He pointed toward a massive desk that sat near the windows. It appeared to be mahogany with curved, carved legs and edges. "That desk belonged to my great-grandfather. He was a writer." Reuben walked over to one of the bookshelves and pulled out an old leather-bound book.

He held it out to me, and I took it. The spine was cracked, but otherwise, the book was in very good condition for its age. I could clearly read the title: *A Wanderer's Dream* by Jacob King.

"What's it about?" I asked, slowly opening the cover. The yellowed pages inside spoke of age and gentle use.

"My great-grandfather considered himself a wanderer through life. Not someone who made his home here, because his home was in heaven. The story is about a man who lost his way, who valued the things of life instead of life itself. He served his possessions instead of God."

"A cautionary tale, huh? How does it turn out?"

Reuben smiled. "In the end he realizes what's really important in life. People. His family. Not the pursuit of ambition."

I closed the cover and handed it back to him. "I'd like to read it someday."

He slid it back into its place on the shelf. "Sure." His tone reflected his obvious skepticism.

"For goodness' sake, Reuben. It's not like we'll be on other sides of the world."

"Maybe so." He shrugged, but it was clear he didn't believe me.

I walked over to the desk and ran my hand across the intricate carvings. Then I gently lowered myself into the old leather office chair. From that vantage point I could look out on the lush green fields. Just a slight turn of my head revealed the Arabians prancing in the rain.

"This is the perfect place to write." The words slipped out of my mouth before I realized I'd said them. I could feel myself flush with embarrassment. "I mean . . . I'm not saying . . ."

Reuben walked slowly toward the desk and faced me. "Please don't feel uncomfortable. You're welcome to come here and write anytime you'd like."

I could see myself sitting here in this lovely house, surrounded by books, words slipping out through my fingers and onto a keyboard. Everything about this room inspired me. I reluctantly rose from the chair and followed him into a comfortable living room with another fireplace. The long windows continued there and into the formal dining room. Images I couldn't control flashed in my mind. A family gathered around the table for Christmas dinner. Children laughing. A wife reaching under the table to take her husband's hand, each of them thankful for the blessings God had given them.

The kitchen was a combination of old and new, perfectly blended. A built-in oven matched the historic charm of the room, while an antique stove, beautifully restored and gleaming, waited for boiling pots of soup and freshly baked loaves of bread. From there, we ventured upstairs to look at the five bedrooms. Two of them were empty and one held storage. The fourth was charming, with antique furniture and touches that seemed distinctly feminine.

"This is my mother's room when she comes to visit," Reuben explained. "The bed, dresser, and rocking chair have been in my family for many years." He ran his fingers across a gorgeous quilt that covered the bed. "My grandmother made this. She was a prolific quilter. You'll find quilts in almost every room."

"It's wonderful. I can almost feel the people who used to live here. My grandmother's house was like this. Every time I went to stay with her, I felt . . . I don't know. Like I was really home. As if the house where I lived with my parents was just a place I visited sometimes."

Reuben smiled. "I know what you mean."

"How could you? You were raised in this house."

"Although I loved the farm, I wasn't always certain I wanted to live here. After college, I moved away. Went to work for a brokerage company in Des Moines. Made a lot of money. Had a nice apartment. Then my father died, so I came home."

"You gave up your career?"

He nodded. "At first I rebelled against the idea. I mean, I had a great job and could buy whatever I wanted. I actually came back planning to suggest Mother sell the farm. But when I walked in the door . . ." He looked away. "When I walked in the door," he said again in almost a whisper, "I knew I was home. I couldn't see myself in Des Moines anymore. You see, ghosts called out to me. Not ghosts from the past. These were ghosts from a future that would never be if I walked away from this farm—from who I really am." He turned to stare at me. "Does that make any sense to you?"

"Of course it does."

He sighed. "I know not everyone is called to live on a farm in the country. If we all did that, our cities would be empty and—"

"We'd have way too much food?"

He smiled. "Yes, I guess we would."

At that moment, I wished I hadn't made a joke. Reuben's

words had touched me and made me uncomfortable at the same time. There was something about this house that pulled at me. My reaction frightened me.

"We probably need to get going," he said brusquely. "We need to get you back to town. You have a lot to do before you leave."

He walked out of the room and started back toward the stairs. "Wait a minute," I called out. "There's another room here. Is it yours?"

"Yes, but it's not much to see. We don't need to—"

"Nonsense. I might as well take the whole tour." I went to the last door and flung it open. I walked into a massive bedroom with more incredible windows that looked out over the farm. Another fireplace sat in the corner. This one was made of some kind of carved stone and had a huge mantel. Old pictures in intricate frames decorated the mantel top, and a large painting hung above it. I recognized the farm immediately.

"This is beautiful," I said. "Who painted it?"

After a brief pause, Reuben said, "I did."

"Are you serious? Why, it's wonderful. You're incredibly talented. When did you—"

"I painted that as a gift for my mother while I was in college."

"Have you done anything else?"

"A few paintings and some sketches. One of these days when I have more time, I'd like to paint again."

"You should." I wandered through the rest of the room, finding a lovely window seat. A perfect place to read a book. For a moment, a picture flashed in my mind. I saw myself curled up on the seat, lost in the pages of a novel. I pushed the image away. "It's incredible, Reuben. I can't imagine coming home to this every night. You're very lucky."

"I feel blessed," he said.

"Do you ever miss your previous life?"

"No. I haven't regretted my decision for one second. I know where I'm supposed to be. That brings me great contentment. God has a plan for my life, and I know this house is where that plan will unfold. Someday, a woman will feel that same call, and we'll build something here that will last forever."

"Forever? That's a long time."

"That's what family is, Wynter. The entire world began with two people. And that's how it will continue until the day we're all called to heaven. I'm standing here now because my great-grandparents had a dream. Years from now, one of my children will be here with his or her family. And on it goes." He came over and put his hands on my shoulders. "How those members come into a family doesn't matter, you know. Family isn't blood. Family is love. Family continues, no matter what. It isn't how you get in. It's how you get out—what you leave behind."

"I know you're right," I said softly. "It's just . . ."

"It's just a shock to find out your parents weren't your birth parents? I know. But the truth is we're all adopted, aren't we? Didn't God adopt us as His own?"

"Yes, He did."

"Well, if it's good enough for Him . . ."

"I know. I'm working on it."

"I understand." He leaned forward and kissed me on the forehead. "Seems to me you were given away by parents who didn't love you to parents who did. That's a pretty big blessing. Something you don't want to throw away."

I didn't respond, just nodded. Being in this house made me feel emotions I didn't know how to interpret. It would take a while for me to figure out what they meant.

We walked out the front door. I said good-bye to Lazarus,

who licked me on the face, and then I climbed back into the truck. The rain had finally stopped, and the sun was beginning to peek out from behind the clouds. By the time we reached town, the skies were almost clear. Reuben pulled up in front of Esther's and stopped, his motor still running.

"Aren't you coming in?"

"Well, I would like to see how Zac's doing," he said. "Maybe I'll just check on him and leave." He glanced at his watch. "It's almost six o'clock. I'll probably go to the restaurant for dinner."

"Can I come with you?"

"Sure, if you want to."

"I won't be in town much longer. As long as Zac is feeling better, we'll probably finish up tomorrow and leave."

He nodded. "I guess you're right. Let's go check on Zac."

I could hear a note of reluctance in his voice. It hurt me to think he might be protecting himself from me. My feelings for him were strong, but fear crouched at the door of my heart. We were so different. Did we have any chance at a future? I couldn't be sure.

We got out of the car and had just said hello to Esther when someone knocked on the front door. Reuben opened it since he was the closest.

"Paul!" he said with surprise. "We were just talking about you earlier today. Come on in."

A young man dressed in the uniform of a deputy sheriff walked into the room. Immediately his eyes locked on me.

"Wynter, this is my friend Paul Gleason."

"Nice to meet you," I said with a smile. "Reuben has told me a lot about you."

Paul didn't respond to my greeting, nor did he return my smile. "You're Wynter Evans?" he asked in a stern voice.

I nodded and looked at Reuben, confused by the deputy's demeanor.

"What's this about, Paul?" Reuben asked, obviously as puzzled as I was.

"It's about the murder of August Metzger, Miss Evans. There is evidence that leads me to believe you have information about his death."

TWENTY

After a few seconds of stunned silence, Reuben finally found his voice. "What in the world are you talking about? That's insane."

"Look, Reuben, we're friends, but I have a job to do. I can't allow you to interfere."

"Would it interest you to know that I've spent a lot of time with Wynter since she got here? I can assure you she didn't have anything to do with killing August."

"I'm not saying she killed him. I'm saying she might be involved. I won't know her level of involvement until I talk to her."

"You mentioned evidence," Reuben said. "What kind of evidence?"

"I can't tell you that."

"Paul, we're friends. Please come down off your official high horse and talk to me."

Paul folded his arms across his chest and stared at Reuben, who glared back at him. They seemed locked in a battle of wills. Finally Paul relented. "We found Wynter's name . . . actually, both of her names, written on a piece of paper in August's billfold."

Reuben flushed red with anger. "What else did you find in his billfold, Paul? Did he have a photo I.D.? Maybe the state of Missouri killed him. What about a fishing license? I know he fished. Maybe the Department of Conservation did it." He shook his head. "This is the dumbest thing I've ever heard."

"Wait a minute," I said. "You said *both* of my names?"

Paul nodded. "Your real name is Emily Erwin, right?"

"Yes, but how would August Metzger know that?"

"Unless you're ready to arrest her, I think you need to leave, Paul," Reuben said through clenched teeth. "I have no idea why August had that information, but that doesn't make Wynter a murderer."

"Of course it doesn't," he shot back. "I'm not saying she murdered him. I'm simply asking questions about some evidence we have. There were papers hidden in August's apartment. Under a loose floorboard. We discovered a file full of items, some of them related to Miss Evans. And a comment written by August that is confusing."

"What does it say?" I said. "I don't understand."

"I'd like you to come down to the station, Miss Evans. I'll be happy to show it to you."

"Does it have to be right now?"

He paused and then shook his head. "No. It can wait for the morning. I want to make it clear that I'm not saying you killed Mr. Metzger. I just have some questions. Please be there by nine o'clock."

"She'll be there," Reuben said. "I'll bring her myself."

"All right. I'll hold you to that." He tipped his hat briefly and left.

We all stood there looking at each other in shocked silence.

"Well," I said, "and here I thought my life couldn't get any stranger."

"I can't believe this," Zac fumed. "What's wrong with that guy?"

I went over and gave him a quick hug. "Just a reminder, my friend. I didn't actually kill August Metzger. Everything will be okay."

"I can't wait to see this so-called evidence," Reuben said. "Why would August have information about you? It doesn't make sense."

I had to sit down. My legs felt shaky and weak. "Actually, it does if he sent me those articles and mailed that note to my father."

Zac came over to the couch and sat next to me. "So you're convinced he left those clippings for you?"

"No, I'm not certain. I'm only saying it's possible. But if he wanted me to look into the kidnappings, why didn't he just come and talk to me?"

"I don't know," Reuben said, "but there's only one person I can think of who might be able to help us figure out what's going on. We need to have our ducks in a row before tomorrow morning. I'm going to call Rae. Maybe she can meet us at the café."

"Don't be silly," Esther piped up. "You tell her to come here. I'll make dinner. Besides, she's very upset about August's death. Having to go out in public might be difficult for her right now."

"Thank you, Esther," I said. "I'll help you."

"Absolutely not. You sit here and rest. You need some peace and quiet." She pointed at Zac. "You will help me."

Zac rolled his eyes. "I hope you're kidding. I can't even get my microwave meals to come out right."

She shook her finger at him. "You need to learn how to cook if you refuse to find a good woman and get married. Besides, you've been lying around for too long. You must start getting a little exercise."

Zac snorted. "I'm not refusing to get married, Esther. I'm just not ready for the commitment."

"When you do meet a good, godly girl, I want her to know you can cook. Come with me."

Zac stood up. "I've been ordered to the kitchen. I suspect it's because Esther thinks you would like to be rid of me so you can talk. But, if she actually forces me to prepare food, you might want to pray. I'm not worried, since I've already survived one poisoning. I'm trusting I've built up an immunity. But you two . . . well, I can't guarantee your safety."

It was obvious he was trying to lighten the mood, and I smiled at him. "I'm willing to take my chances. I trust you, Zac."

He hesitated a moment before giving me a reassuring smile. "Everything will be okay, Wynter," he said. "You know that, right?"

I nodded. "I'm believing that too, but while you're in the kitchen with Esther, you might ask her to teach you how to bake a cake with a file inside."

Zac shook his head. "Actually, they don't use those anymore. I'll probably need some kind of electronic gadget that opens prison doors."

"Get out, Zac," Reuben said good-naturedly.

Zac sighed dramatically. "I hear those words a lot. Well, here goes nothing." He tossed me one more smile before he left the room.

Reuben came over and took Zac's place on the couch. He reached for my hand.

"Like Zac said, everything will be okay," he said soothingly. "I don't want you to worry."

"I'm past worrying. It's like I'm trapped inside someone else's life. I left St. Louis only a few days ago, but it feels like years." I took a sharp intake of breath. "Oh, goodness."

"What's wrong?"

"What if the sheriff's office makes me stay here while they investigate? I can't tell Ed I'm involved in a murder."

"Unless they arrest you, I don't think they can make you stay in Sanctuary. My guess is they'll tell you not to leave the state."

"Unless they arrest me?"

Reuben shook his head. "Wynter, that's not going to happen. Obviously Paul doesn't actually suspect you, but he's found something that needs to be explained. Once we see this so-called evidence, we can confront it and clear everything up."

"I'm interested to see what they have."

"Me too." Reuben stood up and fished around in his pockets. "I left my cell phone in the truck. I'm going to call Rae."

A thought occurred to me. "Maybe we should have told Paul about the man who forced us off the road."

"You're right. After what he said, I totally forgot about it. The truth is, he can't do much. We didn't get a tag number, and there are lots of black trucks in Missouri. I should call my insurance company though." He checked his watch. "Guess that will have to wait until tomorrow. I'll be right back."

"Okay."

As he left, Esther's and Zac's voices filtered in from the kitchen. I felt so close to these three people, and I'd known them only a few days. How strange to leave the place I call home, find myself somewhere new, and feel it's more like home than the place I left. *Home.* That word had started to take on a different meaning. Was St. Louis really home? And what about the people I called my parents? Was my home with them? Even though the shock of discovering they weren't my birth parents had rocked my world, in my heart they were still Mom and Dad. With all their faults, that hadn't changed. I would never know my birth parents, but somehow I couldn't mourn them yet. Someday perhaps, but for now, they were just people who didn't want me.

Reuben's words about home and family had affected me. He was right. Family was important. Families could change the world—for better or for worse. What would the final story be for my family? Would we come out of this situation weakened even further? Or would this strengthen us? Pull us back together? I couldn't answer those questions yet, and I wasn't sure when I would be able to.

Thinking about my dad made me suddenly realize his trip to Jamesport was totally unnecessary. I should have called him right after we left the Fishers, but with everything going on, I'd completely forgotten his quest to dig up information about Elijah.

I jogged upstairs to find my cell phone. After trying a couple of times to get a signal, I decided to join Reuben outside.

He was just coming in when I reached the door. I explained that I was calling my father to tell him he could come home.

"Oh, man. I can't believe I didn't think of that."

"I know. Unfortunately, being accused of involvement in a murder tends to make a person forget things. Hope he won't be angry."

"I'll wait inside while you call."

"Thanks, Reuben. I won't be more than a couple of minutes."

Once on the porch, I punched in my dad's cell number and listened to it ring. It went right to voice mail. Not wanting to tell him about our meeting with Samuel and Naomi through a voice mail message, I left a brief request for him to call me right away. Hopefully, he'd check his messages soon.

I was just starting to go back into the house when my phone rang. Dad.

"Hey," I said when I answered. "I was just calling you."

"I'm on my way back, Emily," he said. "I won't get there until rather late. I need you to wait up for me. I have some news."

"Dad, we found proof that Elijah isn't Ryan. I'm sorry."

There was a prolonged silence, and then I heard him take a deep breath. "Emily, just wait up for me. We'll talk about this when I get there."

"Okay, but I think it could wait until tomorrow."

"Please don't argue. Just do what I'm asking."

A click signaled he'd hung up. Great. Staying up late the night before I had to face an interrogation at the sheriff's office. Perfect.

"Did you get him?" Reuben asked when I came into the house.

"Yes. He wants to talk to me tonight. Wants me to wait up for him."

Reuben frowned. "You told him Elijah couldn't possibly be Ryan?"

I sighed with exasperation. "Well, of course I did." I was immediately sorry I'd taken my frustration out on Reuben. "I'm sorry. I'm just exhausted. I was ready to walk away from all this . . . drama."

He came over and wrapped his arms around me. "It's okay," he said softly. "Everything will turn out all right."

"And how do you know that?" I said, my voice muffled as I leaned into his shoulder.

He pulled back and stared into my eyes. "Because God is with you, Wynter. He loves you, and He'll bring you through. He'll show you the truth."

I walked away and slumped down on the couch. "I don't know why He'd be interested in me. I haven't been very faithful to Him."

Reuben smiled. "You're His child. That hasn't changed. When children make mistakes, parents hope they get it right the next time, but they don't walk away. Parents want their kids to be the best they can be. That's what God wants for you, you know."

I smiled. "I may not have found my brother in Sanctuary, but maybe I discovered something else. A way back to my heavenly Father."

"I'm glad."

"What you said earlier about families—I think you're right. My parents took care of me, raised me, loved me. It may take me a while to get used to the truth about my birth, but I intend to find a way to work through it."

"Can you forgive your father?"

I nodded slowly. "In time. Yes, I'm sure of it. If God can forgive me, I don't have much of a choice, do I?"

"Good. I—"

A knock on the door interrupted him. Reuben opened it. Had Paul come back? Had he changed his mind and decided to haul me down to his office today? I was thankful to see Rae standing on the porch. I suddenly wondered if she also thought I had something to do with August's death. A trickle of apprehension ran up my spine.

As if confirming my fear, she walked straight to me, not even acknowledging Reuben. "Deputy Gleason told me he would be questioning you about what happened to August," she said.

"I . . . I didn't—"

"Oh, honey. I know you didn't have anything to do with August's death. That's the goofiest thing I ever heard." She smiled at me, but I could see the sadness in her eyes. "I'm a pretty good judge of people. You're a good woman. I knew it the first time I met you." She pointed her stubby finger at Reuben. "And that's what I told Paul Gleason. That he was wasting valuable time bothering this young lady when he should be looking for August's killer."

"I agree with you," Reuben said. "He says he has some papers that somehow tie Wynter to August. I can't imagine what he's talking about."

"Me either."

I pointed to the couch. "Do you have a few minutes, Rae? I'd like to ask you a couple of questions, if you don't mind."

She nodded. "A little diversion would be welcome right now."

"First of all, I want you to know how sorry I am for your loss. I understand you and August were close."

She lowered her thick body down onto the couch. "He was a little different. Hard to get to know, but underneath that aloof exterior was a good heart." She wiped away a tear that escaped her eye. "We talked about getting married, but I'm just too independent. Couldn't see myself living with a man tellin' me what to do. Being single, I could take or leave August's advice. But once we said 'I do,' it would be a different story." She sniffed. "Now I wish I'd made a different choice. Somehow, it would make everything a little easier."

Reuben sat down. "Rae, do you have any idea at all what Paul's talking about? What kind of papers would he have that could incriminate Wynter?"

She clasped her work-worn hands together and stared at them, shaking her head. When she looked up, her expression was pensive. "August was a good man," she began, "but he was a conspiracy nut, always seeing demons behind doorways."

"Did he believe someone in Sanctuary was involved in kidnapping babies from hospitals?"

"Oh, dear." She bit her lip and hesitated. "Look," she said finally, "August had friends, people who cared for him. But sometimes I think he felt . . . unimportant. He loved to read up on stories about unsolved crimes. Always had an opinion about them. He ate up those crime shows on TV. Fancied himself an amateur detective. He was constantly calling the police about something. You know that tip line in St. Louis?"

"Crime Stoppers?" I asked.

"Yes, that's it. Well, one of his special cases had to do with babies being taken from Missouri hospitals. He decided someone in Sanctuary was involved."

"Did he say who?" Reuben asked.

Rae shook her head. "No. I told him I had no intention of listening to him accuse one of our friends or neighbors of something so awful, so he kept that information to himself." She gave Reuben a sad smile. "August was abandoned as a baby, you see. His great-aunt raised him only because she felt she had to. It wasn't a happy home. He never got over it. I think the story about stolen babies touched something deep inside him."

Reuben glanced over at me. It was obvious that if my father hadn't taken me from the hospital on the night I was born, I might have suffered August's fate—being raised by someone who didn't really love me. Suddenly I felt a connection to August.

"Why are you asking me about this?" Rae said. "How did you hear about August's obsession with that story?"

I told her about the newspaper articles sent to me, and I mentioned that my father also received a troubling note in the mail, although I didn't tell her what the note said.

"I can see why he gave you those stories," she said slowly. "You're a reporter. I'm sure he planned to contact you about them after you had a chance to look them over. But how would he know your father? I doubt August had anything to do with that."

"You might be right. It was just odd that both things happened right around the same time."

"When did your father get his letter?"

"About a week ago."

"Before you came to town? That doesn't make sense."

"Actually, we contacted Martha over at the library two weeks before we arrived. There was certainly time to send the note to my dad."

Rae shook her head. "But as I said, August didn't know your father."

"Paul said he had both of my names in his billfold. It wouldn't have been difficult to find out who my father was if you had my real name."

Rae's eyebrows shot up. "Your real name?"

I nodded. "I use a different name in my job."

Before Rae had a chance to respond, Zac came into the room.

"I thought you were helping Esther," Reuben said.

"I've been summarily dismissed. Although Esther is too nice to say it, I think she concluded I'm hopeless in the kitchen."

Realizing that Rae and Zac hadn't met, I quickly introduced them.

"Nice to meet you, young man," she said. "I heard you had a pretty bad case of food poisoning. I'm glad to see you're on the road to recovery."

Zac nodded. "I'm still not sure what I'm recovering from. The sickness or the cure."

Rae looked confused, and Reuben told her about Esther's remedy.

Rae laughed. "My mother used the same thing on my sister and me whenever we got sick. Sure keeps you from faking illness to stay home from school."

"I hear you," Zac said with a sigh. "Am I interrupting anything?"

"No, not at all," I said. "We were just talking about August."

Zac sat down in the chair near the couch. "I heard you were close," he said to Rae. "I'm sorry."

She waved her hand at him. "Thank you, Zac. I appreciate that."

"So you don't think August sent that note to Wynter's father?" Reuben asked, steering us back to our previous conversation.

"I have no problem believing August sent you the stories about those kidnappings, but I don't believe he sent that note. My guess is that someone who knows you well enough to know your real name sent it."

I nodded. When Ryan disappeared, there were a lot of letters sent to my family. Most of them were kind, people showing compassion and telling us they were praying for us, but many weren't nice at all. My parents didn't show me the letters at the time, but my mother told me about them years later. Several were written by people who accused my parents of child abuse, believing that if they'd kept a closer eye on my brother, he wouldn't have been kidnapped. A few were sent by religious nuts claiming we were being punished for our sins. There were quite a few with supposed tips as to who had taken Ryan. The FBI checked them all out, but none of them yielded results. Maybe this new note was from someone trying to stir up the past for their own twisted enjoyment.

Like Rae said, some nut that recognized my father's name and decided to torment him.

"Well, at least this explains the newspaper clippings," Reuben said. "But why does Paul think Wynter had some kind of connection with his death?"

"Again, just conjecture," Rae said, her forehead wrinkled with thought, "but maybe Paul found something in August's apartment with your name on it, Wynter. Along with notes about some of his other theories. August had a hard time keeping his thoughts in order. He could have written something that sounded ominous when it wasn't meant that way at all." She shrugged. "That's my best guess. Honestly, I wouldn't worry about it. There's no way they can tie you into what happened to August. I'm just sorry you have to deal with this. You and your family have been through enough."

"Thank you," I said. "I really appreciate your taking the time to come and talk to me. I know you're trying to cope with your own grief. I'm praying they'll find the real person responsible."

"Me too," Rae said, shaking her head.

"You're staying for dinner, aren't you?"

"Better tell Esther we'll have two extra," Reuben said. "Your father will probably be hungry when he gets here."

"I don't know where he called from. Not sure when he'll get in."

"Thank you for asking," Rae said, "but to be honest, I need to be alone right now. Maybe some other time."

I doubted there would be any other time, since I planned to leave town as soon as possible, but I smiled and nodded. We said our good-byes and Rae left. Just as she closed the door behind her, Esther came out of the kitchen.

"Dinner's almost ready," she said. "Was that Rae leaving?"

"She's not really in a social mood right now, I guess."

"Poor thing," Esther said with a sigh.

"Something smells great," Reuben said.

"Trust me. It looks even better than it smells," Zac said. "I'm starving."

Reuben smiled at him. "I'm glad to hear you're hungry. You really are feeling better."

Zac flashed him a crooked grin. "No human being can resist Esther's cooking."

"Help me get the dishes to the table, Zac," Esther said, "and we'll get started."

"So I've been reduced from chef to waiter?"

She nodded. "Guess I wasn't a good enough teacher."

"Don't give up on me. You might make a cook out of me yet."

She gave him a quick hug, and I was surprised to see her eyes flush with tears. "Wish I could, but soon you'll be far away, living in the big city. You'll forget Sanctuary . . . and me."

Zac caught her by the arm as she turned to go back to the kitchen.

"No, Esther. I won't. If you'll let me, I'll come to visit. Maybe even stay the weekend sometimes, if that's okay."

The look on Esther's face tore at my heart. "I would love that, Zac. I get lonely rattling around in this old house."

"I'll be back," he said. "You have my word."

She dabbed at her eyes with her apron and nodded. "We'd better get that food on the table before it's cold."

I caught Zac's eye before he left the room and smiled. The change in him was like night and day. It was amazing. This town had changed me too. I just wasn't sure how. It seemed I'd come to Sanctuary sure of myself and who I was. But now I wasn't certain of anything.

We all gathered in the dining room. Esther had made chicken fried steaks with mashed potatoes and gravy. Fresh green beans, a mixed-fruit salad, and biscuits hot from the oven rounded out our meal. I split a steak with Esther. It was delicious, but I wasn't really hungry and chose to concentrate on the fruit. When I got back to St. Louis, it was back to salads, fruit, and yogurt. Sanctuary wasn't having a good effect on my waistline. My jeans definitely felt tighter.

We finished the meal with strawberry shortcake, one of my very favorite desserts. After helping her clean up the kitchen, Reuben and I decided to carry our coffee out to the front porch so we could wait for my dad. Esther went to her room to knit for a while and then go to bed. Zac also retired to his room. He was definitely on the mend, but I could see the weariness in his face. Food poisoning obviously took a heavy toll on a body.

Reuben and I sipped our coffee and rocked back and forth in the semidarkness, the only light coming from inside the house. We left the porch light off because it would draw bugs. Cicadas sang in the dark. Some people found their songs annoying. They reminded me of summer nights sitting on my grandmother's front porch, and the sound soothed me.

"You haven't told Zac what we found out at Samuel's," Reuben said.

"I know. I couldn't find an appropriate moment. I'll fill him in tomorrow." I sighed. "To be honest, I don't really want to tell him. Saying the words out loud makes it too real. I was so hopeful I'd finally found Ryan."

"I know, Wynter. I'm sorry. I really am."

"I can't imagine what my dad thinks is so important I have to wait up for him," I said. "I'm so tired. What could he have learned in Jamesport that would make any difference? I'm ready to let this go. Why isn't—"

Approaching lights from a car cut off the rest of my sentence. My dad pulled up in front of us and got out of the car.

"Thanks for waiting up for me," he said as he approached the porch. Even in the dim light I could make out the concern on his face.

"Sure," I said, "but as I told you, we know Elijah isn't Ryan."

He came up and stood in front of us. "And how do you know that?"

"We actually saw his birth certificate," Reuben said. "That leaves little doubt."

Dad leaned against the porch railing. "Well, you might be right under normal circumstances."

"What are you talking about, Dad?"

"I talked to a lot of people in Jamesport. For the most part they were pretty closemouthed. Couldn't find out much. But as I was getting ready to leave town, a woman sought me out. Wanted to know if I was the man asking questions about the Fishers. When I told her I was, she asked to speak to me privately."

"How did she know them?" I said.

"This woman, Ruth Yoder, lived next door to the Fishers while they were in Jamesport."

"You asked her about Elijah?"

My dad grunted. "Didn't really have to. She was desperate to share something that had been bothering her for years."

I couldn't see that what this woman had to say would change anything. Elijah was the Fishers' son. Birth certificates don't lie.

"So what did she have to say?" Reuben asked. I could hear confusion in his voice. It was clear he was thinking the same thing I was.

"Ruth told me that the Fishers suddenly left Jamesport after suffering a tragedy. Ruth wanted to stay in touch, but she couldn't find them. About three years after they took off, she ran into someone who had seen them. With their son, Elijah."

"So?" I was beginning to get a little impatient with my father. Tomorrow promised to be stressful, and I wanted nothing more than to get some sleep.

"What was the tragedy?" Reuben asked.

My father took a deep breath before saying, "The death of their only child. Elijah."

TWENTY-ONE

I stared at my father, not certain I'd heard him correctly. "Did you say—?"

"Yes, Emily. The death of their son. Seems Elijah Fisher was walking home from school and some drunk hit him, killed him."

I was trying to process my father's words, but my mind had gone blank. What did this mean?

"The Fishers lied to us," Reuben said.

"If all they did was show you Elijah's birth certificate, they didn't lie," Dad said. "They just didn't tell you the whole story."

"What does this mean?" I asked. "Does it mean . . . ?"

"Yes, Emily," Dad said, his voice breaking. "It means that Elijah is probably Ryan. It's possible you've found your brother."

I couldn't stop the tears that cascaded down my cheeks. After all these years, we'd found Ryan? "Wait a minute," I said, wiping my face with the back of my hand. "I'll bet Nathan's told his brother that we're looking for them."

"But I'm certain they also assured them they had nothing to worry about," Reuben said. "That they'd convinced you Elijah was their natural child."

"What will they do?" I asked. "Will they run farther away, or do you think they might come home?"

"Hard to say," Dad said, his voice heavy with emotion, "but I don't want to take any chances. We need to contact the authorities now. It's time."

"We don't need any kind of massive manhunt," I said. "That would send them somewhere we'd never find them."

"What are you thinking?" Reuben asked.

"Let's talk to Paul. Lay everything out and ask him to help us search for the Fishers quietly. We'll have a better chance of finding them that way."

"Who is Paul?"

"Sorry. He's a deputy sheriff. A friend of Reuben's."

"I don't know, Emily," Dad said. "You want to bring in one deputy sheriff? Don't we need as much help as we can get?"

I shook my head. "I've been around this kind of stuff for a few years now, Dad. Reported on missing person cases. Abducted children. Many times the police don't put information out right away because they need an advantage."

"Maybe that's what they'll do this time."

"Can't count on it. I've seen it go the other way too, and sometimes it ends badly."

"Once you tell Paul what's going on, it will be out of your hands, you know. He may not be willing to do things your way."

"I think he'll listen," Reuben said. "First of all, he's a good man who will see this is the right way to go. Besides, I doubt he'll accept our word about Elijah immediately. That should keep him from sounding an alarm for no reason."

Reuben's logic made sense. I prayed he was right. We were so close. Losing Ryan now was something I couldn't allow.

"Do you really think this deputy sheriff has what it takes to find them?" My father sounded skeptical.

"You can trust Paul," Reuben said. "He's like a dog with a bone when it comes to solving cases. Everyone expects him to be the next sheriff of Madison County."

Dad was silent as he mulled over our suggestions. "Okay," he said finally, "but I'm still a little reluctant to do it this way."

"Look, if Paul doesn't find them by tomorrow evening, we'll call out the cavalry," I said. "But stealth is our friend right now."

"All right. Will he come to us or do we need to go to him?"

"I'll call him right now," Reuben said, rising from his rocking chair. "Let me see what he wants to do."

I sighed. "He'll probably think I'm making this up to get out from being under suspicion."

As Reuben walked a few feet away from the porch to get good reception on his phone, Dad took his place in the rocking chair next to me. "Why are you under suspicion?"

I told him about Paul's earlier visit and his concerns about my involvement in August's death.

"That's ridiculous," Dad fumed. "Are you sure you want this man to help us? He doesn't sound very intelligent to me."

"I think he's our best bet," I said quietly. "I don't want to blow this. We can't alert the Fishers that we're on to them." I smiled in the dark. "Good work, by the way. If it wasn't for your tenacity, I'd have given up and gone home."

"I want Ryan back as much as you do, Emmie. Maybe more."

"Can you imagine what this would do to Mom? If we brought Ryan home?"

"If this boy is your brother, he won't be the Ryan you know."

"What do you mean?"

"I mean that he's lived with the Fishers longer than he lived with us. His personality won't be the same. He won't be . . . our Ryan." Dad sighed. "At least it seems the Fishers are good people. That makes me feel better."

"They may be victims too. Just like Ryan."

"I know. We need to get all the facts before we accuse anyone of kidnapping."

"But if they're completely innocent, why did they leave?" I asked. "They know *this* Elijah isn't their son. Maybe they *think* they love him, but keeping a child that doesn't belong to you isn't love."

My father was silent.

"I'm not talking about you, Dad. Let's stay focused on Ryan."

"All I'm saying is that we should reserve judgment until we have the truth. Right now all I want to do is find my son." Dad rubbed his eyes. "I need to tell him how sorry I am for failing him. For not being the father I should have been. And I need to apologize for the last words I said to him." He dropped his hand and looked over at me. "I guess I'll spend the rest of my life apologizing. To Ryan, to you, to your mother."

"God forgave you a long time ago, Dad. We will too. All you can do is try to make amends and move on. Our reactions belong to us—not to you. I just listened to a sermon that meant a great deal to me. The pastor pointed out that we can't move forward with our lives by looking behind us at the past."

My father didn't respond. We sat in silence until Reuben stepped back up onto the porch.

"Paul's on his way. He wasn't too happy about my call. I think he was already in bed."

"Speaking of being in bed, I wonder if I should wake up Zac," I said. "He doesn't like to be left out of the loop."

Reuben smiled. "You talk about Zac as if *he* were your brother."

I chuckled. "On the way up here, I was ready to strangle him. Now he really does feel like family. Weird."

"He seems like a good kid," Dad said. "I like him."

"Let him sleep," Reuben said. "We'll catch him up in the morning. He's been through a lot."

"Okay, but you can take the blame for it if he gets upset."

"I'll take that responsibility." Reuben yawned widely. "I think we should put some coffee on. We may be up for a while."

"I'll do it," I said. "Won't take long."

I got up and went to the kitchen. After watching Esther prepare coffee in her old percolator, I was pretty sure I could handle it. My coffeemaker at home was certainly easier to deal with, but I actually preferred the taste of the coffee brewed in the ancient pot. I rinsed it out, filled it with water, put the metal basket inside, and added two scoops of coffee to it. Then I put on the lid, set it on the stove, and lit the burner. Just to be sure, I waited around a few minutes until it began to percolate.

By the time I left the kitchen, Reuben and Dad had come inside and were sitting in the living room. Dad was talking about the official investigation into Ryan's abduction.

"Coffee's brewing," I said. "Shouldn't be long."

Reuben nodded distractedly. "Lyndon," he said, "can I ask you something else?"

Dad straightened up in his chair. "Sure. What is it?"

"Tell me again about the man who was blackmailing you."

He took a deep breath, trying to pull up painful memories. I could tell the past was still raw and tender. "He told me he knew the nurse who helped me switch babies that night. Before she died, she told him what she'd done. I guess she felt guilty about it." He shrugged. "At the time, she sure didn't seem to have a problem. In fact, she said she was happy to send Emily to a good home instead of into foster care. I guess over the years, she changed her attitude."

Reuben frowned. "Something about that story bothers me."

"What is it, Reuben?" I asked.

"What kind of a friend is at your bedside as you're dying? Who is the person you share your deepest secret with?"

His question took me aback. I looked over at my father.

"I don't know," he said. "Someone very close."

Reuben nodded. "Like a boyfriend or a husband."

"You might be right," Dad said. "But what does it matter?"

"It matters," I said, answering for Reuben, "because we might be able to discover who this man was."

"It wouldn't change anything."

"I know that, Dad, but if we can find—what was his name?"

"Mac," my father said slowly. "He called himself Mac."

"If we can find Mac, we may be able to prove the link between Ryan and the Fishers." I held my hands out, palms up. "If they're innocent, this could prove it. And if they're not . . ."

"Going after him will definitely bring attention back to Ryan and to us," Dad said. "Do you want to be in the national spotlight again? You saw what happened to that family in Salt Lake City."

"Of course not," I said gently. "But don't you think it's time for the truth? *All* of the truth? The most important person now is Ryan. Proving that the Fishers were unwilling accomplices in his abduction could keep his current family intact."

"It's worth the risk," Reuben said, staring at me. "You're the investigator. Investigate."

"I haven't done a lot of actual investigating, but I'll do my best," I said. "Dad, do you remember the name of that nurse?"

"How could I ever forget? She changed our lives. Her name was Marian. Marian Belker."

"Okay, I'll see what I can find out about Marian. I'll look through Social Security death records. Old obituaries. Maybe I can find something that will lead us to Mac."

"She worked as a nurse," Dad said. "Can't you check hospitals in Illinois to see if she's listed?"

I nodded. "Sure, but I'm not certain that will tell us what we need to know, although it might at least give us her last known address."

The smell of coffee reminded me about the pot on the stove. "Reuben, why don't you help me with the coffee?"

He stood up and stretched. "Sounds good. I'm so tired I can barely keep my eyes open."

I headed toward the kitchen, and he followed me. "Where are the cups?"

I pointed toward the cabinets. "Over there. You get cups and saucers, and I'll get sugar and cream."

"You got it."

I found the tray Esther used for carrying coffee and food. I put the sugar bowl on it and got the cream out of the refrigerator. Reuben brought the cups over to me.

"That was really sharp," I said, "thinking about Mac's relationship with Marian Belker. It should have occurred to me."

He put the cups down on the tray. "No, it shouldn't have," he said, taking my hand. "You've been through a lot of emotional upheaval. Right now, you're just trying to hang on." He raised my hand to his lips. "I'm really proud of you."

"What are you talking about? I haven't done anything to be proud of."

He kissed my hand. "You're wrong. Most people would be a basket case by now, but you're keeping yourself together. You're still kind and generous. Even with your father. After what he told you, you could have gone ballistic. Ordered him out of your life. Shut him out completely. But instead, you're trying to work through it. Understand him."

I shook my head. "Don't get ahead of yourself. After this is over, I'll probably have a complete nervous breakdown."

"I don't believe that. But I do believe you'll find a way to make your relationship with your father and mother stronger than ever. That's the kind of person you are. I'm also confident you'll have your brother back soon." He kissed me gently. "You're a very strong woman, Wynter. Stronger than you realize."

"I hope you're right." I gazed into his eyes. "But if I decide somewhere along the way to fall into a million pieces, will you help pick me up and put me back together?"

He smiled and kissed my nose. "Always."

We were interrupted by a loud knock on the front door. Reuben quickly grabbed another cup and saucer, picked up the tray, and we both hurried to the living room. We got there just as Paul Gleason was coming in the front door.

"I'm not sure what I'm doing here," he said with a scowl. "Couldn't this wait until morning?"

"No," Reuben said. "As I told you on the phone, it's important. There are some things we've kept from you. Things you need to know." He pointed toward the couch. "Have a seat. This could take a while."

Paul glared at him. "So you've been lying to me?"

"Not lying, really. After we explain, I hope you'll understand why we kept quiet."

Paul glared at him. "If we weren't friends—"

"I know. You'd throw me to the floor, slap handcuffs on me, and haul me off to jail forthwith."

Paul's annoyed expression relaxed a bit, and the corners of his mouth twitched. "Hardly," he said. "I was thinking more of walking out on you."

"Just give us a few minutes. I think you'll change your mind."

"Does it have anything to do with August Metzger's death?"

"Good question. I wish I had the answer."

Paul walked slowly toward the couch, his reluctance showing in every step he took. After he sat down, I poured him a cup of coffee and put the cream and sugar within his reach. As he picked up his cup, I had to wonder if this was a mistake. Ryan was so close. The voice from my dreams echoed in my head. Would I finally be able to answer his calls for help, or would this decision send him out of my reach forever?

TWENTY-TWO

"So that's what's going on," Reuben said. "Everything we know."

Paul sat silently through Reuben's detailed recounting of Ryan's disappearance, my discovery of a picture that led me to believe he might be in Sanctuary, and everything that had taken place after that. When Reuben finished, Paul just stared at him. What was he thinking? Did he believe us?

"I'm trying to understand this," he said finally, "but it's difficult." He turned his eyes to me. "Why didn't you just contact us when you got here? We could have investigated immediately and saved everyone all this upheaval."

"Because I wasn't certain the boy in that picture was Ryan. It was just a photograph. Not enough to go on. My family lived for years under a microscope. Opening that up again for no reason . . . I couldn't take that chance. I had to be sure."

"After Wynter arrived," Reuben said, "and realized the kind of town Sanctuary is, she didn't want to bring us unwanted attention. As you're aware, we have some residents who don't need the media to show up here."

"If Elijah Fisher really is Ryan Erwin," Paul said solemnly, "there may not be any way to stop that."

"But why?" I asked. "The case is cold. No one cares about it anymore. Isn't there a way we can just settle things quietly?"

Paul shook his head. "I don't think so. I can't cover up something like this."

"Even if it has nothing to do with August's death?" Dad said.

"I'm not so sure that's true," Paul replied slowly.

Reuben carefully studied his friend. "What do you mean? Do you have reason to suspect otherwise?"

Paul leaned against the back of the couch, his features tense. "Look, the file full of papers we found in August's room contained copies of newspaper articles. Some of them had to do with the abduction of babies from Missouri hospitals." He locked his gaze on me. "Others had to do with the kidnapping of your brother, Miss Evans."

I was stunned by this revelation. August had kept my real name in his billfold, but it hadn't occurred to me that it was associated with Ryan.

"I'm sorry," I said. "I just don't understand."

"I don't either," Paul said firmly. "Is there something else you aren't telling me?"

My father and I looked at each other. I saw the warning in his expression. Before I could say anything, Reuben spoke up.

"Someone sent the same clippings to Wynter while she was here—the ones about the babies, I mean."

Paul frowned. "Why? Why was August interested in these cases? Is that what got him killed?"

The three of us stared at him silently. What could we tell him? What *truths* should be avoided?

"Look, Deputy," my dad said quietly. "I don't want to drag up things that aren't important to this situation."

"If you want me to help you, you need to tell me everything you know," Paul said. "If it doesn't pertain to the case, I'll keep it to myself."

"If you want complete honesty from us," I said, "we want the same thing from you."

Paul raised an eyebrow. "What do you mean?"

"What was it in August's papers that made you think I had something to do with his death?"

Paul leaned forward and picked up his coffee cup. It was obvious he was stalling. After a couple of sips, he set it down again.

"For crying out loud, Paul," Reuben said with exasperation. "I promised Wynter and her father that you would listen and help us. Wynter's not a criminal. She's an innocent person who lost her only sibling as a child. She's a victim, Paul. Can't you see that?"

Reuben's passionate pleading seemed to have an effect. Paul sighed and relaxed back against the couch. "I don't know you, Wynter, but I know Reuben. And I trust him." He studied me for a moment. "I'll be as candid as I can, but you must understand that I'm in a rather difficult position. I work for the sheriff, and he's tough. If I say or do something to impede the investigation of a murder, I could get into big trouble."

"We would never ask you to do that," Reuben said. "You should know me better than that."

Paul nodded. "I do."

"Please, Paul," I said, "tell me why you thought I was involved with August's murder."

He sighed deeply and ran his hand through his dark hair. "August Metzger lived in a small room he rented from a couple

I don't think you've met. The Andersons live about four blocks away from The Oil Lamp. He had very little in earthly possessions, but underneath a floorboard, we found a box with papers, the ones I mentioned. We also discovered his journal. In that journal, your name was mentioned several times. Most of the entries are just your name, along with dates. Some passages don't make sense. Must be some kind of shorthand only August understood. But the day before he went missing, he wrote '*In fear for my life. Wynter Evans must know the truth.*'"

I gasped. "Know the truth about what?"

Paul shook his head. "That's the million-dollar question, isn't it? He obviously thought you knew something, and because of it, his life was in danger."

"Wait a minute," my father interjected. "What if he was saying that his life was in danger, and he wanted to *tell* her the truth about something?"

Paul nodded. "That occurred to me."

"Look, Paul," I said. "I can't explain August's notes, but I need you to find Elijah before I lose him for good. And without red lights and sirens, please. We can't allow the Fishers to get spooked."

I breathed a sigh of relief when he nodded in agreement. "We'll tread carefully. I don't want to accuse them of something they didn't do. Nor do I want them to disappear if they do have your brother. There are a lot of small rural towns in Missouri. A few are like Sanctuary—private and closed off. Getting lost in one of them is easier than you might think."

"Then how do we proceed?" Reuben asked.

Paul frowned at him. "You don't. I do. I'll visit Samuel Fisher myself. I'm sure he knows where his brother is. Maybe the threat of becoming involved in a kidnapping case will convince him to tell me the truth." He pulled a small notebook from one pocket and a pen from another one. "Reuben, who are Nathan and Anna Fisher close to in Sanctuary?"

Reuben rattled off several names. The only ones I recognized were Jacob Troyer, the pastor of Sanctuary Mennonite Church, and Sarah Miller, the teacher at the small private school.

"Why don't you meet me in the morning about nine?" Paul said. "We'll talk to these folks. Then, unless we have the information we need, I'll drive over to Nathan's place." He nodded at me. "We'll find Elijah, Wynter. He can't be that far away."

"Thank you. Does this mean you don't suspect me anymore?"

Paul rewarded me with a half smile. "You're off the hook . . . for now. Just remember that I have to go wherever the clues take me. I have no other choice."

"I understand, but I can assure you that I had nothing to do with August's death."

"I'm pretty sure you didn't, but the best way we can keep you out of this is to find his killer. And some motive would be helpful. Right now, I have no idea why anyone would want to murder this man. He might have been a conspiracy nut, but he seemed perfectly harmless to me." Paul stood up. "I've got to get going. It's been an unusually long day. I suggest you all get some sleep." He pointed at Reuben. "I'll see you in the morning."

"Sounds good." Reuben got to his feet. "I'll walk you to your car."

"Wait a minute, Paul," I said. "I need to ask you a question."

"And what's that?"

"You said August had a journal."

"That's right."

"Did he have a distinctive way of forming the letter *T*?"

Paul frowned as he considered my question. "As a matter of fact, he did. The top line was extra long. Extended across the rest of the word."

I nodded. "The person who sent the newspaper articles wrote the same way." I reached into my pocket and took out the note I'd kept with me so it wouldn't disappear along with our other clues. I handed it to Paul. "You might want to compare this note to the handwriting in the journal."

Paul took the paper I offered him. "I will. Thanks."

Dad and I said good-bye to Paul. As soon as he and Reuben were outside, I turned to my father. "I hope this was the right thing to do."

"We had no choice. We've got to do everything possible to bring Ryan home."

"At least we can be certain August sent the articles to me *and* the note to you."

"Well, it certainly sounds like it," Dad said, "but we can't be completely sure until Paul compares the handwriting."

"I guess, but I'm already convinced. Paul confirmed August had copies of the newspaper articles, so at least we can put that question to rest."

Dad shook his head. "Of course that only brings up an even more important question. Why did he send these things? Are they related in some way?"

"I have no idea," I said. "You know, Paul seemed to realize we weren't telling him everything."

"Honestly, Emily, I really don't see that what happened at that hospital so many years ago has anything to do with this situation."

"It might not, but this isn't the time to protect ourselves."

My father didn't respond, just stared into his coffee cup.

"Dad, why would August have news reports about Ryan's abduction? Could he—"

"Be Mac?" My father sighed. "Believe me, it crossed my mind, but I don't think so."

"Why? You never met him."

"Paul said he rented a small room from some family in Sanctuary. Money was important to Mac. He blackmailed me for years, and I'm fairly sure I wasn't the only one. I sincerely doubt someone like Mac would end up in a little rented room in a small Mennonite town. Doesn't make sense. Besides, didn't you say August was a cook in a local restaurant?"

I nodded.

"Mac was a low-down blackmailer, but he seemed intelligent. He never did anything to give himself away. Never made a false step. His vocabulary was extensive. He certainly didn't appear to be the kind of person who would be happy with a job like that. And as far as the note, why would Mac send it? He wouldn't want us to find Ryan. I think this August person may have accidently stumbled across something that got him killed."

"That makes sense."

Dad gave a sigh. "Look, if we decide there's a good reason for me to tell Deputy Gleason about your birth and what I did, I will. If it would help us find Ryan, I'd crawl over broken glass. But until we know it's necessary, I'd rather keep that to myself."

"You know, it's possible once we find out the truth, we may also discover Mac's real identity."

Dad nodded. "But I doubt it." He shook his head. "I still don't believe he had anything to do with Ryan's disappearance. Never did."

"I don't think we can rule it out though."

My father's face turned crimson with anger. "What will it

take to get you to let this go? Mac had nothing to do with your brother!"

"You don't have to yell at me."

"I-I'm sorry. It's just—"

"If Mac was involved, you'll blame yourself."

Dad gazed at me with tears in his eyes. "Of course I will. If I'd told the police about Mac when Ryan was abducted, maybe we would have found him."

I got up and went over to the couch, putting my hand on my father's arm. "Dad, the police told you it was Burroughs who took Ryan. There wasn't any reason for you not to believe them. You didn't do anything wrong. Let yourself off the hook."

He put his hand over mine. "I'm afraid there are a lot of things I'm *on the hook* for, honey. Honestly, I don't think I'll ever be able to forgive myself for all the mistakes I've made."

"I understand that you believed you were doing a good thing the night I was born, even if you didn't do it the right way. I thought about what you said about Mom too. You're right. Her past history might have made it impossible for you to adopt me."

"I knew she would be a wonderful mother. Her . . . problems had nothing to do with being able to love you and take care of you. If they had, I wouldn't have made the decision I did. Wouldn't have put either one of you in that situation."

"To be honest, I don't know what I would have done in your position." I paused and took a deep breath. "But I know your heart was in the right place. You and Mom always made me feel loved and accepted."

"Except when I started drinking. With everything else I did wrong, that's the one thing I regret the most. I let the pressure overwhelm me. I let all of you down."

"I was thinking about Mac," I said. "What if you had refused to let him blackmail you? If he'd really followed through on all his threats, we would have had to deal with the truth back then. As a family. Maybe it would have made a difference."

"I thought about that." His voice faltered. "But we could have lost you, Emily. You weren't ours . . . legally. I couldn't do that to you—or to us."

"Maybe I'll find something when I look into Marian Belker's death. Where and when she died. It might lead us to finding Mac."

Dad shook his head. "I'm certain Mac wasn't his real name, and he's probably long gone by now."

"Still, wouldn't you like to know who this guy was?"

"Of course. I'd love to see him face justice."

"That could bring everything out in the open, Dad. I thought you didn't want that."

Dad kneaded his temples, and I realized how weary he looked. "I don't know, Emily. We just have to let it play out the way it will. If we can keep your mother from any more pain, I'd like to do that. God knows I've caused her enough."

"So you're convinced Elijah is Ryan?"

"I think it's entirely possible, but to be honest, there's still a little doubt in my mind."

"You're afraid Burroughs really did kill him."

Dad rubbed his hands together like he was cold, but it was warm in the room. "I was certain Burroughs murdered Ryan, although down through the years, I guess there was always a small seed of uncertainty. I wondered more than once if Ryan could possibly be alive somewhere, but the police were so certain, I was afraid to hope."

"I never completely believed he was dead. I've been hearing

him for years in my dreams. Calling my name. Asking me to find him."

My father stared at me with wide eyes. "Why didn't you tell me? You never said anything."

I shook my head. "I was afraid. Besides, we haven't really had much honest communication, have we?"

"No, we haven't. And that's my fault too. I've been keeping secrets for so many years I'm not sure what the truth is anymore." His face was twisted with emotion. "But the one thing I never lied about was how much I love you, your brother . . . and your mother."

"You still love Mom?"

"Always. I never stopped."

"What about Angela?"

He shrugged. "I married her because I was desperate for a family. I felt so lost and alone."

"And now you've lost her too."

"Our marriage wasn't right, Emily. Not from day one. I was willing to do the right thing—stick it out—but then she found someone else. Someone who wasn't still in love with his wife."

Dad's declaration astounded me. I was still trying to come up with a response when Reuben came through the front door.

"Are you all right?" he asked when he saw my face.

"Yeah. Fine."

"Well, at least we know who sent those newspaper clippings, and it looks like August also sent the note to you, Lyndon."

"But we don't know why," I said.

Reuben glanced down at his watch. "Look, it's after two in the morning. I think we all need to get some sleep. Paul will be back in the morning, and we'll take it from there."

"I've got a long ride back to the motel," Dad said. "I need to get on the road."

Reuben frowned at him. "I live right outside of town, Lyndon, and I have plenty of room. Why don't you stay the night with me? Of course you wouldn't be able to change your clothes."

"Actually, I'm fine," Dad said. "I packed a bag for Jamesport just in case. It's still in the car."

"Great. Just follow me. You'll get a lot more rest this way."

"Thanks, Reuben. I appreciate it."

Dad looked over at me. "Guess I'll see you in the morning, honey."

"Okay. And thanks, Reuben."

"No problem." He came over and gave me a quick hug. "Have faith," he whispered in my ear. "We'll have the truth soon."

"I know," I said quietly. "See you in the morning."

After they left, I carried our cups and saucers to the kitchen, rinsed everything out, and left them on the counter.

Before going upstairs, I checked the front door to see if it would lock. There was a knob on the inside, so I turned it and was relieved to hear a click. Maybe Esther didn't believe in locking her door, but knowing someone who didn't belong had slipped inside the house at least twice convinced me we needed to be especially careful.

I turned off the light in the living room and went upstairs. As I passed Zac's room, I could hear him snoring. His door was open, so I poked my head inside. The reason I hadn't seen any of the cats around this evening quickly became evident. All four of them were on the bed, snuggled up against Zac's body. I smiled and closed his door. Tomorrow I'd bring him up to date on everything that had happened after he went to bed. I still hadn't told him about our visit with Samuel.

When I reached my room, I should have dropped right into bed. It had been a long day, and tomorrow promised to be another one. But something kept rolling around in my head, so I grabbed my laptop, settled onto the fainting couch, and started doing a little research. An hour later, I'd uncovered something interesting. There was nothing I could do about it at three in the morning, so I closed my computer, changed into my pajamas, and crawled into bed.

When I finally fell asleep, once again I heard Ryan calling my name.

But this time his voice was much louder.

And closer.

TWENTY-THREE

"Wynter? Are you awake?"

It took effort to open my eyes. My body screamed that it needed more sleep. I rolled on my side to see the clock by my bed. Eight o'clock.

A knock on the door. "Wynter, can I come in?"

I recognized Zac's voice. "Wait a minute," I called out. I got out of bed, found my robe, and went to the door. He was standing on the other side, dressed and looking concerned.

"Sorry, I was starting to worry."

"It's only a little after eight, Zac."

"I know, but when I got up to go to the bathroom last night, I heard voices downstairs. It was after midnight. What's going on?"

I swung the door open and motioned him inside. "Why didn't you come down?"

"I heard your dad. Figured maybe it was family stuff. Didn't want to horn in."

"You wouldn't be *horning in*. I don't have any secrets from you anymore."

He laughed. "You're just feeling guilty because I may have been poisoned for your sake."

"You're probably right. And I'm glad you're feeling better."

"Thanks. So now what, Sherlock?"

"How about you go away and let me take a shower? I'll meet you downstairs in about thirty minutes and bring you up to date."

"Don't you have an appointment to keep this morning?"

"So that's why you woke me up."

"I didn't want to see you hauled out of here in handcuffs. Would upset my digestion, and there's been enough of that."

"Actually, our deputy friend is coming here at nine, but not to drag me off to the slammer. He's going to help us find out where Elijah and his family have gone."

Zac's eyebrows shot up. "Are you serious? And how did this magical transformation take place?"

"All in good time, my friend. Now scoot."

"Okay, okay. Hope Esther's making some of those melt-in-your-mouth biscuits. I could eat them every day. Not sure what I'm going to do after we go home."

"You had your chance. She was willing to share her culinary secrets."

He laughed, got up from the bed, and left. I hurried around, took a quick shower, and was downstairs about forty minutes later.

After saying good morning to Esther, I joined Zac in the living room, where he was sipping coffee and waiting for me. First I told him about our visit with Samuel and Naomi, then filled him in on last night's events.

"Wow," he said when I'd finished, "a guy gets a little sleep and misses out on all this? I may never sleep again."

"Don't say that," I said with a yawn. "I'm beat."

"So now what?"

"I get a cup of coffee."

Zac made an impatient noise. "I mean, what do we do today?"

"Well, Reuben, Deputy Gleason, and my dad are going to check with some people in town who know the Fishers. See if they can figure out where they are. If they don't turn up something solid, Paul's going to drive to Samuel Fisher's farm and rattle his cage a bit."

One of Zac's eyebrows shot up. "And just how does he intend to do that?"

I shrugged. "Maybe Paul can bring up things like impeding an investigation or aiding a kidnapper. I don't know, but he seems like the kind of guy who won't take no for an answer. I suspect Samuel won't last long under real pressure."

"I hate to bring this up, but what about the station? How long are we going to be able to keep Ed on ice?"

"I don't know, Zac. Right now, I just don't care. We're so close."

"I know."

"You should go back."

Zac's eyebrows shot up. "Without you? No way."

"Look, there's no sense in your losing your job because of me. I'm running out of excuses for Ed. I've been thinking about telling him the truth. Let the chips fall where they may." I smiled at Zac. "You've been such a good friend, but it's time I started thinking about what's best for you. I'm going to take the blame for all of this. I want you to call Ed and tell him you're coming back today."

Zac was quiet for a moment. Then he shook his head. "No. I won't do it. Coming here—being with you—has given me much more than any job ever will. I've not only made a good friend, but I think I've rediscovered something else I never thought I would—my faith." He gave me a tremulous smile. "So you see, no matter what happens, I'm ahead. A job's a job. I got hired at KDSM, and I can get hired somewhere else. I'm not leaving. I'm seeing this through to the end."

"Oh, Zac. Are you sure?"

He nodded. "I've never been more sure of anything in my life. I want to be here when you find your brother."

"And if I don't?"

"Then I want to be here to help you through that. Either way, I'm not leaving."

"Here I've tried to keep myself from making emotional attachments, and suddenly I find myself with a new friend. How weird is that?"

"Hey, my new friend turned out to be a reporter—and a woman. No one is more surprised than I am."

We both laughed, and I let go of his hand. Then I dug around in my pocket for my phone. "Well, guess I might as well get it over with. This should be interesting."

"Good luck."

I took my cell phone outside. Not wanting to be disturbed in case Reuben and Paul showed up while I was talking, I walked around the side of the house. Thankfully, I had enough bars to make the call. As my phone dialed the number of the station, I noticed something odd in the grass. I quickly hung up before the call went through and looked closer. A narrow patch alongside the house had been planted with something. Bricks formed a border around the small garden. The scent coming off the plants made it clear Esther was growing mint. But the plants right under the window were crushed, and some of the bricks used to create the border had been moved and stacked on top of one another. Someone had been looking in the window. I stood on my tiptoes and stared inside. I could clearly see the living room and Zac sitting in a chair, waiting for me.

I stepped back and stared at the bricks. Who had been watching us? And why? I started to put the bricks back where they were supposed to be but then thought better of it. Maybe leaving them where they were would be smarter. When Paul and Reuben arrived, I'd tell them about it. With any luck, perhaps our peeper would come back and we could catch him.

I walked quickly back toward the front of the house, hoping the person who'd been spying on us wasn't watching. I didn't want him to know I'd discovered his makeshift perch.

I sat on the edge of the porch and redialed the station number. The receptionist put me through to Ed. When he answered, I said a quick prayer, took a deep breath, and let the truth tumble out unfettered. All I could do was hope it made sense and Ed would understand.

I'd just hung up when I saw Reuben's truck coming down the street. I jumped up and hurried inside.

"They're here," I told Zac.

"Did you get Ed?" he asked.

"I wish I could give you better news. He wasn't happy. We've got until the end of the week to finish the story and get back. Then he wants to meet with both of us." I shook my head. "I'm sorry, Zac. I may have lost us both our jobs."

Zac shrugged. "There are other jobs. I'm not worried. But I'm sorry for you. I know you were counting on that anchor spot."

I smiled at him. "As strange as it sounds, it doesn't seem very important anymore."

"What if we don't find Ryan by Friday?"

"Then you'll go back, and I'll take whatever punishment Ed thinks is right."

"You know I'm not going anywhere, right? I've come too far with this thing to bail out now."

"He'll probably fire you."

"Then he fires me. I'm not leaving."

At that moment the door opened and Reuben walked in, my dad on his heels. "Paul's not here yet?"

"Not yet."

Esther came into the room and greeted Reuben and Dad. "How about some breakfast?" she asked.

Zac jumped to his feet. "Sounds good to me."

I laughed. "Food always sounds good to you."

He gave me a quick wink. "As long as it's not Italian or anything chocolate."

My dad looked confused, and I shot Zac a warning look. Since we really didn't know if there was something wrong with the fudge, I couldn't see bringing it up to Dad. If he thought someone had tried to poison me, he might decide I needed protection. And right now, I didn't want to deal with an overprotective father.

"No Italian food or chocolate on the menu," Esther said with a smile, "but I have some nice biscuits with sausage gravy."

Zac patted his flat stomach. "Just what the doctor ordered."

We followed Esther into the dining room and sat down at the table. Esther nodded at my father. "Would you lead us in prayer, Lyndon?"

I expected my father to refuse, but to my surprise he bowed his head. "Father, we thank you for this food and for the warm hospitality of this house. We pray blessings back on this gracious lady, and we ask for your help in finding the truth about my son. Please forgive us for our past weaknesses and mistakes and restore that which was lost. Thank you for second chances. In the name of Jesus we pray. Amen."

I had to blink away tears. I'd forgotten that my father used to pray every night at dinner before Ryan went missing. Hearing him again brought back a flood of memories. Good ones. Memories I'd pushed into the recesses of my mind.

"Thank you, Lyndon," Esther said. "That was lovely."

"Yes. Yes, it was," I said softly.

Dad's small smile told me he was pleased that his prayer had touched me.

"Zac tells me your deputy sheriff friend is coming over this morning," Esther said to Reuben. "Does it have anything to do with August's death?"

"Not really," I said. "Remember when I first came here and you asked me if I was missing anyone?"

Esther nodded. "Yes, you mentioned your brother. I've been praying you would find him again. Does your friend know where he is?"

"It's possible. He's following a lead. I hope you'll keep praying for us."

Esther smiled. "I certainly will. Wouldn't it be wonderful if you found your brother after all these years?"

"Yes. Yes, it would."

Reuben glanced at his watch. "Paul should have been here by now."

"Maybe he's doing some investigating on his own," I said.

Reuben frowned. "Maybe, but he's always been pretty prompt. I hope nothing's wrong."

I wanted to tell Reuben, my dad, and Zac what I'd found during my time on the computer last night, but with Esther in the room, I wasn't sure I could. We'd only been eating a few minutes when she got to her feet.

"Please forgive me," she said, "but I need to get a couple of pies in the oven for tonight. If I don't do it now, they won't be set by supper."

I nodded at her. "What about your breakfast?"

She pointed at her almost empty plate. "I must confess the truth, I suppose. I had two biscuits before you came downstairs." She wrinkled her nose, tickled by her admission. "I couldn't possibly eat another bite."

Zac chuckled. "If I'd been in the kitchen with you, there wouldn't have been a bite left to serve."

"Please, Esther," I said, "do whatever you need to do. We can manage by ourselves. We'll take the dishes into the kitchen when we're done."

"Thank you, Wynter. I appreciate that." She left the table and went into the kitchen.

Grateful for the chance to share my findings but aware Paul could arrive any minute, I quickly explained about my research into Marian Belker. "I found something very interesting," I said, keeping my voice down. "Dad, you said Mac told you he was with Marian when she died?"

He nodded. "Yes."

"Well, that's interesting because I used the station's account and searched through Social Security records. There's no documentation that shows a Marian Belker dying in Missouri around the time Mac first contacted you."

Dad frowned. "Maybe they weren't living in Missouri."

I shook my head. "You said her middle name was Rose, right?"

"Yes. I remember that specifically because she first introduced herself as Rose. But when I wrote her the check, she asked me to make it out to Marian, since that was her first name and Rose was her middle name."

"There's no record of any Marian Rose Belker dying during the years in question."

"I don't understand," Dad said slowly. "Mac said—"

"Mac lied, Dad," I said. "I have no idea why. Maybe Marian told him what happened, and he used it against you without her knowledge."

"Or maybe Mac was working with her," Reuben said. "Perhaps the person really behind the blackmailing scheme was Marian."

My father shook his head. "Call me naïve, but it just doesn't fit with the woman I met that night in the hospital. At first she didn't even want the money. I had to talk her into it. I would swear she was more concerned with giving you a good home, Emily."

"People change, Dad. Maybe she decided the money was important after all."

I could see Dad turning this idea over in his head, but he wasn't having an easy time of it.

"Well, here's something else," I said. "While I was looking up information on Marian, I ran across a Joseph Edgar Belker who died three years ago. His widow was Marian Rose Belker."

"So Rose was married?" Dad said.

"Sounds like it. I tried to do some checking on her after that, but it's like she dropped off the edge of the world. No records of addresses or anything else."

"Could her husband have been Mac?" Reuben asked.

"I think it's possible. But why would he say she'd died?"

"Because if I thought she was alive and contacted the police, they'd be able to find him," Dad said. "For some stupid reason, I accepted what he told me. Mostly because I couldn't believe Marian would have anything to do with blackmailing me."

I shrugged. "I'm not sure what happened or what this information means. It's just another part of our very confusing puzzle. But it certainly provides a twist to the situation."

"So Marian . . . or Rose, is alive," Zac said. "But she might not have anything to do with Ryan's kidnapping."

"If Marian's husband was Mac, then August certainly wasn't. So why did he have information about my brother hidden in his apartment? And why did he send me the clippings and mail that note to you, Dad?"

"We're still keeping this information from Paul?" Reuben asked.

"For now," I answered. "Until we see a solid connection. Since we know for certain he wasn't Mac, we have no reason to tell Paul the details of my birth."

"But as I said, if at any point there seems to be a need," my father said firmly, "I'll tell him everything."

"Could you get in trouble?" Reuben asked.

Dad shook his head. "I don't know, but Ryan comes first."

I looked around the table. "You're all okay with keeping my secret? For now anyway?"

Everyone nodded except Reuben.

"What are you thinking?" I asked.

"What if Joseph Belker really was Mac?" he asked, his forehead wrinkled with concern. "Doesn't that bring up a lot of new possibilities?"

"I don't know," I said. "There are still so many unanswered questions. Let's concentrate on finding Ryan. Maybe he can tell us who Mac is—or was."

Reuben nodded. "I hope he can, but we should probably keep trying to find out everything we can on our end."

Someone knocked on the front door, and Zac jumped up. "I'll get it."

I grabbed my cup and downed the rest of my coffee. Then I took the carafe and refilled my cup. Making it on so little sleep was going to take lots of caffeine.

"Good morning," Paul said as he came into the dining room.

"Good morning," Reuben answered. "How about some breakfast?"

"Thanks. I already ate. Some coffee would be nice though."

I pointed to the extra table setting. "Esther set a place for you in case you were hungry. Your cup is right there. We thought you'd be here before now."

Paul walked around the table and sat down, picking up the empty cup and filling it with coffee. After a little cream and sugar, he took a big gulp. "We stayed up too late last night. I can barely keep my eyes open."

"So what's up this morning?" Dad asked.

I held my hand up. "Before we start on that, I have something I want to tell you." I told Paul about the bricks outside the living room window.

"Why didn't you mention that earlier?" Reuben asked.

I rolled my eyes. "We were busy talking about other things. Didn't get a chance."

"Did you see any footprints?" Paul asked.

"I didn't think to look," I said. "But I can tell you there are some now. Mine." I sighed. "Sorry. I was so busy trying to figure out what our Peeping Tom could see through that window, I wasn't thinking about footprints."

"Would that really have helped?" Dad said.

Paul shrugged. "Not unless the person who stood there had unusual shoes or an odd foot size. Then it might help to narrow the field."

"Maybe I didn't completely ruin everything," I said. "Why don't you take a look before you leave and see if there's anything that might help us discover who is so interested in what we're doing?"

Paul took a sip of coffee and nodded. "I will. But before I do that, there are a couple of things you need to know. First of all, as near as we can tell, the handwriting on Lyndon's note matches August's perfectly. I haven't had time to get a handwriting expert to look at it, but there's no doubt in my mind that August wrote that note."

"We were pretty sure he did," I said. "So that's settled. What's the other thing you wanted to tell us?"

Paul smiled. "The reason I was late. I was following up on something."

"And what was that?" Reuben asked.

Paul shrugged. "Oh, nothing too important. I found Elijah."

TWENTY-FOUR

Dad choked on his coffee at Paul's announcement. "Where is he?"

"He's at Anna's cousin's house in De Soto."

"How did you find him?" I asked. "Shouldn't you pick him up before they take off again?"

Paul raised his hand. "Everyone relax. The Fishers aren't going anywhere. Their plan is to stay where they are until you" —he pointed at me—"leave town."

Dad said, "But that means—"

"It doesn't mean anything yet," Paul interrupted. "The Fishers definitely don't want you looking into how they got Elijah, but according to Samuel, he isn't Ryan Erwin."

"You talked to Samuel?" I said angrily. "You may have tipped them off. He thought we bought his story about the birth certificate. Now he has no reason not to tell his brother we're on to him. They'll grab Elijah and run."

"Samuel was our only link to finding Elijah. He knew exactly where his brother was hiding. And as far as tipping off Nathan, he has no intention of telling his brother that we know where they are."

"And why is that?" Reuben said sharply. "I'm with Wynter. They could disappear. We might never find them."

"No, they won't. Samuel Fisher cares about his family, but he also cares a lot more about himself."

"I don't understand," I said.

Paul grinned. "Let's just say that Samuel's crops aren't all legal."

Reuben's mouth dropped open. "Are you saying . . . ?"

Paul nodded. "Samuel's growing pot."

"Wow," I said. "I guess when you leave the Mennonite Church, you go downhill fast."

"Naomi, his wife, is a good Mennonite. She didn't know anything about it. Samuel's the black sheep of the family."

"Does Nathan know about Samuel's special harvest?" Reuben asked.

Paul shook his head. "I'm certain he doesn't. If he did, he'd probably turn his brother in."

"Wait a minute," Reuben said, frowning, "you can't just ignore what he's doing."

"Oh, I didn't. I took some pictures of the plants with my phone and told Samuel they all need to be out of there and destroyed by tomorrow. If they're not, I'll arrest him."

"But is it right to let him get away with that?" I asked. "You're an officer of the law."

"Yes, I am. And I made a decision. A few pot plants or finding your brother. Samuel's operation, which was very small anyway, has been shut down. We know he won't warn Nathan and Anna that we're looking for them because if he does—"

"He goes to jail," I said. "Of course, your superiors would want to know why you waited so long."

Paul shrugged. "That's a chance I'll have to take. Your brother has been missing almost ten years. I think that's long enough."

"I don't know how to thank you, Paul."

"Well, I hope it helps," he said, "but remember that Samuel still says Elijah isn't Ryan. And he should know."

"Not a very reliable witness," Reuben said doubtfully.

Paul nodded. "I agree, but why would he lie at this point? Doesn't make much sense."

"I can't believe we've come this far and this boy might not be Ryan after all." My dad's voice was so faint I could barely hear him. He'd given a lot to find the truth, even telling me something he knew could tear us apart forever. I fought back feelings of frustration.

"So what do we do now?" Zac asked.

"I'm going there to talk to them," Paul said. "You all need to stay here."

"But they don't know you, Paul," Reuben said. "You think they'll open up to you because you're a deputy sheriff? They won't. Conservative Mennonites believe in government through the church and don't have much trust in worldly authority. Although they'll treat you with respect, they won't trust you."

Paul sighed. "There's not much I can do about that. No matter what they believe, I'm the law, and they'll have to answer to me."

"You're not leaving me behind," I said forcefully. "I've got to know the truth."

"I understand how you feel," Paul said slowly, "but it might not be a good idea."

"What do you mean?" I tried to speak calmly, but I couldn't control my emotion, and my voice trembled. We were so close. How could he deny me the chance to finally bring Ryan home?

I felt Reuben's hand on my shoulder. "Wynter, it's best if you stay here. You could make things more difficult. You're too close to this."

I pulled away from him. "Ryan is my brother, not yours. You can't stop me from going."

He paused for a moment. "Please, Wynter," he said finally. "I'm trying to protect you. Stay here." He frowned at Paul. "Why don't you let me go with you? The Fishers know me. Even though they don't recognize me as their mayor, we have a very good relationship."

I watched as Paul chewed on Reuben's suggestion. Finally he said, "Okay. But I intend to walk out of that meeting with the entire truth. I want to know who Elijah is—or was. He's not their natural child, and he certainly didn't grow in their garden. That young man came from somewhere, and I'm not going to stop until I know exactly where that was."

He stood up. "Let's go. It will take us a couple of hours to get there." He nodded toward me. "I know this is difficult, Wynter, but we'll contact you when we know something. Just wait for us, okay?"

Although I wanted to fight them, to argue my case, in my heart I knew they were right. I'd jumped out of Reuben's truck when we went to Samuel's. Obviously, I wasn't completely in control. Although it was difficult to give in, I nodded. "All right. But please don't let them get away again. Bring this to a close, no matter what you find out."

"What about me?" Dad asked. "I know my son better than anyone. If that boy is Ryan, I'll know it."

Paul stared at him, biting his lip.

Dad stood up and walked over to Paul. "One other thing to consider. I look almost exactly the same as I did when Ryan went missing. A little older, maybe, but my son would definitely recognize me."

After a few more seconds of silence, Paul nodded. "I might not take you in with me at first. You'd have to wait in the car until I think there's a reason to bring you inside. Can you accept that?"

"Yes, absolutely. You're in charge."

"Okay. Let's get going." He turned toward Reuben. "Are you ready?"

Reuben didn't respond, and I noticed the trepidation in his expression.

"What's wrong?" I asked.

"I just remembered that Lazarus is in my truck. I promised Rae I'd bring him by this morning for his shots." He waved his hand. "I'll just cancel the appointment. Not a problem. We can drop him back off at the house on our way out of town."

"You can take him with us, if it will help," Paul said. "He can stay in the car."

"Don't be silly," I said. "I'll take him to Rae's. It's better than sitting around here doing nothing."

"Maybe we could do some interviews while they're gone," Zac said.

I nodded. "You're right. With everything going on, I almost forgot about our story. After Ed's warning, we've got to finish this assignment. It just might save our jobs."

Zac grunted. "I'm all for that."

"We'll take Lazarus with us," I said. "Maybe folks will open up more with him around."

"I appreciate this, Wynter," Reuben said.

I sighed. "I think you're using Lazarus to distract me, but I'll do it. He's a great dog."

Reuben smiled. "Yes, he is. He'll love spending time with you."

"We need to get going," Paul said.

I went over and gave my dad a hug.

"If it's him, I'll bring him back to you," he said.

Overcome by emotion, all I could do was nod.

I watched as Dad followed Paul outside to the car.

"Here are the keys to my truck," Reuben said. "Thanks for taking care of Lazarus. I know he already loves you."

I smiled at Reuben. "I love him too."

He put his hands on each side of my face and gazed into my eyes. "When I get back, we need to talk. Seriously. Lazarus isn't the only one with deep feelings about you."

He kissed me quickly and left, the door slamming behind him.

"Wow," Zac said. "Things are moving pretty fast, aren't they?"

I nodded. "Yes, and I'm not sure what to do."

"What do you want to do?"

I stared at Zac for a moment, trying to come up with an answer. Finally I said, "I don't know. I have these strong feelings in my heart, but my head keeps telling me we're from two different worlds. My life is in St. Louis. His is on his family's farm."

"I'm certainly not an expert on relationships, but I've heard that love always finds a way." Zac smiled. "You know, you're not the same person who drove us into Sanctuary. You've changed."

"In what way?"

"It was like you had all these walls around you, protecting yourself. It was almost impossible to get around them. Now those walls are coming down. I would say this place has had a great effect on you."

"And you. You're not the same smart aleck you were when we first got here."

His eyebrows shot up. "Does that mean I'm just a different kind of smart aleck?"

I laughed. "That's exactly what it means."

Zac chuckled. "You know, my mother says God doesn't lead

us through our heads. He leads through our hearts. So I guess you should follow your heart."

I sighed. "I know my heart is saying something, but I haven't sorted it all out yet. Guess I'll keep trying." I glanced at my watch. "It's almost ten. I should take Lazarus to his appointment. Will you be okay on your own?"

He nodded. "I'll help Esther clean up from breakfast, and then I'll get my equipment ready so we can tape some interviews when you get back. Do I need to make any calls?"

"I don't think so. We'll just do the best we can. Anyone we can't see today, we'll schedule for tomorrow."

"And then?"

I shrugged. "And then we'll see. If nothing comes of the meeting with the Fishers, if Elijah isn't Ryan, we'll leave tomorrow afternoon."

"And if he is?"

I shook my head. "I can't think past that, Zac. I really can't."

"I understand." He stood up. "I'm going to start clearing the table, then I'll locate Esther and see what else I can do to help her."

"Okay." I started for the door but stopped halfway there. "Uh, it might help if I know how to find Rae's office."

"I'll ask Esther. Hang on."

He disappeared into the kitchen and was only gone a few seconds before returning. "Go one block past The Whistle Stop and turn right. Keep going about a mile. The vet's office is on the right side of the road. There's a big sign that says 'Pet Sanctuary' out front."

"Wonder why Rae doesn't have an office closer to town."

"Esther says her office is on the same property as her house. Guess she likes it that way."

"Okay. Well, I'm off. Be back in a while."

Zac nodded and trotted back toward the kitchen while I went out the front door. Sam and Frances were lying on the porch. I took a moment to pet them. Maizie and Clyde were probably roaming around somewhere.

It was a brisk spring morning, and the air was invigorating. Reuben's truck was parked right in front of the house, and Lazarus sat in the driver's seat, looking as if he was ready to put the truck in gear and take off. He smiled when he saw me and scooted over to the passenger side, no doubt anticipating our ride together. Little did he know he was getting ready for shots. I wondered if that knowledge would change his happy expression.

I opened the door and got in. Before I could start the engine, I was immediately greeted with a sloppy doggy kiss on the cheek.

"Why, thank you," I said. "Hope you still want to kiss me after your appointment."

Lazarus responded with another wet kiss. When I started the truck, he turned toward the window. I rolled it down so he could hang his head out.

After leaving town, I watched the speedometer. Just about the time we'd reached a mile, I spotted Rae's office. Sure enough, there was a large red wooden sign next to the road that read "Pet Sanctuary." Below those words was an arrow pointing to the right. I turned and followed a dirt road all the way down to the office. It was obvious it had once been a barn, but it had been completely renovated into an attractive facility.

After parking the truck, I got out and looked around for a leash. I finally found it stuck between the seats, pulled it out, and attached it to Lazarus's collar. He gave me an offended look, but I had no idea if he'd actually follow me once I let him out of the truck. The last thing I wanted was for him to take off. Better safe than sorry.

As we walked toward the office, I noticed a large house about a quarter mile down the road. Two stories, white with black shutters—it was beautiful. If Rae owned the vet's office, the house and all this land, she was wealthier than I would have guessed.

The front door was unlocked, so we walked in. No one was in the waiting area. The office was rustic but clean. Pictures of dogs, cats, horses, and even cows covered the walls. There were padded benches across from the front counter, so I sat down to wait. Lazarus jumped up next to me and put his head on my lap. I stroked his soft head, hoping Rae would show up soon. I'd just decided to go looking for her when she came into the room.

"Well, there you are, Lazarus," she exclaimed. "Wondered when you were going to show up."

Instead of cowering from her, Lazarus jumped off the bench before I could grab his leash and ran over to Rae. They greeted each other like old friends.

"Guess he's not afraid of coming here," I said. "You must be a very special veterinarian to get that kind of reaction from your patients."

She laughed. "I have some scaredy-cats. They're not all like this guy." She gave the dog a big hug. "I think he knows I saved his life. I can't explain it, but I'm as sure of it as I can be. He's always acted this way toward me."

"He's a great dog, isn't he?"

She nodded. "Very special. I'm glad he's got such a wonderful owner." She looked around and frowned. "Where is Reuben today?"

"He had an errand, so I volunteered to bring Lazarus in to see you."

"Glad you did. Do you want to come back to the exam room? You can stay with him if you'd like."

"Sure. Sounds good."

I followed her through a door behind the front counter and into a hallway with three different rooms. Rae ushered us into the first one we came to.

"You can have a seat," she said, pointing to a chair in the corner. "I'll be back in a minute with his shots."

I nodded and sat down, holding on to Lazarus's leash.

"He doesn't really need the leash," Rae said. "I've never known him to run off."

"Thanks. I wasn't sure. I didn't want to have to explain to Reuben why I lost his dog."

Rae grinned. "You don't need to worry about that. This dog is joined to Reuben at the hip. Never seen a man and a dog as close as these two. Does my heart good."

"Makes me wish I had a dog."

"I've got two strays in the back looking for homes," she said. "Just say the word."

"Sorry. I live in an apartment, and sometimes I work up to twelve hours a day. I'm afraid it will be a while before I can actually take care of a dog. Mr. Henderson is enough company for me right now."

"Okay, but if you change your mind, let me know."

I bent down and looked Lazarus in the face after she left the room. "It's not going to hurt you to keep this leash on until I'm convinced you'll be good," I whispered. "I'm not taking any chances, buddy."

Another lick revealed he wasn't too concerned about my declaration. Tired of sitting, I got up and checked out the room. A diploma mounted on the wall declared that Mady Rae Buettner had completed a degree in Veterinarian Medicine from Jefferson College in Missouri. It was an impressive piece of paper, but something about it caught my eye. It was a real diploma, but the area with her name looked odd. I'd done some research into faked documents for a story once, and something was definitely wrong with the certificate. Rae's name had been typed on something else and then added on later. Strange.

I'd just started to sit down again when I noticed some boxes on the counter next to me. They looked familiar, but I couldn't remember where I'd seen them before. I picked one up. It was plain and white, but there was a sticker on the side that said *Syringes*. Without thinking about it, I peeled back the sticker. Then I opened the box. It held syringes, but the last time I'd seen a box like this, it had contained several pieces of fudge.

As I tried to understand what I was seeing, my eyes went back to the diploma. *Mady Rae Buettner.*

"Oh no. It can't be."

A noise from behind startled me, and I dropped the box.

Rae stood there with another syringe in her hand, staring at me. "It can't be what?" she asked softly.

"Mady Rae Buettner. The initials. You're Marian Rose Belker."

TWENTY-FIVE

Rae slowly closed the door behind her and put the syringe on the counter. "Well, I guess denying it won't do any good, will it? I was hoping you'd never find out."

"I . . . I can barely believe it."

She gave me an odd smile. "I was at the hospital the night you were born, you know. I gave you to a good home and kept you from a life lived in and out of foster homes. The same kind of life I had."

"I don't understand. What are you doing here?"

She sighed. "I originally came here to make sure your brother was safe. But then I decided to stay. Sanctuary is a place where someone like me can start over. A safe place." She glowered at me. "Until you came here, that is."

I glanced toward the other door. The one we'd come through. Rae opened a nearby drawer and pulled out a handgun. "Get back over there by Lazarus."

When I didn't move, she yelled, "Now!"

I scurried back to the chair and sat down. Lazarus looked

back and forth between us as if trying to figure out what was going on.

"I don't understand," I said. "Did you kill August?"

"It was an accident. When I found out you were coming to town, I told him the truth about everything. I thought he'd understand, but it was a mistake. The day he died we were fighting about it. He wanted me to tell you everything. I got mad and pushed him. He fell and hit his head on that exam table. I tried to save him, but I couldn't."

"So you just dumped him off by the side of the road?"

She sighed. "I was going to bury him, but someone found him before I had the chance. He was so heavy, I couldn't drag him far enough into the woods. If I'd buried him faster, everyone would have believed he'd left town."

My mind raced, trying to figure out what to do next. Was killing August really an accident? Was she planning to kill me too? I was painfully aware there wasn't anyone who could help me. Reuben, my dad, and Paul were on their way to confront the Fishers. Zac knew where I was, but there wasn't any reason for him to come after me. Somehow I had to keep Rae talking while I figured out what to do next.

"You said August wanted to tell me *everything*. What do you mean?"

"No questions," she said angrily. "I've got to decide what to do with you."

"Listen, Rae or Marian, whatever your name is, I think you owe me an explanation. I want to know what August wanted to tell me."

She pointed to the examination table. "Get on the table. Now."

She waved the gun around, and I prayed it wouldn't go off

accidentally—or on purpose. Leaving Lazarus, I climbed up on the table, trying not to think about this being the place where August died. The table wasn't very long, so my legs dangled off the end.

"Lie down," she barked.

"That's ridiculous. The table's too small."

She took a step closer, keeping the gun trained on me. "Let your legs hang off."

I did what she asked. She opened a drawer in a cabinet next to the table and pulled out some kind of heavy strap.

"Now put your arms over the sides."

She tied one end of the strap around one wrist and then reached under the table for the other one. She tied my hands together and then wrapped the end of the strap around the pole that held the table up in the middle. I pulled against my bonds, but there was no way I could get my hands free. The position of my arms strained my shoulders, and every time I moved, it caused pain.

"I use these to hold animals to the table while I operate. They're strong. You won't be able to break them."

"What are you going to do?"

"I . . . I don't know. I need to think."

"Rae, you did something nice for me when I was a baby. You're obviously not a bad woman. You say you didn't mean to kill August. It's not too late to turn yourself in. You might get off with a light sentence. Please think about what you're doing."

She made a noise that sounded like a strangled sob. "No, they'll send me away."

"I don't think—"

"I killed my husband," she said, her voice breaking. "I made the mistake of telling him what happened the night you were born, and he decided to blackmail your father. I begged him not to, but he wouldn't listen. Then he decided we could make money by stealing babies out of hospitals. No one would suspect a nurse. He made me take them, and then he sold them. Fake adoptions to people who would have a hard time adopting, like your parents."

"And how did he *make* you do that, Rae? You didn't have to listen. You could have said no. Turned him in."

She slumped against the counter, defeat etched into her face. "You don't understand. He was all I had. All I would ever have. He . . ." She shook her head. "I can't explain it. He had the power to make me believe he was right and I was wrong. Even after all these years, I still feel it." She took a deep breath. "He finally stopped for several years. I thought everything would be okay. We could live a normal life. But then he said we needed more money. He was going to start again. That's why I had to kill him. There wasn't any other way to stop him."

Although I could have pointed out that a long prison sentence would have brought his activities to an end, I thought better of upsetting her now. Maybe her regret would keep me alive. Still, I had to ask one thing. I couldn't help myself.

"Why did he take Ryan? He couldn't have gotten much money for him."

"Revenge. To punish your father for stopping the payments. It made Joe furious. A friend of his knew the Fishers. Their son had died, so Joe met with them. Told them Ryan was in an abusive home and needed to be placed somewhere safe. Joe told them it was a legal adoption but that Ryan's parents might come looking for him to do the boy harm. He warned them to take Ryan someplace where no one would ever find him. So they came to Sanctuary. After Joe died, I came here too. I was so

relieved to find out Ryan was okay. Happy. And he is, Wynter."
She gave me a small smile. "And I kept tabs on you too. Watched
you grow into a fine young woman. When you changed your
name and started working at the news station, I knew I'd done
the right thing."

I wanted to scream at her. Tell her that she and her husband
had destroyed our family. But I fought to control my anger. Rae
was obviously crazy. The only way I could protect myself was
to keep her calm.

"If you cared so much about Ryan, why didn't you tell the
Fishers the truth? Why didn't you help him to get home?"

She shrugged and stared off into space. After a few moments,
she said, "I was afraid. Joe was gone; I was safe. And Ryan
was happy with the Fishers." She glared at me. "They're good
parents. Why can't you leave him alone?"

I had to bite my tongue. Making her angry wouldn't help
me now. I tried to gather my thoughts. "What about the other
children?" I asked. "The babies you took. Do you know where
they are?"

"No. Joe never let me know where they went. After he died,
I searched through all his papers, but I never found any information. I assume the new parents still think their children were
legally adopted, but I don't know that for sure. Each time Joe
got their money, we moved away. Joe told them he was retiring
and they accepted that. I have no idea if any of them ever figured out there was something wrong with their adoptions, but
if they did, they probably kept it to themselves. By that time,
they loved that baby like it was their own." She shook her head.
"That was Joe's biggest insurance policy. He knew love would
keep him safe. And he was right."

It took everything I had to choke back the fury that rose inside me for the real parents who were living their lives wondering what had happened to their children. Rae seemed to have no concern for them at all. It was also clear she had no problem spending the money her husband gained through the pain of innocent victims. It explained where the financing had come from to buy all her properties. She seemed to have no ability to understand right from wrong.

"Look, I know it was wrong," she said, as if she knew what I was thinking. "That's why I finally stepped in. Stopped him. Couldn't let it go on anymore."

I felt sick to my stomach at her twisted logic. "What about Ryan? Why didn't he try to come home?"

She shrugged. "Joe convinced him your parents didn't want him. That they'd arranged for him to live with someone else. Believe it or not, children that age are very susceptible. I guess there were things going on in your family that made Joe's lie easy to accept."

Between our family dynamics and Joe's ability to manipulate, Ryan had been thrust into a perfect storm of insecurity and lies. He never stood a chance.

"We called the authorities, Rae. They're on their way to get Ryan right now. It's only a matter of time before they connect the dots back to you."

She stared at me with raised eyebrows. "It doesn't matter."

A wave of panic washed through me. The only way she could keep her secret was to dispose of me. Was that her intention?

"I realize you'll tell them the truth," she said. "But I intend to be a long way away from here before you get the chance."

"You—you're not going to kill me?"

She scowled at me. "I'm not a murderer. I had to stop Joe

because he was hurting people. Babies. But I brought you into the world, Emily. There's no way I could harm you."

"Then why am I tied up?"

"I'm going to put you and Lazarus into my storm shelter. No one will think to look for you there for a while. It will give me enough time to get away."

She turned around and opened a cabinet door. Removing a vial of something, she took out a box of syringes, selected one, and began to fill it with the liquid in the vial.

"What's that?" I couldn't keep the fear out of my voice. Marian Belker, aka Mady Rae Buettner, was certifiably nuts. I didn't trust her ability to administer drugs without making a serious mistake.

"Relax. It's just something that will put you to sleep for a while. It's not the same thing I put into the fudge."

"You made my friend Zac extremely ill."

She grunted. "That fudge wasn't for him. He had no business eating it."

"You could have killed me."

She shook her head. "It couldn't have killed anyone. Just make you sick so you'd go home. I've been trying to get you out of Sanctuary for quite a while, but you wouldn't take the hint. If you'd just left—"

"I'm not leaving my brother."

"I know that," she said slowly, "but I wonder if you've thought much about him. Elijah has a good family. Your interference will devastate him."

"*My* interference?" I asked, stunned by her level of denial. "*Your* interference destroyed a family, took my brother out of his real family, and caused everything that's happened."

"That was Joe, not me."

I could tell Rae had closed an emotional door. Her reactions were becoming flat and unemotional. She approached me with the syringe in her hand.

"Please don't do this," I pleaded. "What if something goes wrong?"

"You should be fine. I've never used this on a person before, but I don't think it will do any permanent damage. You'll just go to sleep."

Without another word, she pushed up my sleeve and jabbed the needle into my arm. I cried out in pain.

"What do you mean I *should* be fine?" I said. "You're not sure?"

Rae shrugged. "We always have to warn our patients that any kind of medicine could have side effects." She gave me a strange smile, and terror coursed through my body. No matter what she'd said earlier, this woman wasn't convinced the drug she was shooting into my body wouldn't kill me.

After emptying the contents of the syringe into my arm, she tossed it into the trash. Then she came over and removed the straps from my hands, but not before picking up her gun again.

"Get on your feet," she ordered. "I need to get you into the shelter while you're conscious. I don't want to carry you down the stairs."

I pushed myself into a sitting position. My shoulders hurt from being restrained, and my arm throbbed from the shot Rae had given me. When I tried to stand, I discovered my legs had gone numb. I almost fell, but I caught myself by grabbing the edge of the exam table.

Rae shoved the gun into my side. "Get going," she ordered. "Now."

"What about Lazarus?" The retriever was watching us carefully, almost as if he were trying to determine exactly what was going on. Too bad he hadn't been trained to attack. It would certainly be helpful now.

"He's coming with us."

After making certain the feeling had returned to my legs, I bent over and picked up his leash.

"Out the back door."

Lazarus and I obeyed Rae's instructions. We walked down a hallway to another door that led outside. Rae pointed to a pair of metal doors on the ground near the back of the clinic. They belonged to an old storm shelter.

"Since I have a basement in my house, I've never used this shelter. It will come in handy now though."

She stepped around me, still keeping the gun pointed at me. Suddenly, the first rush of drowsiness hit, and I fell to the ground. When I hit the dirt, I accidentally let go of the leash. Instead of staying by my side, Lazarus gave me a long look and then bolted away, running across the yard toward the road. I tried to call his name, but my voice was so weak, I couldn't make a sound.

As darkness started to overtake me, I could see Rae fling the metal doors of the shelter open. Then she grabbed me by my shoulders. I attempted to wrestle myself out of her grasp, but she was too strong. She pushed me down some old wooden stairs. I fell on moist earth, surrounded by the dank smell of mold and mildew. Next to me were a couple of suitcases. August's. I thought I heard Rae say something about being sorry, and then everything went black.

CHAPTER

TWENTY-SIX

"Can you hear me, Emily?"

I tried to shake the fog out of my head, but it clung to me like tendrils from a spider's web.

"Dad?" I choked out. "Is that you?"

"Yes. We're here."

I realized I was lying on the ground. Turning my head, I could see the clinic and the doors of the shelter that had been flung open. "Where is she? Where is Rae?"

My father stroked my head. "They caught her trying to get out of town. She's in custody, honey."

"Oh, good. She's—"

"Marian Belker. Yes, we know."

"How . . . ?"

"We'll talk about it later. Right now, we need to make sure you're okay."

"I'm fine. She gave me a shot. Made me sleepy."

I heard Dad say something, but I couldn't quite make out the words. Someone spoke back to him. It sounded like Reuben, but I couldn't be sure.

"We called an ambulance. It's on the way."

"Don't be silly. I'm okay." I tried to sit up, but the world swirled around me in a kaleidoscope of colors and shapes.

"Just take it easy, Emily," Dad said.

As I stared up into his face, the dizziness seemed to be fading somewhat. "How . . . how did you find me?"

"Lazarus, Zac, and Janet Dowell," Dad said with a smile. "Zac was looking through his notes and the research you two did, and he remembered something."

My mouth was so dry I couldn't seem to get my lips apart, so I just nodded at my father.

"The night you asked Rae questions about August, she mentioned feeling bad for you because of everything your family had been through. But no one had told her about Ryan. As Zac was wondering how she could have known, Janet knocked on Esther's door. The other night when she took her dog, Murphy, outside, she saw someone looking through Esther's window. The person ran away, but she was pretty sure it was Rae. At first, she didn't think much of it, but after a while, it began to bother her. She came over to tell Esther about it, and Zac overheard their conversation. By then, he'd already realized something was wrong. He called Paul on his cell phone and told us to come back. Then he drove over to the vet clinic looking for you."

"How did he figure out where I was?"

"It was Lazarus. Zac looked all over for you. He was about to give up when Lazarus came running up to him. He led Zac to a mound of dirt and started barking and pawing at it. Zac cleared away the dirt, discovered the shelter, and found you. He'd just pulled you out when we got here."

"Oh, the bricks," I said. My tongue felt like it was too big for my mouth.

"I don't understand, honey."

"I just realized. The bricks under the window. They were piled high. For a short person. It was Rae."

Dad chuckled. "It doesn't matter anymore, Emmie. Rae, or Marian—whatever you want to call her—won't hurt anyone else."

I heard Zac call out. He ran up next to us. "Here it is," he said, handing my dad a vial. I recognized it immediately.

"That's it," I said. "That's what she gave me."

"I don't know what this is," Dad said.

At that very moment, the sound of a siren split the air. An ambulance pulled up the clinic's driveway, and an EMT jumped out. Dad quickly explained the situation to him and handed him the vial.

"It's ketamine, a sedative used by doctors and veterinarians during surgery," the EMT said. "It shouldn't cause any permanent damage."

"Thank God," Dad said a little breathlessly.

"It wouldn't hurt for us to check you over though, miss," the attendant said. "Just to make sure."

I sat up, this time without the cobwebs and weird colors. "Thanks, but I'm feeling much better."

"Are you sure? We're already here." His worried expression made me smile.

"I'm sure."

He came over anyway, knelt down, and checked my vitals. Then he snapped the lid shut on his medical kit.

"Just rest today. You'll start feeling better in a couple of hours." The EMT looked at my dad. "Keep a close watch on her. If she's still groggy by this evening, take her to the emergency room and have them take a look at her."

Dad nodded. "I'll do that. Thanks for your help."

The EMT patted me on the shoulder, got up, and ran back to the ambulance. We watched as they pulled away.

"I want you to take it easy, Emily. And you will go to the hospital if you're not feeling better in the next few hours."

"Really. I'm fine. I'd just like to get up off the ground, if you don't mind."

"You sit there just a little longer. I don't want you passing out."

I grabbed his arm. "Dad. Elijah. He's . . . he's Ryan. Rae . . . I mean, Marian confirmed it."

My father smiled. "Once we realized who she was, I knew you'd found him. I'm so proud of you, sweetheart. It's because you refused to give up."

Suddenly something came at me from my left side. As a wet tongue washed the side of my face, I grabbed Lazarus around the neck and hugged him.

"Good boy," I said, burying my head in his fur. "You're such a good boy."

"You're awake." Reuben sat down on the ground next to me. "I was so worried. Afraid that crazy woman had hurt you."

"It was Rae," I said. "She was behind all of it." I looked up at my father. "Her husband blackmailed you, Dad. And she poisoned the fudge, Zac. The idea was to make me sick so I'd have to go home."

"What fudge?" Dad asked.

"We'll explain it later," Zac said. "It's not important now."

I pointed toward the shelter doors. "She killed August, although she said it was an accident. His suitcases are down there."

"We know," Dad said. "We already found them. Now let's

get you home and cleaned up, honey," Dad said. "Then we'll talk some more. You've been through a lot."

Even though I felt like I wanted to tell them everything I'd discovered, my head was starting to pound. I looked down and realized I was covered with mud, and I smelled.

"Good idea. Help me up."

Dad put his arms around me and pulled me to my feet. Reuben took one arm while Dad held on to the other. With their help, I made it to Reuben's truck.

"You drive her back," Dad said to Reuben. "We'll follow behind you."

Reuben put his arms around me and lifted me into the seat. Dad kissed me on the cheek and closed the truck's door. Then Reuben went to the other side of the truck, ordered Lazarus into the cab, and climbed in after him. Lazarus immediately scooted up next to me and put one paw on my leg. I put my arms around him.

"Thank you, Lazarus," I whispered.

He rewarded me with another kiss on the face. I suddenly became aware of how filthy I really was. "Oh, Reuben. I'm getting your seat all dirty."

"I don't care about my truck, Wynter. I'm just so thankful you're all right."

For the first time I realized how haggard and worried he looked. "I'm fine. Really."

Reuben put his face in his hands. When he removed them, there were tears in his eyes. "It's my fault. I'm the one who sent you to Rae."

I reached past Lazarus and grabbed his hand. "Reuben King. That's ridiculous. It's not your fault at all. You had no idea Rae was dangerous."

"But I should have known. I should have realized . . ."

I smiled at him. "That the town vet was a crazy woman who kills people? Don't be silly. Marian was adept at lying. Not only to others but to herself." I looked down at Lazarus. "We were all fooled—except for Lazarus. When she tried to put him in the storm shelter with me, he took off. He knew I needed help, and he went to find it." My declaration was met with another wet kiss on the cheek.

Reuben looked deeply into my eyes. "Maybe it's time I was bold enough to follow his lead. I love you, Wynter. I know you might be thinking it's too soon for me to say it, but almost losing you made it clear I can't let you go back to St. Louis without knowing how I feel."

I smiled at him. "Wondering if I was going to come out of this alive made me rethink some things too. I love you too. Feeling this strongly about someone is new to me, so I might need some time to adjust."

Reuben held up his other hand. "No problem. All I heard is that you love me. I can live with that. For now."

I grinned. "Any man who doesn't mind a woman smearing mud all over his truck is a man I can see a future with."

He nodded. "Again, the truck's not important. And, speaking of trucks, when Rae was stopped on the road out of town, would you like to know what she was driving?"

"A black truck with tinted windows?"

He nodded. "August's truck. I didn't recognize it when she tried to run us off the road. He rarely drove it. Walked everywhere. He kept it here, parked in her garage. If it matters, I don't think she was trying to kill us. She wanted you out of town before you discovered her secret. If you were injured or got sick, she figured you'd go back to St. Louis."

"But I didn't know anything about her. If she'd kept quiet and hadn't told August what she'd done, we would have finished our interviews and left."

"We owe a lot to August. I wish he was still around so we could thank him. He sacrificed himself for the truth."

"She said they got into an argument and he fell and hit his head."

Reuben glanced over at me. "Do you really believe that?"

"I don't know what to believe. I'm comfortable letting the police sort everything out." I took a deep breath, hoping a shot of oxygen would help to clear my mind. "Reuben, what about Elijah . . . I mean, Ryan? I've got to see him."

"Did I hear you say that Rae admitted that Elijah is Ryan?"

I nodded, tears filling my eyes. "I've found my brother, Reuben. After all these years . . ."

I felt like a dam broke inside me, and I began to sob.

"It's not going to be easy, Wynter," Reuben said gently. "Ryan's spent most of his life with the Fishers."

"I know," I sputtered. "And they had no idea who he really is. Rae's husband told them Ryan was an abused child who needed to be kept away from his parents. They weren't trying to hide him from us. They were trying to protect him. I'm sure Samuel and Naomi were doing the same thing."

"This is going to be really hard for Nathan and Anna."

"I know, but at least we found him. Now we can tell him the truth. That Mom and Dad weren't trying to get rid of him, and that we looked everywhere for him. Even if he feels more connected to the Fishers, he'll finally know we've always loved him."

Reuben smiled. "That's a great way to look at it."

I leaned back against the seat. Lazarus put his head on my shoulder and I stroked him.

"I should have caught Rae's comment about my family," I said. "I've just had so much on my mind, it went right past me."

"God bless Zac for remembering. We owe him and Janet a great deal. They started us in the right direction. Thank God we knew where you were."

"I would have regained consciousness eventually and climbed out."

"Maybe," Reuben said with a frown, "but Rae covered the storm shelter with a mound of dirt. I had no idea there was a shelter there—nor did anyone else." He looked over at me, his eyes full of tears. "It's possible you couldn't have opened those doors, Wynter. The dirt made them too heavy. If we hadn't found you . . ."

A chill went through me. Was it possible I could have actually died?

I kissed Lazarus on the head. "Lazarus came back from the dead, and he may have kept me from dying. Quite a special dog."

Reuben reached over and patted the beautiful golden retriever's head. "Yes, he is that."

I closed my eyes and we rode back to Esther's in silence. There was so much going through my mind. The pieces of our crazy puzzle had finally come together. They'd begun to form a picture I could understand, although there were still a few questions I had no answers to. Would finding Ryan become a big story in the media? Would my father get in trouble for exchanging babies in a hospital twenty-three years ago? How would my mother respond to all of this? And what about Ryan? Did he still love us? Had he recognized me when I talked to him in the restaurant?

I could tell that the effects of the drug were wearing off. My body wanted to rest, but my mind was going a hundred miles a minute.

"Here we are," Reuben said suddenly.

I looked up and saw Esther and Janet waiting on the front porch. We'd just parked the truck when Dad pulled up next to us in his car, Zac in the passenger seat.

"Where's Paul?"

"Back at the station, questioning Rae."

Reuben jumped out of the truck and came around to my side. He opened the door and put his arm around me. "Step out slowly. Don't move too fast."

I laughed. "I'm not an invalid, Reuben."

"I know that, but I don't want you to get dizzy again."

I swung my feet around and Reuben lifted me down. Lazarus jumped out behind me, staying right by my side.

"Thanks be to God, you're okay," Esther said as we approached.

"I'm fine," I said. When we reached the porch, I put my arms around Janet. "Thank you so much," I said, my voice breaking. "You helped to save my life."

"Oh, my goodness," she said breathlessly. "I just wish I'd said something sooner. Maybe things wouldn't have gotten so serious."

"Oh, Janet," Esther said, "just take the girl's thanks and feel good about it. You're a hero!"

I let Janet go and was tickled to see her blush. "I'm just glad to have helped you," she said quietly. "For once, butting into other people's business turned out to be a good thing."

"You can butt into my business anytime," Esther said with a smile. She gave her friend a big hug. "I'm so thankful to have a wonderful friend like you."

Janet didn't answer, but I could tell she was pleased. "I'd better get back home," she said, still red from all the attention she was getting. "Murphy needs to be fed."

"You feed him and then get back over here," Esther said. "You're invited for dinner tonight. We need to celebrate Wynter's rescue. You be here at five-thirty. We'll eat at six."

"Thank you. I'd love to."

Esther nodded. "Good." She turned her attention to the rest of us. "Now, let's get this young lady into the house. My goodness, she's filthy. Let's get you out of those dirty clothes."

I let Esther guide me upstairs. After making sure I was steady on my feet, she took my muddy clothes while I got in the shower. The hot water felt wonderful. I stood under it, allowing the water to wash away the grime while my mind sorted through the thoughts that bombarded me.

My father's decision on the night I was born was made out of grief over losing a child and compassion for his wife. What he'd done, he'd done out of love. Because of it, I'd found a family. It wasn't a perfect family, but I doubted that anything like that really existed. The world was full of imperfect people. And maybe that was good enough. We had a hard road ahead of us. My mother would have to confront the death of her natural daughter, and all of us would have to find a way to deal with the past.

I couldn't help but think about the child who didn't live. She felt close to me. Like a sister. My tears mixed with the water that coursed down my body. Who was she? What kind of person would she have been? Would she have liked me? Was I the kind of daughter she never got the chance to be?

Then there was Ryan. Would he want anything to do with us, or would he choose to walk away? We'd lost so many years, but with a little love and understanding, maybe we could make the most of the time we had left.

Through everything that had happened, one thing had become clear. God had been there the entire time. Never leaving me. Never disappearing. Whatever happened, my relationship with Him had changed. My life had stopped in one moment of time, and now it would begin again—in another moment. This moment.

I prayed right then and there, asking His forgiveness for putting other things in front of Him and recommitting my heart and life to His will for me. The water that washed me felt like a baptism, and by the time I got out of the shower I felt different. Lighter.

As I dressed, I understood that the days ahead would be full of difficulties and blessings. But with God's help, I was ready to face whatever I had to. The path God had for me lay ahead, and I couldn't wait to find out where it led.

CHAPTER
TWENTY-SEVEN

"Before they get here, I wanted to make sure you don't have any other questions." Paul was in street clothes, and I marveled at how different he looked. Although he wasn't here in an official capacity, we'd asked him to stay until they arrived. He was the one who had explained the truth to the Fishers. Then he'd set up this meeting. It had been four days since Marian Belker forced me into the shelter under her clinic. Today was the day we'd all been waiting for.

"Tell me exactly what Ryan said when you spoke to him," Mom said.

My mother, whom I'd seen as fragile, had been a source of encouragement and strength since learning the truth about the past. Dealing with the death of her biological daughter wasn't easy, but her love for me hadn't changed at all. As she told me, "You are my daughter, Emily. Nothing in this world could change that." And although she had every right to be angry with my father, instead, she seemed touched by his attempt to protect her from sorrow. During my father's confession, Mom actually asked him to forgive her for turning her back on his pain. "I should have been there for you, Lyndon," she'd said. "Instead, I needed someone to blame. I'm sorry it was you."

"At first he denied he was Ryan," Paul said. "But after I explained what really happened—that you didn't give him away, and that you did everything you could to find him, he finally opened up. The Fishers were stunned. They'd believed Joe Belker's lies that Ryan was an abused child who needed protection. They never heard the news reports about Ryan's abduction, so they just named him after their dead son and moved him into their family. Belker was right in his belief that sending Ryan to live with a conservative Mennonite family would keep him away from prying eyes.

"By the time the Fishers moved here, the stories about Ryan had pretty much subsided. Even if someone could have recognized him from past newscasts, no one made the connection between the boy in the pictures and a Mennonite boy living in a small town. People weren't looking in Sanctuary. It was the perfect cover."

"But he said he wanted to see us?" Mom asked. Paul had already assured her on this point several times. It was obvious Mom was nervous.

"Yes, he does. Very much. Ever since he saw you in the restaurant, Wynter. He recognized you immediately. In fact, he followed you. Watched you, trying to decide what to do."

I nodded. "I saw him outside Esther's the first night I was in town. Although I didn't notice him again, I had the feeling I was being watched."

"That's because you were. Ryan wanted to talk to you, wanted to contact you, but he was afraid the Fishers would get in trouble, and he loves them very much. They're very nice people, and they feel awful for everything you've been through."

"This must be hard on them too," I said.

Paul nodded. "Yes, it is. But they want the best for Ryan—and for you."

"How could Joe Belker do something so evil?" Mom asked. "Taking our child because Lyndon refused to pay any more blackmail money?"

Paul shrugged. "It was strictly revenge. He targeted Ryan, and when he finally caught him alone, he took him. Called himself Bill Martin. Ryan was convinced he was a neighbor. I guess Belker was very persuasive." He shook his head. "The Belkers were quite a couple. No sense of right or wrong. But in the end, Marian's lack of conscience betrayed Joe. In her mind, killing him made sense. She did it because she didn't want to steal any more babies. She still sees herself as misunderstood. Someone just trying to do the right thing."

"I thank God Zac survived one of her attempts to do the right thing," I said. "If he'd eaten all that fudge, he might not have made it."

Paul nodded. "She took a chance putting that candy in your room. Anyone could have gotten into it. You might have mentioned it to Esther when you found it."

"I guess she was so desperate she was willing to try anything."

Esther and Reuben had gone to The Oil Lamp for lunch so we could be together as a family. Oddly, with them gone, I felt as if some of my family were missing.

"That's true." Paul shook his head. "I don't know if she will ever take responsibility for her actions. But it's in the state's hands now. They'll decide what to do with her."

"I feel sorry for August," I said. "When he found out the truth, he tried to help."

"If he hadn't been so reluctant to betray Rae, he might have saved his life," Paul said. "He hoped that by sending you those clippings you would find a way to link them back to Rae. And the note he sent to you, Lyndon, was designed to bring you to Sanctuary. I'm not sure why. Maybe he thought you'd recognize Marian. He hoped one of you would put the pieces together so he wouldn't be the one responsible for her arrest. Even with everything she'd done, he still loved her."

"We know now why Marian didn't stay for dinner the night she came over to Esther's," I said. "When she found out you were coming, Dad, she was afraid you'd realize who she was."

My father shook his head. "I'm afraid August and Marian were both wrong about that. I can't remember what she looked like twenty-three years ago. There's no chance I would have recognized her now."

"Will Marian be charged with two murders?" Mom asked.

"I have no idea. Illinois and Missouri are trying to decide who gets her—and for what. It will take some time to sort everything out. The important thing to realize is that she can't hurt you anymore."

"And what about Ryan?" I asked. "Will our story end up in the press?"

"I don't know that either. Everything has been turned over to the authorities. What happens after that is up to them. I think you have to be prepared for anything. Besides Ryan's abduction, there's the kidnapping of seven babies to deal with. Searching for them will certainly garner national press. You need to discuss the possibility of media attention with the Fishers and together decide what to do. The best thing might be to go into hiding. I know they'd rather not leave their farm." He gave me a quick smile. "Maybe you could take Ryan back to St. Louis for a while. Give yourselves some time to get reacquainted."

"That might be a little difficult," I said. "I'll only be there a couple more weeks. You see, I'm moving."

Paul's eyebrows shot up. "Moving? I thought you'd stay near Ryan now that you've found him."

I smiled at him. "Well, if he stays in Sanctuary, we'll be very close."

"You mean . . . ?"

"Yes, I'm moving here. Esther is putting me up. I've decided to do some writing. And there's a certain farmer I want to spend some time with." I sighed. "If you'd told me a couple of weeks ago that I'd walk away from my job at the station, I'd have said you were crazy. But now I can't imagine going back."

"And Zac?"

"He's staying at KDSM, but he's promised to visit. Esther is still determined to teach him to cook."

Paul laughed. "I'm glad you're coming back, Wynter. Sanctuary would miss you."

I looked over at my mother and father. Mom's eyes kept darting to the front door. She'd been waiting a long time for Ryan, and today that waiting was coming to an end. I saw my father reach over and take her hand. She grabbed on to him like a drowning woman finding a life preserver. When they looked at each other, it was as if time hadn't passed at all. My father was still the handsome man my mother had fallen in love with, and Mom was still the young, beautiful girl who turned heads when she walked down the street. Maybe others could see the changes age had brought, but at that moment, I only saw them the way they'd been when Ryan and I were young.

"Actually, you can call me Emily," I said. "I don't think I need Wynter anymore. She's retiring."

He smiled. "Nice to meet you, Emily."

"And I'm happy to meet you, Paul."

The sound of a horse's whinny came from outside. Mom stood to her feet and Dad followed her.

"Are you ready?" Paul asked.

I laughed lightly. "We've been ready for a long, long time."

When the door opened and Ryan stepped inside, he caught my eye and smiled. Tonight I'd sleep sweetly, and the voices in my head would be silent. As my parents approached him, the shadows we'd gathered for years were swept away in an instant, and together we walked into a future full of light, love, and promise.

ACKNOWLEDGMENTS

My thanks to the awesome Mark Bogner for his help in creating KDSM, a fictional news station in St. Louis. Mark is the kind of guy who is driven to help people, whether he's warning them about the weather or peering into their ears as a hearing instrument specialist. The stars in your crown will be many, my friend.

Thanks to my wonderful daughter-in-love, Shaen, for reading through this story and helping me punch it into shape. Love you, honey.

To my son, Danny: Thank you for taking me "through the mines" since I couldn't get there myself. I love you.

Love and hugs to my "Inner Circle": Mary G., Larry, Tammy, Michelle D., Cheryl, Rhonda, Susan, Karla Lynne, Mary S., Michelle M., Bonnie, JoJo, and Zac. And o Zac: Still waiting for that ponytail! LOL!

To the incredible Kim Sawyer: Thank you for allowing me to

use your kitties in my book. I love them all. And thank you for letting me spend time at the beautiful King's Inn. It was such a privilege.

As always, thanks to Raela Schoenherr and Sharon Asmus. I'm so blessed to have you both in my life—even when the edits are so extensive it makes me think about changing my name to Gertrude and moving to Canada, eh?

And most of all, my thanks to God, who has given me this wonderful opportunity—and kept me from becoming Canadian.

Nancy Mehl is the author of fifteen books and received the ACFW Mystery Book of the Year Award in 2009. She has a background in social work and is a member of ACFW and RWA. She writes from her home in Missouri, where she lives with her husband, Norman, and their Puggle, Watson. Visit her website at www.nancymehl.com.

If you enjoyed *Gathering Shadows,* you may also like...

As the Mennonite town of Kingdom, Kansas, is plagued by strange incidents and attacks, three young women have their faith in God and their community tested to the limits. Will they all survive the dangerous road ahead?

ROAD TO KINGDOM by Nancy Mehl
Inescapable, Unbreakable, Unforeseeable
nancymehl.com

Widow Andrea Wilson and her young son sought temporary refuge in the Amana Colonies, but will the peace she finds there convince her to stay?

A Shining Light
HOME TO AMANA
judithmccoymiller.com

More Romance and Intrigue

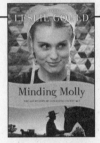
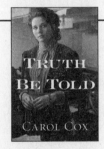